D1378003

THE SEARCH
FOR THE BUDDHA

OTHER FIVE STAR WESTERN TITLES BY MICHAEL ZIMMER:

Johnny Montana (2010)
Wild Side of the River (2011)
The Long Hitch (2011)
City of Rocks (2012)
Beneath a Hunter's Moon (2012)
Río Tinto (2013)
Leaving Yuma (2013)
The Poacher's Daughter (2014)

AMERICAN LEGENDS COLLECTION,
BOOK 4

MIAMI GUNDOWN

A FRONTIER STORY

MICHAEL ZIMMER

FIVE STAR
A part of Gale, Cengage Learning

GALE
CENGAGE Learning·

Farmington Hills, Mich • San Francisco • New York • Waterville, Maine
Meriden, Conn • Mason, Ohio • Chicago

GALE
CENGAGE Learning®

LIBRARY OF CONGRESS CATALOGING-IN-PUBLICATION DATA

Zimmer, Michael, 1955– author.
    Miami gundown : a frontier story : American Legends Collection Book 4 / by Michael Zimmer—First edition.
        pages cm
    ISBN 978-1-4328-2847-9 (hardcover) — ISBN 1-4328-2847-9 (hardcover)
    1. Cattle drives—Florida—Fiction. 2. Frontier and pioneer life—Florida—Fiction. I. Title.
PS3576.I467M53 2014
813'.54—dc23   2014018201

First Edition. First Printing: September 2014.
Published in conjunction with Golden West Literary Agency.
Find us on Facebook– https://www.facebook.com/FiveStarCengage
Visit our website– http://www.gale.cengage.com/fivestar/
Contact Five Star™ Publishing at FiveStar@cengage.com

Printed in the United States of America
1 2 3 4 5 6 7 18 17 16 15 14

For Mary Zimmer
A Cracker at Heart

FOREWORD:
THE AMERICAN LEGENDS
COLLECTIONS

During the Great Depression of the 1930s, nearly one quarter of the American work force was unemployed. Facing the possibility of economic and government collapse, President Franklin D. Roosevelt initiated the New Deal program, a desperate bid to get the country back on its feet.

The largest of these programs was the Works Progress Administration (WPA), which focused primarily on manual labor with the construction of bridges, highways, schools, and parks across the country. But the WPA also included a provision for the nation's unemployed artists, called the Federal Arts Project, and within its umbrella, the Federal Writers Project (FWP). At its peak, the FWP put to work approximately six thousand five hundred men and women.

During the FWP's earliest years, the focus was on a series of state guidebooks, but, in the late 1930s, the project created what has been called a "hidden legacy" of America's past— more than ten thousand life stories gleaned from men and women across the nation.

Although these life histories, a part of the Folklore Project within the FWP, were meant to be published eventually in a series of anthologies, that goal was effectively halted by the United States' entry into World War II. Most of these histories are currently located within the Library of Congress in Washington, D.C.

As the Federal Writers Project was an arm of the larger Arts Project, so too was the Folklore Project a subsidiary of the FWP. An even lesser known branch of the Folklore Project was the American Legends Collection (ALC), created in 1936, and managed from 1936 to 1941 by a small staff from the University of Indiana. The ALC was officially closed in early 1942, another casualty of the war effort.

While the Folklore Project's goal was to capture everyday life in America, the ALC's purpose was the acquisition of as many "incidental" histories from our nation's past as possible. Unfortunately the bulk of the American Legends Collection was lost due to manpower shortages caused by the war.

The only remaining interviews known to exist from the ALC are those located within the A.C. Thorpe Papers at the Bryerton Library in Indiana. These are carbons only, as the original transcripts were turned in to the offices of the FWP in November, 1941.

Andrew Charles Thorpe was unique among those scribes put into employment by the FWP-ALC in that he recorded his interviews with an Edison Dictaphone. These discs, a precursor to the LP records of a later generation, were found sealed in a vault shortly after Thorpe's death in 2006. Of the eighty-some interviews discovered therein, most were conducted between the years 1936 and 1939. They offer an unparalleled view of both a time (1864 to 1912) and place (Florida to Nevada, Montana to Texas) within the United States' singular history.

The editor of this volume is grateful to the current executor of the A.C. Thorpe Estate for his assistance in reviewing these papers, and to the descendants of Mr. Thorpe for their co-operation in allowing these transcripts to be brought into public view.

An explanation should be made at this point that, although minor additions to the text were included to enhance its effect, no facts were altered. Any mistakes or misrepresentations resulting from these changes are solely my own.

Leon Michaels
December 17, 2012

SESSION ONE

Boone McCallister Interview
Fort Worth, Texas
November 15, 1937
Begin Transcript

If that machine is running, I've got something I want to say right up front, and that is that I did *not* feed David Klee to an alligator.

That damned rumor has hounded me my whole life. It's been up and down the cattle trails between Texas and Kansas half a dozen times. It's followed me as far north as Cheyenne, as far west as El Paso, and as far south as, well, hell, as far south as Punta Rassa. But it ain't true.

Dave Klee was killed by a 'gator, all right. That part is factual enough, and it's also a fact that I was there when it happened. But I didn't throw him in. Truth is, I was the one who pulled Dave's body out of the swamp that night, and did my best by him until we were driven off by his brothers, cousins, and assorted kin.

I suppose you already know all this happened back in 1864, while I was bossing my first cattle drive. I was eighteen at the time, and young for the position, but Pa had handed me the job on the day he was pulling out for the north with a herd of his own—over three thousand head of Florida longhorns, carrying

11

not only our own Flatiron brand, but cattle from several of the neighboring ranches as well.

I can still remember Pa's voice that mid-spring day, made all the more poignant because it would be the last time I ever heard it. We were on the holding grounds north of the Pease River when he handed me a note made grimy from the hands of who knew how many strangers as it made its way to the Flatiron range.

"One of Turner's men just gave me this," Pa said in a voice made low and gravelly by weariness.

Pa believed strongly in the Cause, and had been pushing herd after herd north to help feed the Confederacy ever since the war's beginning. All that hard, unrelenting toil had taken a heavy toll on him. He was honed down to scarecrow dimensions, with blossoming gray in a beard that had once been as black as the bottom of a cast-iron skillet, and sagging lids above his work-worn eyes. Pa wouldn't even talk about slowing down, though. He claimed the South's armies were gill-full of men who would like nothing better than to do just that, but who knew they couldn't without weakening the fabric of our new nation. Then he'd start north again, just as quick as he could pry another herd out of the scrub.

That day on the Pease, Pa handed me the note without further explanation. I unfolded it and read it right there, the two of us sitting our horses side-by-side as a mottled river of tallow and horn and brindled hide flowed north before us. The letter read:

To Jefferson McCallister, Flatiron Ranch, Pease River.

Sir, I have need of cattle numbering the amount to fill the hold and deck of a moderately sized schooner, which I have received word will soon dock at Punta Rassa. If you can fulfill this contract for a delivery of no later than March 30th, I am in a position to offer the sum of $35 per head for full-grown beeves, *payable in Spanish doubloons upon arrival. If unable to provide the numbers requested, please advise by post.*

It was unsigned, but we both knew who had sent it. Refolding the note, I tucked it inside a vest pocket. I didn't ask Pa what he wanted me to do about it. He wouldn't have given me the letter if he didn't expect me to fill the contract.

"You reckon a couple of hundred head?" I asked.

"Two hundred and fifty might be better, but take whatever you can find. That scrub over west of Turkey Creek ain't been all the way combed out yet. Was it me, I'd start there." He turned quiet for a moment, his gaze fixed on the flat plane of the horizon. Then he said: "Get the gold, Boone. Don't let that slick-talkin' son-of-a-bitch con you into taking script. Bring the herd back if he tries. There are soldiers in Mississippi and Tennessee who can use that meat a hell of a lot more than a bunch of Cubans."

I knew it galled Pa to sell even a shipload of cattle to outside markets—in this case, Havana—but we all knew how tough it was going to be to start over after the fighting was finished, no matter which side won. The gold I'd get in Punta Rassa for those two hundred and fifty head would be the seed money we'd need to rebuild the ranch to what it had been before the war.

"I will," I said.

He nodded tiredly, then gathered his reins. "The Flatiron is yours until we get back. Keep it safe."

I said again that I would. Then we briefly shook hands, and Pa galloped off to join the herd. That was the last time I ever saw him, sitting ramrod stiff atop his flat, English-style saddle, his mount gouging up little clods of soil from beneath its hoofs. The sharp, pistol-like cracks of the cow hunters' whips and the excited barking of the drovers' dogs as they flanked the moving herd was comforting in its familiarity, and I found myself wish-

13

ing that I was going with them. As the cattle streamed past, I raised my hand in a farewell salute to the men who were helping move the herd north. I had four brothers in that crew, and there were two of them that I'd never see again, either. That damned war was a mean one. I guess they all are, but the Civil War was a lot more personal for some of us. Me included.

Anyway, that note from a Punta Rassa cattle buyer named W.B. Ashworth was the reason I was trailing my own small herd of beeves toward the Gulf of Mexico that day. Toward a small fortune in gold, too, $35 a head being about five times what we normally got for a cow.

Although the worst of the fighting was up north, running a herd to Punta Rassa, even a paltry bunch like ours, wasn't going to be any picnic. By '64, there were Federal patrols scouring that whole region, looking for cattle and caches of salt to supply their own armies, not to mention Confederate troops to tangle with. At first I figured that was why we were all feeling so unsettled as we neared the end of our journey, and why I kept looking over my shoulder every little whip-stitch with such a sense of dread. As if there were something lurking back there— something mean and hungry, with a full set of teeth. Even though we didn't talk about it, I knew the others were feeling it, too, so, after a couple of days of trying to ignore our growing unease, I finally sent a man out to scout our back trail. Meanwhile, I kept the herd moving along at a good clip. I knew we were melting off what little fat those scrubby longhorns had started the drive with, but I was anxious to make our delivery, then get out of there before the Union garrison at Fort Myers caught wind of us.

We were still three long days out of Punta Rassa—using a roundabout way to get there in order to avoid the bluebellies that infested that area—when I sent my man back. It was nearly dusk of the same day before he returned. The guy I'd chosen was a beefy Cuban named Pablo Torres, and I could tell from his hunched shoulders and downcast demeanor that the news he brought wasn't going to be to my liking. Pulling my horse away from the drive, I loped back to meet him.

My ramrod that trip was Casey Davis. Seeing me leave the herd, then spotting Pablo coming in at an angle from the direction of the Caloosahatchee River, Casey wheeled his mount and rode to join us. We met in the settling dust a quarter of a mile behind the herd. Pushing his broad-brimmed straw sombrero back on his head, Pablo mopped the sweat from his brow with a dirty sleeve.

"It is as you most feared," Torres said in a dust-cracked voice.

"Yankees?" Casey asked.

"Worse . . . bandits."

"Rustlers," I breathed, and Pablo nodded solemnly.

"How far back?" I asked.

"A few miles, but no more." He hesitated, then went on: "I stayed hidden in the trees and did not let them see me, but they know where we are. I think they only bide their time now."

"Waiting until we get closer to Punta Rassa," Casey said. "Letting us do the hard work, then they'll swoop in like vultures, stampede the herd, take what they can grab quick, and hightail it for the coast while we lose time gathering up what they scattered."

I saw it the same way. It was a common practice during those turbulent war years, and for quite a while afterward, too. "Did you get a good look at them?" I asked Pablo.

"Not so good, no, but I recognized their leader." He paused again, his eyes shifting uneasily from me to Casey, then back again. Finally he said: "No man rides a horse like Jacob Klee. He makes that little Cracker pony of his look like a dung beetle."

I swore quietly. I suppose I shouldn't have been surprised that it was Klees trailing us—they'd been a thorn in the

15

Flatiron's side ever since we moved onto the upper Pease River in 1848—but the last I'd heard, the bulk of the clan had scattered into the swamps early in the war to avoid Confederate conscripts.

I probably ought to add here that most of Florida's cow hunters and salters had been exempted from the draft because of our efforts to supply the South's armies. Most Klees lacked that exoneration, however, largely because the only cattle they dealt in had been stolen from someone else's range, a fact the draft board was well aware of.

With most of the good men away fighting Yankees, the cattle ranges all through Florida were just about overflowing with hardcases. But the Klees, well, they were their own little entity in that part of the world. Scattered like weeds across the southern half of the state, and probably three-quarters of them as crooked as a stream of piss in a high wind. Old Judah Klee was the patriarch of the clan, and about what you'd expect, with his wild long hair and a white beard halfway to his belly button. Jacob and Jubal were his middle-aged sons, not quite as shaggy as the old man, but just as ornery. As far as I'm concerned, the whole bunch was as underhanded as snake-oil salesmen, although, in time, some of those Klees would rise high in state politics, while others became lawyers and judges and county sheriffs and such.

Before Judah moved his extended family into the southern swamps, the Klees had squatted along the western shore of Lake Okeechobee in an almost fortress-like compound of run-down shacks and sagging *chickee* huts. In fairness, I'd never personally seen the place, but I didn't doubt the word of men who had. More than one had insisted that those lake-front hovels smelled worse than open privies, and I was inclined to believe that, too. Of course, when it comes to a Klee, I might be biased.

Dave Klee was one of Jubal's boys, one of the good ones, folks would say after his death, although I'd ask you this . . . if Dave Klee was so good, what was he doing with his uncle Jacob, skulking after our herd like a pack of slobbering wolves?

I'll tell you what, just knowing those boys were behind us sent a chill dribbling down my spine.

"How many?" I finally got around to asking Pablo.

"I think seven," was his vague reply. "Seven or eight. I could not get close enough to be sure."

"If they're going to hit us, it'll be soon," Casey said tautly. "We're getting too close to Punta Rassa for them to put it off much longer."

I nodded grim accord, but didn't immediately reply. In my mind I was picturing the route that still lay between us and the coast. Or at least what I knew of it. Although I'd been to Punta Rassa numerous times over the years, Pa had always avoided that land south of the Caloosahatchee because of its proximity to the Big Cypress Swamp, and the general marshy terrain that made travel there so difficult. It was a tough country to tramp under any circumstance, but pushing a herd of longhorns through those jungle-like forests, populated with water moccasins, rattlesnakes, and alligators, made it a nightmare of struggle and fatigue. The only reason I'd taken that herd so far south was because of the damned Yankees that Mr. Lincoln kept sending us.

I don't know how common this knowledge is, but with the Mississippi and most of the Confederacy's coastal ports closed off by the Union blockade, Florida was about the only source of meat the South had any more, and Lord knew we were sending a bunch of it up there, cattle and hogs both. But now that the North was transferring more troops down our way, reoccupying forts they'd abandoned at the beginning of the war—like Fort Myers, a couple of hours' ride east of Punta Rassa—the stakes were rising dramatically. I wasn't worried about Pa making it through with his three thousand head. He'd push that herd straight up the central part of the state, following the highlands into Georgia where the Federals hadn't yet ventured, but the odds for me and my crew were a bit tighter. And now, as if prowling Yankees, poisonous snakes, and hungry 'gators weren't enough, we had Jacob Klee and his gang to contend with.

Turning to Casey, I said: "We're not going to wait for them to jump us. We're going to take the fight to them."

"Suits me," Casey growled. "What do you want to do?"

"You remember that little thumb where we found the chestnut that time?"

"I ain't likely to forget."

I don't guess either of us would. We'd been on a drive to Punta Rassa with Pa and a small crew of drovers when Casey and I discovered the place. This was just after the war broke out in '61, and times hadn't seemed quite so perilous then, although I suspect we were just naïve in our thinking. At any rate, we were still north of the Caloosahatchee, following it southwest toward the lower ford at Fort Myers, when Casey and I crossed the river on a lark one evening after bedding the herd down for the night. Although we'd told Pa we were going to hunt for fresh meat, maybe some turkeys or a young deer to supplement the tough beef and beans we'd been eating, we were mostly just out on a ramble, a couple of young bucks filled with energy and aimless ambition.

We'd swum our horses across the river at a spot not too far from the herd, then ambled south toward the Big Cypress. I had my rifle resting across the saddle in front of me, a fine percussion Sharps in .54 caliber—a carbine, rightly, although I called it a rifle—while Casey toted Pa's shotgun. It was Casey who first spotted the horse, standing among the scattered palmettos and Spanish bayonets a couple of hundred yards away. We pulled up warily.

"That horse don't look so good," Casey declared after a few seconds, and I couldn't argue the point. The chestnut was swaying weakly back and forth, its head drooped low, its saddle hanging partway down its side with one stirrup dragging in the grass. And then the horse just keeled over.

"Son-of-a-bitch," Casey squawked, his head rearing back in surprise.

After a few seconds, I said—"Let's go take a look."—and lightly tapped my marshtackie's ribs with the sides of my stirrups. [*Ed. Note:* Marshtackie is a Southeastern term for a small, fleet-footed horse, similar in size and heritage to the Western mustang.]

The horse was—or had been—a fine, tall gelding, although it was ribby and full of ticks when we found it. Its left shoulder swarmed with buzzing flies, and its mane and tail were knotted with burrs and twigs. Despite the saddle hanging across its rib cage, there was no rider nearby. A bullet hole under the crawling flies confirmed the animal's cause of death; the drying blood and presence of maggots in the wound told us it had been shot quite a while before, then probably wandered out here on its own to die.

The horse had stopped on a spit of dry land that curved into the marsh like a giant thumb, although with an entrance barely twenty yards across. We did a quick search, but didn't find anyone, and didn't want to linger with darkness closing in. Jumping to the ground, I stripped the saddle—one of those Texas rigs with the tall horn and a high cantle—from the chestnut's back, while Casey loosened a lightly rusted, slightly shortened Model 1841 military musket, what we used to call a Mississippi rifle, from beneath the bedroll. Then, being just fifteen and easily spooked by thoughts of the supernatural, we lit out of there like we had goblins on our tails.

Several of us went back the next day for another look, but didn't have any better luck locating the rider. Satisfied that we'd done all we reasonably could, Pa ordered us on to Punta Rassa. Although we asked around town after we got there, nobody could recall a tall chestnut gelding, or a man toting a sawed-off Mississippi rifle. By the time we were ready to head back home, Pa declared the rifle as belonging to Casey, and I got the Texas rig.

As best as I recall, that afternoon when Pablo told us we were being trailed by Jacob Klee and some of his boys, we weren't too far away from that curling spit of land, and I told Casey to get the herd moving toward it.

"If we can reach Chestnut Thumb before dark, we can hold the cattle there with just a couple of hands," I said. "That'll free up the rest of us to fight, if Jake Klee wants to push it that far."

Casey nodded curtly and wheeled his horse toward the retreating herd. Pablo hesitated uncertainly, until I told him to go with Casey. I held my own mount back, eyeing the flat palmetto plains that stretched away to the east and north, dotted with distant hammocks of oak and hackberry that reminded me of stumps, although I knew the bigger trees in those groves could tower seventy-five feet or more above the ground, with enough lumber in just one of them to build a small house. [*Ed. Note:* Hammock is a Southern term, referring to confined growths of hardwood vegetation on ground usually somewhat higher than the surrounding terrain; they tend to be relatively small in size, generally no more than a few hundred yards in circumference.]

There was no sign of Jacob Klee or his men, but I knew that didn't mean much. Not in that Southern wilderness, as wild in those years as anything the American West would ever produce. There were too many places to hide, too many ways a group of determined men could slip in undetected, especially on something as unwieldy as a herd of longhorns.

My muscles were drawn tight from the prospect of a raid. I was young then, and unafraid as only the young can be, but anyone who has ever worked cattle knows what a burst of unexpected gun play can do to an unruly herd, especially one just recently yanked from the scrub. A stampede in that swampy morass south of the Caloosahatchee could cost us half our drive.

Letting my gaze sweep the distant horizon a final time, I pulled my marshtackie around and spurred after the herd. It was late enough in the day that I had to pull the broad brim of my gray slouch hat low over my eyes against the westering sun. Thick dust mantled the plain, and the cattle's lowing rose in protest to the quickened pace. We didn't have any dogs—Pa had taken all of them, including my own merle, Blue Boy, to help with the larger herd—but the sharp cracks of our whips, snapping above the bony spines of the resistant herd, were enough to keep the cattle contained and on the move. I unfurled my own twelve-footer as I came up behind a lagging roan steer, popping it sharp as a gunshot above the animal's tail to startle it after the rest of the herd.

My mind was only half on the task at hand as we pushed toward Chestnut Thumb. I was trying to take stock of the situation, weighing our odds and options. Although our situation wasn't the best, it could have been worse. I had eight men in my employ. Besides Casey and Pablo, there were Casey's younger cousin, Artie Davis, plus Roy Turner, Ardell Hawes, Dick Langley, Calvin Oswald, and Pa's slave, Negro Jim. [*Ed. Note:* Although the n-word of the 19th Century didn't have the same negative connotations as it does today, the editor of this edition of the transcript has decided to substitute the word Negro in its place.]

That was about the same number of men that Jacob Klee had, although with one notable difference. With the exception of Negro Jim, all of my hands were young, ranging in age from fifteen to eighteen, and were considerably less experienced in the ways of warfare. They were good men, don't get me wrong about that. Every one of us had been born on the cattle ranges of Southwestern Florida, raised in times of danger and strife. I didn't have any doubts whatsoever that they would fight with the best of them. To be honest, what worried me most were the decisions I knew I was going to have to make in the next few hours, and the fear that even the smallest miscalculation on my part could cost the life of one or more of my men, all of whom I considered friends. That's a chunk of responsibility to set on the shoulders of an eighteen-year-old; hell, it's a lot to hand to any man, no matter how much experience he has.

Negro Jim was riding point that day, and I urged my marshtackie up alongside his gray mule to outline my plans, sketchy as they were. He nodded solemnly as I spoke, although never taking his eyes off the herd.

"I reckon that sounds like something your daddy'd approve of," Jim replied after I'd finished.

I didn't say anything, but I was relieved by the old slave's inferred approval. Negro Jim had fought in the last two Seminole Wars with my pa, both of them scouting first for General Harney, then for Colonel Loomis during the Third War, what the locals called the Billy Bowlegs War. Jim knew his way around a battlefield, and would have found a way to let me know if he didn't agree with my plan, or saw any major flaws in my strategy.

I've always called Negro Jim old, but he really wasn't. Probably fifty or so in those years, and only aged and stolid in the eyes of a bunch of rowdy teen-agers. Jim had been a part of the Flatiron for as long as I could remember, the first of the four slaves that we'd eventually own, and Pa's right-hand man until us boys got old enough to shoulder more of the responsibilities.

I knew Jim would fight, too, if he had to. The stories Pa told of him and Jim and my ma withstanding a three-day siege during the Second Seminole War can still send a shiver up my spine. But I wouldn't ask him to participate if I didn't have to. It was never a good thing in the South to arm a Negro against a white man, even a bunch of egg-suckers like those Judah Klee had spawned.

As I reined away from Jim, I spotted Roy Turner loping a chunky sorrel in my direction, and slowed my own pony to allow him to catch up. Roy was Frank Turner's youngest, and in more or less the same boat as I was when it came to his father's ranch. Roy had also been left behind while his pa and brothers went up the trail with my pa. The Turners owned the Slash T, and ran cattle over all that land between the Kissimmee River and Arbuckle Creek, east of the Flatiron range. Being headstrong and hot-tempered, Roy didn't waste any time getting to the point.

"Casey says Jacob Klee and some of his boys are following us, and that we're going to fight."

"I figured we would, unless you've got a reason not to."

"Not a damned one," he returned hotly.

Like the Flatiron, the Slash T had also been hit hard by rustlers since the war's beginning, but things had taken a definite turn for the worse since the Federal reoccupation of Fort Myers. Where before we'd maybe lose a few head at a time, in recent months we'd been having bunches of twenty or thirty head at a time vanish, as if snatched into the sky by hungry gods.

A lot of those losses could be laid at the feet of Union troops, who were stealing our cattle in ever-increasing numbers for their own armies under the sweep of Lincoln's Confiscation Act. [*Ed. Note:* Although the Confiscation Act of 1861, signed into law by President Lincoln on August 6th, was designed primarily to appropriate slaves held by Southern property owners, thereby preventing the use of black labor in order to free up able-bodied white men to fight the North, all Confederate property was deemed admissible; acts of confiscation increased with the war's duration.]

Those things the Yankees wanted but couldn't steal, they bought from men like Jacob Klee. Some said even old Judah Klee himself would occasionally fork a marshtackie and venture out of the swamps to steal some cattle or hogs, just to keep his hand in the game.

We were pushing pretty hard that day I'm telling you about, what with the light running its string and the Thumb still several miles away. We were following a winding thread of dry land bordering the northern rim of the Big Cypress, the country on either side of us becoming increasingly marshy the farther we went. The dust took on a reddish tint as the sun eased down atop the horizon, and the cattle bawled raucously at our unfamiliar urgency. The steady cracking of our whips and the grit-thickened voices of the cow hunters kept the herd moving along at a swift trot, although I knew not a popper touched a hide. [*Ed. Note:* A popper is the tip of a bullwhip, sometimes consisting of a small amount of lead sewn into the leather to give the instrument extra crack.]

Every one of us on that drive had been handling bullwhips since we were old enough to stand on two legs. It was the hallmark of the Florida cow hunter, where the lariat of the wide open spaces of the West was too easily tangled in the swampy scrub of the Southeast. The whips were used for the ear-splitting cracks that gave the herd both incentive and direction. In more sedate times we would have had catch dogs to help us work the herd, thick-chested curs born of the swamps and marshes, and as bred to the art of cow hunting as the men they assisted.

The sun was nearly gone by the time we reached the Thumb,

just a crown of gold set down on the horizon. I sent Jim and Roy ahead to turn the herd onto the narrow spit, then ordered the right flankers to move up and help. As soon as the last cow had been driven through the narrow opening at the Thumb's base, I had two of the boys string picket ropes from one side of the entrance to the other, tying the makeshift gate off on sturdy palmettos.

While they were doing that, Casey and Roy made a quick circuit of the Thumb looking for alligators—a big 'gator could pull even a moderately sized cow under without much difficulty if they caught the bovine unaware—and Jim eased his mule into the herd to shy out the two pack horses we'd brought along to carry our grub and supplies, which included our long guns and extra ammunition. Dick Langley and Ardell Hawes caught the horses and led them forward, although we left the packs in place. I didn't know how long we were going to be there, or what Jacob Klee and his boys might have in mind, and I wanted to be ready in case we had to make a run for it.

Jim dismounted and began passing out rifles and shotguns, and Artie jumped down to help. As a rule we didn't carry our long guns while working cattle, as they had a tendency to get in the way, although we naturally wore our revolvers. They were a tool, like a knife or a hoof pick, and didn't do anyone any good packed away where they couldn't be easily reached.

After collecting my Sharps, I laid it across the saddle in front of me and reined out of the way of the others. Then I slid the strap of my leather shooting bag over my left shoulder so that it hung down on my right side, just above the Colt Navy revolver Pa had given me for my fourteenth birthday. The bag was a holdover from my muzzleloader days, although minus the powder horn. It's where I kept extra ammunition and some small tools and cleaning supplies while in the field. It took only a few seconds to slip a linen cartridge into the Sharps' breech, then press a musket cap down over the nipple.

Although still light in the west, dusk seemed to be settling all too quickly over the countryside. The night sounds were already in progress—frogs and insects and the piercing screams of limpkins that could rattle a man's nerves if he didn't know what they were. From the direction of the Caloosahatchee, a wolf's lonely howl floated across the scrub. Calling the others close, I quickly outlined my plans, then ordered Calvin Oswald and Dick Langley to stay behind with Jim to guard the herd—Calvin because he was the youngest at fifteen, and Dick because, although only a few months shy of his eighteenth birthday, he had a wife and newborn son back at his cabin at Lake Istok-poga.

"Them cows ain't likely to drop off into the swamp, so all you'll probably have to do is keep them from slipping out on this side and making a break for the river," I said. "The rest of you can come with me."

I paused briefly, noticing the taut anxiety of their expressions, the grim resolve in their eyes. My gaze strayed briefly over our collection of firearms. Although we all had pistols, not everyone owned a long gun. I had my Sharps, of course, another gift from Pa, this one for my tenth birthday, with my name and the date engraved on the brass patch box, and Casey had his shortened Mississippi rifle, picked up not one hundred yards from where we were sitting our saddles that night. Pablo had a pair of revolvers and a shotgun, and Roy Turner and Ardell Hawes each carried sturdy, full-stock muzzleloaders of traditional Kentucky design—most of our guns in those days had to be loaded from the front; my Sharps and Artie's modified Joslyn were the only breechloaders in the crew—but Calvin just owned his handgun, and Dick Langley had only a single-barreled shotgun in addition to a twin-barreled percussion pistol. [*Ed. Note:* McCallister is probably referring to the Joslyn Model

1855 Navy version here, in .58 caliber.] Negro Jim had the double-barreled shotgun Pa had given him during the Indian Wars, although he'd never admit ownership where a white man might overhear him.

All in all, our armament wasn't half bad, but I knew Klee's men would have better. Outlaws usually did.

The flesh along both of my arms was tingling as I led my crew back onto the narrow ribbon of dry ground we'd been following toward the coast. I'll admit the country wasn't exactly the way I remembered it from when Casey and I found the chestnut there in '61. It seemed a lot swampier, for one thing, with sloughs on every side, and the main trail had narrowed to less than eighty yards across. In some ways that was going to work to our advantage, as it would force Jacob Klee and his men within range of our guns. On the other hand, it wasn't going to give us much wiggle room, if we needed to wiggle in a hurry.

You might be asking yourself why we all seemed so hell-bent on a fight that evening, but I can only argue that you weren't there. I will say this. Even with all the jabbering I've done so far, I don't think you can really understand what we were up against. There wasn't one of us there who had any doubt whatsoever about Jacob Klee's intentions. If it wasn't our herd he and his boys were after, they wouldn't have been so far south of the Caloosahatchee, swatting mosquitoes and dodging rattlesnakes and water moccasins and short-tempered alligators the whole way. Nor would they have been following us, hanging back like Pablo said, but never very far away. No, they were after our cattle, and we didn't intend to let them have them. At least not without a fight. And if we were going to tangle, I wanted it to be where the Flatiron had some control of the situation, and not have a raid sprung on us unexpected.

It was fairly late by the time Jacob Klee and his men showed up. Twilight hung over the plain like a fog, and bats hogged the sky. I had my men spread across the trail with our rifles and shotguns in full view. The Klees advanced similarly, armed to the teeth with an assortment of long guns, all of them out in the open and ready to buck. As they drew close, I remembered Pablo's words from that afternoon.

No man rides a horse like Jacob Klee. He makes that little Cracker pony of his look like a dung beetle.

Most of those Cracker ponies, what we called marshtackies, were small, finely proportioned animals, descended from stock left behind by Spanish explorers. Like the Western mustang, marshtackies had evolved over the centuries to suit their environment. They are quick, sure-footed, and as swamp-savvy as any old-time Seminole. Marshtackies are the horse of choice for those who make their living prying longhorns out of the scrub. They generally run about thirteen to fourteen hands, but Jacob's horse was a lot shorter. Probably no more than eleven hands. [*Ed. Note:* A hand equals four inches, the approximate width of a man's palm laid side-by-side up a horse's foreleg and ending at the withers.]

A lot of people made fun of Jacob Klee and his tiny horses, but a lot more were angered by it, and not just his rough handling of the bit, but the loads he'd pile on them. I'm guessing the man weighed close to three hundred pounds by himself. Include a brace of revolvers, a rifle, plus his saddle and tack, and it added up. Just for comparison, three hundred pounds is about half what a full-grown scrub cow weighed in those days. Folks sympathetic to the Klees—and there were those, too—said the reason Jacob preferred shorter mounts was because of his arthritic knees and massive calves, not to mention having to haul all that bulk into his saddle, but most of us weren't inclined to forgive the man for his selfishness.

Jacob hauled up about sixty yards away, and his men quickly

fanned out to either side of him. As soon as they did, I realized
Pablo had either miscounted their numbers, or hadn't seen
Jacob's whole crew. I counted an even dozen men in the rapidly
fading light, half again our number, and I've got to admit my
throat went as dry as an old cornhusk. A strained silence hung
over the trail for perhaps a full minute. Then Klee shouted:
"Clear the way, McCallister! We're coming through!"

You might consider my reply reckless. "Go around!" I yelled.

Even from so far away, I clearly heard the grumbling that followed my response. Finally Jacob held up a hand, and his men
fell silent. "I'll not suffer the whims of a fool, nor the howling of
pups. It's a free country, and I mean to pass."

"You've been trailing us for two days or more," was my
return. "You've had plenty of time to go around, if that was
your intent."

"Where I go and how fast I get there is still my business,
youngster. Don't think the name of McCallister cuts any sign
with me."

I hesitated, and in the silence Artie said: "Maybe we ought to
pull back, Boone. Let 'em pass to the north."

"Bullshit!" Roy Turner bristled. "That's just what them
skunks want, to get ahead of us. Then they can set up an ambush
somewhere down the trail where we ain't expecting it."

"They can rush us from the back just as easy as they can
from the front," Artie argued.

"Hush," Casey chided. "Boone's bossing this outfit. It's him
that will decide."

Well, it was a McCallister herd, for a fact, and no denying the
decision was mine to make, but I'll confess my resolve was
starting to buckle. I would have given just about anything to
ride back and ask Jim what he thought I should do, but asking a
Negro for his opinion on anything simply wasn't done in those
days. Glancing uncertainly at Casey, I said: "Maybe Artie's

right. Let's pull back and let them pass, but keep our guns handy, just in case."

"Dammit, Boone," Roy hissed through clenched teeth, but Casey cut him off before he could get started.

"Come on, boys, let's give those murdering cut-throats the trail," Casey said, and I couldn't tell from his voice or his words whether or not he agreed with me.

I waited until everyone had pulled back alongside Negro Jim and Calvin and Dick, then raised my voice for Klee and his boys to hear. "The road is yours, Jacob. Pass on by, but don't stop where we can see the light of your campfire tonight, or we're liable to come calling."

That brought only rough laughter from the Klee faction, and I began to wonder if I'd done the right thing. Some men would see wisdom in my retreat from the road, but others would view it as weakness, with the belief that if I did it once, I'd surely do it again. Jacob Klee would fall into that latter category.

As Klee and his men kicked their mounts forward, I reined out of their way. I watched warily as the gang fell into line behind their corpulent leader. Although they carried their rifles out where they would be quick to swing into action, I wasn't especially alarmed, as we were doing the same. Still, I was caught off guard when the man riding immediately behind Jacob let his shotgun fall over the crook of his left arm and pulled the trigger.

A gray-white cloud of powder smoke blossomed from its muzzle, center-punched by a flash of smoky yellow and a bright, arching stigma of crimson. Buckshot screamed past my left shoulder, and someone behind me hollered in pain and surprise. Then all hell broke loose, with guns banging out on every side and men yelling and cursing as they either sought shelter or fled.

Spilling from my saddle, I slapped my marshtackie's rump

with the barrel of my rifle to drive it out of the line of fire, then threw myself to the earth, lead whistling past my ears all the way down. Even though my view from the ground was hampered by clumps of palmetto and Spanish bayonet, I managed to squeeze off a single shot before the rustlers could scatter and take cover.

The Sharps slammed back firmly against my shoulder, spitting out its own dingy brume that briefly obscured the flat plain in front of me. Working swiftly, I lowered the trigger guard to expose the rear of the chamber and inserted a fresh linen cartridge from my shooting bag. As I slapped the lever closed, I could feel the soft tear of cloth as the upper edge of the breech sliced off the rear of the cartridge, like a pair of scissors snipping off the tip of a fine cigar. With the powder inside the chamber exposed, I thumbed a fresh cap over the nipple, then eared the hammer back to full cock. Altogether it probably didn't take me twenty seconds to reload, yet by the time I was ready to fire again, the field in front of me was empty. There wasn't a Klee in sight.

Cursing under my breath, I rose cautiously to my knees. As soon as I did, a shot rang out from the scrub on my left, the bullet whump-thumping a foot or so above my head in that peculiar whine anyone who has ever been a target on the plains will instantly recognize—and anyone who hasn't, I'd wager, never will. I swung instinctively toward the billowing cloud of gunsmoke that was scooting through the palmetto like a feral hog, and shouldered my rifle. Although most of Klee's men had vanished into the gloaming, I spotted one of them darting into the scrub about eighty yards away, and snapped off a shot before he could disappear. My bullet raised a startled squawk and a hearty obscenity, although I was fairly sure that I'd missed. I'll have to admit, though, that his response brought a satisfied grin to my mug.

31

After that last shot, an unearthly silence enveloped the flat, as if the normal night sounds had been struck mute. I reloaded by feel, keeping my eyes rolling across the empty plain. Hearing the scud of boots coming up on my right, I started to swing in that direction, but it was only Casey, coming through the palmetto in a bent-over run that reminded me of an armadillo scurrying for the woodpile.

"Dang it, Boone, are you OK?"

"Yeah, I'm fine. How about you?"

"I ain't bleeding nowhere obvious, but I sure as hell figured you for a goner, the way you tumbled out of your saddle. We all thought you'd been shot plumb center."

A self-conscious grin tugged at my lips. "No, just scared and in a hurry. Is anyone hurt?"

"Artie got his arm punched by a chunk of buckshot, but it ain't bad enough to kill him. It sounds like a couple of cows got hit, too, from the way they're bawling."

I could suddenly hear the cattle again, above the tentative croaking of frogs, and realized that life was returning to normal in the scrub. From where I was crouched, the cows' lowing didn't sound panicked, like it would have if one or more of the animals had been seriously injured. All in all, I figured we got off pretty lucky.

"Did you see where they went?" Casey asked.

"No, I was hoping you did."

"I guess me and the boys were too busy ducking to pay much attention, although Calvin said he thought a bunch of 'em made a run for those trees yonder." He nodded toward a hammock about three hundred yards away, looking like a column of black coal propping up a violet sky.

"Did he say how many?" I asked.

"He didn't."

I was still squinting in the direction of the hammock, trying to decide what our options were, when a sound unlike anything I'd ever heard before rose from the scrub to our left, near where the man I'd taken my last shot at had disappeared—a piercing screech raking at the dark belly of the sky. I've heard panthers shriek in ways that can curdle your blood, especially when they're close by and it's after dark, but this was far more harrowing than that. Then a single pistol shot came from the direction of the scream, followed by an abrupt silence, so deep it felt like we'd been dropped to the bottom of a lake.

"Jesus Christ," Casey gasped. "What was that?"

I was so startled, I didn't even attempt a guess. From the Thumb, I heard Roy calling for Casey, his voice taut with fear.

"We're here!" Casey shouted. "We're both here. Boone's all right."

"Stay where you are and watch the herd!" I bellowed on the tail end of Casey's reassurances, then gave my ramrod a troubled glance. "You reckon it might be a trick to draw us away from the cattle?"

After a pause, Casey shook his head. "That sounded too real to be fake."

As if in agreement, Jacob Klee's voice echoed from the distant hammock. "Davey! Davey Klee, are you OK?"

"Son-of-a-bitch," I swore softly. Then, after a pause: "I guess we'd better go take a look."

"Are you crazy? If we cross paths out there with Jacob or his men, it'll mean a fight for sure."

"It's already a fight, Case. Come on, I want to see what's going on."

Staying in a crouch, we swiftly made our way through the palmetto, me up front and Casey tight on my heels. I had an idea of where the sound had come from, and didn't slow down until we were fairly close. Finally dropping to one knee, I waited for Casey to come up beside me. The edge of the slough lay directly in front of us, its shore crowded with cat-tails and ferns and clumps of sedge, a maze-like collar I found myself reluctant to enter.

"We don't have to do this," Casey whispered as if reading my mind.

"No, but I guess we will." I thumbed the Sharps' big side hammer to full cock, then cautiously eased into the bracken flanking the slough. My scalp was twitching like it wanted to jump off my skull and take flight, and when I look back on that evening now, I'm not so sure it didn't have the right idea.

Although we hadn't wasted any time getting there, I was no longer in a hurry. Moving through the tall grass, planting each foot with care as my eyes probed the deeper shadows surrounding us, I tried to shut out the self-doubt that dogged my every step. After about twenty yards, I felt Casey's hand on my arm.

"Hold up, Boone," he whispered, then nodded toward the smooth black water of the slough. "What's that?"

Following the direction of his gaze, I spotted a patch of white cloth floating several yards out. At first I couldn't make out what it was. Then something seemed to twitch unnaturally beneath the fabric, and I grunted as if punched hard in the kidneys. "It's a man."

"Oh, hell, it is," Casey breathed.

I took my hat off long enough to pull the shooting bag off my shoulder, then handed that and my rifle to Casey.

"What are you doing?"

"Whoever it is, he's moving. I'm going to go fetch him in."

Casey's grip tightened on my arm. "You smell that?"

I hesitated, shaking my head. The fact is, I couldn't smell much of anything after all the gunsmoke I'd inhaled. Yet when I concentrated, I was able to pick out a couple of familiar odors, filtered through the thick, sulphury stench of burnt powder that lingered over the plain. One of those smells was blood, which I knew didn't come from either me or Casey. The other was a heavy, musk-like odor I remembered all too well from past excursions into the swamps.

"That's a 'gator."

"You damned well better believe it's a 'gator," Casey said earnestly. "Close by, too."

My gaze returned to the patch of white fabric floating on the water's surface. Once again, I thought I saw it move. Or was that only a trick of the poor light and my own jittery imagination? Then I heard a groan, followed by a faint splashing as an arm moved in the water, and I said: "I've got to get him out of there, Casey. We can't just walk away."

"You think Jacob Klee would do the same for you?"

I knew the answer to that without even pondering it. He wouldn't. But I wasn't Jacob Klee, and I hoped never to become like him. I said just about that same thing to Casey, then pulled my arm free. "Keep an eye out for that 'gator," I said.

"Dammit, Boone, I ain't never gonna see that 'gator in this light. I probably couldn't see him if it was full-on noon, not if he came at you from below."

"I ain't got a choice, Case," I replied tersely. "Just watch close, and if you see so much as a ripple, sing out."

"The only ripple I'm going to see is the one you make when that reptile pulls you under," he replied glumly. Moving up to the very edge of the slough, he propped my Sharps against his hip where it would be easy to grab, then shouldered his own rifle. The ratcheting of the Mississippi's big lock as it was thumbed all the way back sounded like the tolling of a distant bell in my ears.

There was a lot of shouting off to the west, from the direction of the hammock where Jacob Klee and his boys had taken shelter, but I couldn't make out who it was or what he was saying. Later on, Artie would tell me it was Jacob, trying to get a fix on the men who weren't with him in the trees, and wondering who had screamed. Jacob may have been curious, but I noticed he wasn't in any great hurry to venture out of his snug little hidey-hole to investigate.

Dropping my gun belt in the grass, I stepped gingerly into the slough's black water. It was March, and cooler than you might imagine for being so far south. Or maybe that was just my own gut-numbed feelings as I inched toward the still floating body. The water rose quickly at first, then seemed to level off about hip-deep. Thick mud sucked at my boots, threatening to pull them off even as it slowed my progress to an awkward plod.

My eyes swept the smooth surface of the water, following the gentle, outward flow of ripples that marked my progress, looking for any that weren't of my own making. Inexplicably my teeth began to chatter, and I began making small, inane noises far back in my throat. I've seen alligators pull dogs, colts, even full-grown cattle under water, dragging them beneath the surface in what the 'gladers call a death roll, until their quarry drowns and can be hauled back to the big reptile's underwater lair. There, the carcass is left to rot, the bones cleaned at leisure. I've also seen the half-eaten corpse of a man who had been caught by one of these wily beasts, then dragged ashore by a companion after the 'gator had been killed. Those were the memories that were most vivid in my mind as I moved deeper into the slough.

Although I could logically tell myself that this couldn't have been a very big 'gator, otherwise it wouldn't have left such a valuable prize floating so close to shore, I was having a hard time convincing my legs of that. Logic can seem like a foreign creature at times, and is often at odds with what a man feels deep in his guts, and what I was feeling that night wasn't going to be quelled by something as wimp-kneed as rationalization.

Fact is, I had fear racing up and down my spine like a child's yo-yo, puckering more parts of my anatomy than I care to acknowledge. I think if I'd heard so much as a frog croak nearby, I would have shot straight up out of that slough like I had rockets on my boots, instead of spurs. [*Ed. Note:* Although a seemingly modern toy, references to yo-yos can be traced back as far as 500 B.C.] Luckily the nearby brush remained deathly quiet, and although it seemed like hours, it probably wasn't even a full minute after stepping into the water that I was able to grab that guy's collar and start hauling him to shore.

As strange as it may seem, I believe I was more frightened coming back than I was going out. I was sure as heck moving a lot faster, and making more noise than a smart man ought to with 'gators nearby. To be honest, if I'd lost my grip on the guy's shirt, I'm not sure I would have gone back for him. Fortunately I didn't, and it wasn't long before I was clambering ashore, Casey reaching out to help me drag my grisly cargo onto the bank.

Safe on dry ground, I fell forward onto my hands and knees with my heart clattering like one of those old Singer sewing machines. After catching my breath, I scooted back on my hands and knees to peer into the slack face of the man I'd rescued. That was the first time I realized who it was.

I think I've already mentioned that David Klee was Jubal's boy, not Jacob's, although the way all those Klees ran together, it was often difficult to remember who belonged to whom. I knew Dave pretty well, though. He used to work the docks at Tampa before the war, punching cows up that long, cypress-wood pier from the holding pens onto the decks of Gulf-bound cargo ships. At one time or another, he'd worked for most of the cattle buyers around Tampa, and was generally well-liked by the cow hunters who sold their herds there. Folks used to say Dave would someday be a man to be reckoned with, and a lot of people believed he would eventually become an independent buyer, maybe even have his own dock and scow. Of course that was before the war brought everything between the Ten Thousand Islands and Tampa Bay to a grinding halt, forcing the cattle trade toward smaller ports along the coast like Punta Rassa and Punta Gorda, and smaller, faster sailing vessels.

I reckon if any Klee could have done it, it would have been Dave, but I knew as soon as I looked into his face that night that he wasn't ever going to punch another cow across anyone's wharf, let alone his own.

"Sweet Lord," Casey breathed. He was staring at what remained of Dave's right leg, not that there was much to it. I noticed that the spurting blood from a severed artery was already starting to lessen. Meeting my eyes, Casey said: "This boy's dying, Boone."

I gave him a sharp look, but didn't say anything. Dave's eyelids were fluttering, and I wasn't sure that he couldn't hear what we were saying. Leaning close, I said as gently as possible: "Dave. Dave Klee."

The lids quivered some more, then peeled back. "Did . . . did I get him?"

"Did you get who?"

" 'Gator, big . . . big ol' boy. I think I. . . ." His right hand was moving clumsily over the empty holster at his waist, and I remembered the solitary report I'd heard immediately after his scream.

"You must've got him," I said. "He ain't around now."

Dave nodded weakly. "Good, it's good I . . . I killed the sumbitch, 'cause he sure as hell killed me."

I started to tell him that he was wrong, that the wound wasn't all that bad and that he'd likely pull through once we got some bandages on it, but then changed my mind. Although it may

38

sound cruel, I'm glad I didn't lie to him that night, his last on earth.

"Your uncle's still out there," I said. "I reckon he'll take you home, if that's where you want to be buried."

Dave laughed softly, nearly choking when the sound hung up in his throat. Then he closed his eyes and turned his head away. Thinking he was going to say something else, I waited for him to go on. It took a moment to realize he'd already passed on.

"Sweet Lord," Casey repeated, sitting back on his calves. "What just happened here, Boone?"

"I reckon a man died," I replied, feeling kind of cut adrift myself as I stared down at the waxen figure before me.

"Davey!"

Casey and I both flinched. That was old Jacob Klee himself—I would have recognized that dull, bass bellow anywhere—and he wasn't very far away, either. Scrambling to our feet, I slid the shooting bag over my shoulder, then quickly buckled the gun belt around my waist. Casey handed me the Sharps.

"Davey, god dammit, where are you?" the old man thundered.

"We'd better scoot," Casey said in my ear. "You know that old goat ain't coming in here alone."

I nodded agreement. "Go on. I'll be right behind you."

"Boone."

"He's over here!" I shouted, and Casey jumped as if he'd just sat down on a prickly pear pad.

"What are you doing?" he demanded.

"Hold on," I whispered.

"Where?" Jacob demanded.

"Next to the slough, about twenty yards east of that dead cypress tree. Follow the shore. You can't miss him."

Well, we were backing off even as I spoke, and as soon as I was done, we spirited out of there as fast and quiet as we could. We hadn't quite made it all the way back to the Thumb when I heard the roar of a man's voice, filled with rage and raw anguish. It lasted just a few seconds, before fading off like a wolf's howl, but I shivered as if caught in a cool draft.

"Damn you, McCallister!" that old man ranted. "Damn you to hell. You'll pay for this. I'll make you bleed, boy. I'll make all of you bleed, until there's no more McCallister blood left to spill. Do you hear me? Do you hear what I'm promising you? On the Good Book, boy. I'm swearing it on the Lord's own words."

"That old bastard is as crazy as a limpkin," Casey whispered.

"He's sure mad right now."

Jacob's threats went on like that for quite a while, long enough for me and Casey to make our way back to the Thumb's entrance, where the others were waiting with their guns handy. In time the words began to grow fainter, and I realized Klee was retreating toward the hammock. There was no lessening of the bitter rage that infused his words, though; it stained the night like bile from a punctured gut, and affected everyone there that night, even though the threats were directed only at me. At least in the beginning. In time they would grow to include all of us, but no matter how twisted the story became, I was always the ringleader, always the core of evil that hatched the dirty deed.

Eventually the old man's words faded out altogether, and we began to stir uncertainly. Coming up beside me, Ardell Hawes said: "He's hurting pretty bad right now, Boone, but he'll cool off."

"Sure," I replied, and I won't deny the shakiness of my words. "He'll cool off."

But I didn't believe it. Not even then. I don't think any of us did.

Excerpted from:
Scrub Cattle and Cracker Horses:
A Brief Description of the Florida Frontier
by
Anne Nichols
Host Publishing, 1979

Distant horizons and dusty cattle trails evoke images of the American West in the minds of many, but those scenes might just as easily apply to Florida during that state's raucous frontier era. In a land of mouse-ear hats, space travel, and thriving citrus orchards, it's difficult to imagine an era of hard-riding cowboys, range-war lynchings, rowdy cow towns, and six-gun justice, but Florida's unique history supplies all of that, and quite a lot more.

Florida's "scrub" cattle share a common heritage with the longhorns of Texas and California fame, as all of these herds were initially brought to the New World aboard Spanish galleons. . . .

The first recorded history of cattle in Florida came with Ponce De Leon's efforts to colonize the Charlotte Harbor area in 1521. . . . [After] an attack by the Calusas Indians, De Leon's expedition fled to Cuba, leaving behind several head of Andalusian cattle. These animals eventually joined with herds from other failed attempts to settle the peninsula, and gradually evolved into the Florida longhorn of today.

Organized cattle ranching began in 1565 . . . [and] by the latter half of the 19th Century, Florida was the nation's leading exporter of beef, shipping large numbers of scrub cows to markets in the Caribbean. . . . The state currently ranks in the top fifteen for cattle production. [*Ed. Note:* In 2006, Florida ranked 12th in the number of cattle owned, combining beef and dairy breeds.]

41

★ ★ ★ ★ ★

Traits [of scrub cattle] include a smaller body, with most females and steers averaging between 400 and 600 pounds, although mature bulls can reach 800 pounds or more. Unlike their distant Texas cousins, the horns of Florida's scrub cattle are shorter, probably due to the state's denser foliage. Considered "wiry" by most standards . . . colors range from white to black, but a brindled tan or sorrel seems to be most common. . . .

Open range continued in Florida until the instigation of a fever tick [Texas fever] eradication program in the early 1920s, nearly 40 years after most Western ranges were closed by barbed wire.

SESSION TWO

It was two more days of hard travel from where Dave Klee was killed by an alligator to a stand of sand pines some miles east of Punta Rassa, where I intended to hold the herd until a deal could be arranged with Ashworth. We were so near the coast by then that I could smell the briny scent of the Gulf, wafting inland on a westerly breeze, and the harsh cries of shore birds as they circled overhead.

Loping my marshtackie up alongside Jim's gray mule, I used the handle of my bullwhip to point out a broad clearing amid the pines a couple of hundred yards to the south. "We'll hole up in there for the night, but don't light any fires," I told him. "How much food do we have in our packs?"

"That don't need fire fixin'? We got cold grits and a little of that side pork we could eat raw, I s'pose."

I couldn't help wincing at the older man's suggestion. I've eaten raw meat, including bacon, more than once, but it was never anything I enjoyed. "Hand out the grits, but keep the pork hidden," I said. "It won't kill anyone to go to bed hungry."

"They ain't gonna like not havin' a fire to gather 'round after dark."

"They'll live," I predicted, then wheeled my 'tackie around the front of the herd to where Dick Langley was riding right point that day.

Except for Jim, whose experience I wanted up front on the left, between the herd and the deeper swamps to the south, I

43

tried to regularly rotate the crew through the various positions of a cattle drive. Swing riders flanked the herd and kept it moving in a straight line; drag riders brought up the rear, swallowing dust and cursing the boss, which was me on that trip, although I've ridden drag enough to appreciate their bellyaching. But it was the point riders whose job was most vital. They were the ones who kept the herd on course, making sure it didn't veer off or become bogged down in deep jungle or quicksand. That's why I always kept Jim up front, and made sure the others knew they were to follow his advice if Casey or I wasn't around. Jim couldn't give orders, of course. None of the hands would have accepted that from a slave, but I think everyone there realized that old Negro had more range experience than all the rest of us combined.

Riding alongside Dick, I nodded toward the tall pines. "We'll bed 'em down in there."

Dick nodded his OK. "They ought to be wore down enough by now not to scatter."

He was probably right—we'd been pushing pretty hard the last few days, eager to get the herd into Punta Rassa and complete our transaction—but I wasn't going to tempt fate by taking any unnecessary chances. Not this close to the end of the drive.

"They might be, but keep a tight guard on them, anyway," I said. "We're close enough to Fort Myers now that I swear I can smell Yankee."

Chuckling, Dick said: "Likely you just stepped in some cow shit this morning. Nothing scraping off the bottom of your boots wouldn't fix."

"That's a possibility, too," I acknowledged, forcing a grin I didn't really feel. Reining off to the side, I studied the northwestern horizon while waiting for Casey to come up. Fort Myers, and the little community that had sprung up around it, was too far away to be seen from where we were, but I was concerned that the dust churned up by our herd—or too many sharp, popping cracks from a cow hunter's whip—could reach the eyes or ears of someone from the fort. Especially if that person was outside the post, away from the usual noises of the village and garrison.

Casey had already spotted Jim and Dick bending the herd toward the clearing, and although I suspect he'd likely guessed my intentions, he asked anyway: "That where you plan to squat for the night?"

"Figured we would. It's solid ground and the grass is good. I'll ride into Punta Rassa after dark and hunt up Ashworth. If everything's all right, we'll run the herd in at first light tomorrow. With a little luck, we'll be back in the scrub before those damned Yankees at Fort Myers start blowing their morning bugles."

"You going in alone?"

"Yeah . . . why? Do you want to come along?"

"No, not me, but you ought to take Punch. Have a doctor look at that arm of his."

Punch was Artie Davis, Casey's cousin, who'd caught a round of buckshot in our little skirmish with Jacob Klee and his boys back at the Thumb. We'd started calling him Punch that same night, after Casey kidded him about being punched in the arm with a chunk of lead. The name had stuck, but no one was joking about it any more. The flesh around the wound was starting to look red and angry, and I decided Casey's idea to take Punch into town with me was a good one, even though I doubted we'd find a doctor. I'm not certain Punta Rassa ever had its own physician, but I knew it hadn't since the war's beginning. Any man with even a rudimentary knowledge of medicine had long since been conscripted into the military.

"I'll do that," I told Casey. "Let's get the herd settled first.

Pass the word that I don't want anyone using their whips any more than they have to until we've put some more distance between us and Fort Myers. I've already told Jim not to build a fire."

He glanced my way curiously. "You feeling edgy, Boone?"

"I'm not going to breathe easy until we're all back in the scrub," I admitted.

Casey nodded soberly, then loped after a red steer that was trying to slip away from the herd. I pulled off to one side, keeping a worried eye on the thick dust the herd was churning into the sky. Although a stiff breeze off the Gulf was keeping the clouds low among the tops of the palm trees, I couldn't help a certain amount of apprehension, as close as we were to Myers.

The cattle were tired and didn't cause any problems as they slowly fanned out among the trees and began to graze. The grass was about as good as any we'd seen since leaving the Flatiron, bright green from the moisture of the Big Cypress and knee-high to a tall horse. The herd would do well there, and likely settle down to chew their cuds as soon as darkness fell. If something didn't come along to spook them overnight, they'd probably still be bedded down when the sun came up the next day.

We gathered on the north side of the herd after sundown to wolf down a supper of cold grits and some strips of raw cabbage palm Ardell had brought along in his packs. Poor fixings by most accounts, but not too bad if you're hungry, and we were all about half starved. You'll find most teenage boys can put away a heap of food at mealtime, and, save for Jim, we were no exception.

We washed our meal down with water from our canteens, and you might be surprised to learn that I probably used a canteen as much in Florida as I did running cattle up the trails from Texas. I'll not deny there is a lot more water per acre in the Peninsula State, but that didn't mean much to a cow hunter stuck out in the middle of a flat, dusty plain, an hour's ride from the nearest creek.

With dusk turning thick as gumbo around us, I told Punch to grab our rifles and follow me. He didn't waste time asking foolish questions, but just hauled his modified Joslyn and my Sharps from one of the packs and met me at the edge of the pines.

There's a reason there weren't any settlements—nor many cabins, for that matter—south of the Caloosahatchee in 1864. It was because in those days, all of that land east and south of Punta Rassa was nothing but a woolly tangle of black-water marshes, sloughs, mangrove hammocks, and outright swamps—tentacles from the Big Cypress pushing up into the belly of the state's cattle ranges.

Still, you could find your way through even that morass if you were smart enough to let your horse do most of the navigating. It was dangerous, though. Twice we had to rein around hissing 'gators we couldn't see in the ink-like darkness, and once the nearly overwhelming, cucumber-like smell of a water moccasin became so powerful I thought my horse was going to start pitching—not the reaction you're looking for in that kind of an environment. Yet we eventually made it, breaking free of the scrub several hours before midnight to circle the nearly empty cattle pens east of town.

Keeping our rifles unslung, we made our way cautiously down Punta Rassa's broad, sandy thoroughfare. We rode light in our saddles, and kept a wary eye on the line of stores fronting the town's single street. We were watching mostly for signs of Federal presence—U.S.-branded horses at the hitching rails or blue-clad troopers strolling the boardwalk—but save for a solitary 'coon hound rumped down in the dirt next to the livery, the place seemed as deserted as a bone orchard. In fact, several of the businesses were boarded up as if in anticipation of a hurricane, and the buggy posts were all bare.

"Where'd everybody go?" Punch asked uneasily. Although Punta Rassa was relatively new as a cattle town, with the Union's blockade at Tampa Bay, it had become a major shipping point for a number of Caribbean ports. Early on, the town had been as rowdy as Dodge City or Abilene would be at their worst, but I guess Punch hadn't been there in a while, what with most of our cattle going north since the war's beginning.

"I reckon everybody's either off fighting Yankees, or hiding from them in the swamps," I replied distractedly, drawing rein before a false-fronted building near the far end of the street. In the dim starlight I could just make out the faded lettering painted across the fake second story. *Müller's Mercantile*. Then below that: *Groceries and Dry Goods*, and finally, in smaller script: *Werner Müller, Prop.* Although the windows were dark, I thought the place looked occupied.

"This way," I said to Punch, guiding my mount down a dark alley between the store and the rough-hewn log walls of a boarded-over shipping office. There was an empty corral behind the mercantile, and we tied our horses there. I glanced furtively over my shoulder before knocking at the rear door. I'd known old Werner Müller since I was knee-high to a water bug, but damned if I didn't feel like a skulking thief that night. It made me mad, to tell you the truth, and still does when I think about how we had to live in our own country during the Yankee invasion.

We waited on Müller's rear stoop for several minutes, until I sensed someone staring at us through a small but judiciously placed gap in the curtains. Stepping back where I could be better seen, I loudly whispered: "Mister Müller, it's Boone McCallister . . . Jeff McCallister's son."

I heard a low voice from behind the darkened panes, uttering what sounded like my name, then the mouse-like scratching of a key turning in its lock. The knob rattled loosely, the door squeaked inward, and an aged voice emerged from the shadows within. "Come in, come in, young ones, before the bluebellies see you."

We quickly stepped inside, and Müller hastened to close the door. I heard the muffled thud of the bolt sliding into its socket, but couldn't see a thing in the darkness.

"A man any more cannot be too careful," Müller explained a little breathlessly. "You boys wait here, while I go to find a lamp to light."

Punch and I stood, silent and tense, as the whisper of the old man's bare feet retreated over the hardwood floor. A few seconds later I heard the smack of steel on flint, and a couple of heartbeats after that, a warm glow flowed into the room where we stood. Giving Punch a nudge with my elbow, we entered a tiny parlor to find Werner Müller waiting for us next to a pewter floor lamp with a decoratively fringed green shade. He was holding a small handgun tight against his leg, almost hidden within the folds of his nightshirt.

"Alone, are you, Boone?" he asked, eyeing Punch suspiciously. "Your father, he is not also here?"

Müller was the son of German immigrants who had come to Florida just after the turn of the century. Although he claimed to barely remember the scenes of his youth, his speech remained heavily influenced by his Deutsch ancestry. Words like "there" or "father" came out closer to "der" and "fadder". Some people had difficulty understanding him. I usually didn't.

"There's just the two of us, Mister Müller," I said, "but we've got a herd stowed in some pines east of here."

"A herd! Cattle you have brought again to Punta Rassa?"

I nodded, briefly debating whether or not to tell him about W.B. Ashworth's offer. I finally decided against it, but soon wished I hadn't. It might have been helpful to have the elderly Dutchman's opinion on what had been going on around Punta Rassa since the Yankee reoccupation of Fort Myers.

Tipping my head toward Punch, I said: "This is Arthur Davis. He's Big Ed's boy, and Casey's cousin."

"Sure, sure, I know Big Ed. And young Arthur, him I have seen, too, when his father used to ship cattle from here."

"We call him Punch on account of his arm got punched by a round of buckshot a few days ago. I was hoping you'd take a look at it. We don't have any medicine, and I think it might be getting infected."

Müller's shaggy brows bobbed in concern. "An infection would not be a good thing for him to have, Boone." Motioning Punch forward, he pulled a fragile-looking parlor chair out from the table with instructions for the younger man to sit down. "So a look I can have at this buckshot you got," he said.

The lamp was a double burner. Using a splinter of pine pitch, the storekeeper ignited the second wick. The room brightened immediately, illuminating the doubt in Punch's eyes, the apprehension in Müller's.

"Go on," I said, giving the young drover a gentle shove. "Mister Müller knows what he's doing."

"Let us hope I do," the older man amended solemnly. "Come, young fellow, don't be so afraid. I am not some savage to take a hatchet to your scalp." He looked at me and shook his head. "Stands up to a man firing buckshot and never flinches, I will bet, but to face an old shopkeeper like myself, armed with only a needle and thread and a pinch of sulphur to cleanse the wound, and like a little boy he becomes. And you, Boone, don't you be smiling so big. You would be no braver, I think."

"Probably not," I admitted, but kept my grin in place—more at Punch's wall-eyed expression of distress than the older man's admonitions.

"Your father, Boone, and Big Ed?" Müller asked the question absently, bending forward to ease the ripped fabric of Punch's sleeve away from the wound.

"They're on another drive," I said.

"They're bound for the railhead in Georgia, if the Yankees ain't blowed it apart yet," Punch nervously blurted.

I found myself wishing he'd kept his mouth shut, and that I had, too. The fewer people who knew about Pa's activities, the better, I thought, and that included trusted friends like Werner Müller.

"And these cattle that you bring to Rassa?"

Speaking quickly, before Punch could let anything else out of the bag, I said: "Just a small herd. We're looking for a buyer."

The older man offered me an understanding glance, then turned his full attention to Punch's arm. Pulling away the dirty bandage, he clucked his tongue at the angry red flesh underneath. "I think maybe this shirt should come off, young man."

Punch gave me a chary look, but then shrugged and slipped out of his old linsey-woolsey, peeling it over his head like a smelly rind, although attentive to his injured arm. While he did that, I dug a couple of coins from my pocket and dropped them on the table for Müller. The clatter of gold caught the attention of both men.

"As soon as Mister Müller is finished with your arm, come on down to the cow pens," I told Punch. "You'll see my horse. Wait for me there."

"You are leaving?" Müller asked in surprise.

"Yes, sir. I've got some business to take care of before it gets too late."

Müller nodded and moved away from the table. "Come, then, I will show you the way."

I followed him into the first room; a small kitchen and dining area, I saw. The light from the twin wicks illuminated a stack of dirty dishes in a dry sink, a netting of cobwebs from the exposed rafters. Recalling that Müller's wife had died nearly five years earlier, I felt a sudden pang of sympathy for the older man.

At the door, Müller said: "Them Yankees, you watch for them, Boone, you hear?"

"Yes, sir, I will." After a brief hesitation, I added: "I was wondering how you were fixed for merchandise?"

"It is a store that I run here, is it not?"

"I know, but everybody says there ain't anything useful coming into the state since the blockade."

Müller sighed and nodded. "*Ja,* there is truth in those words, young one. Go and look at my shelves and you will see more empty than full. But a few things I have. What do you need?"

I pulled out a list that I'd put together back home. "We're needing flour and kerosene, coffee, sugar, some quinine, if you've got it. We could use some sulphur powder, too, but mostly what we need is gun powder and lead and as many caps as you can spare, musket size and smaller, for our pistols."

I stopped as the shopkeeper began shaking his head.

"Some of that stuff, maybe a little I've got, but no gun powder or caps of any kind, and not so much lead, either. Medicine, none of that I've got. What little there is goes to the army. The flour, too, goes to the army, but some cane sugar I have, and kerosene." He chuckled. "Plenty of kerosene. I guess the army does not use lamps so much."

"Probably not," I agreed. "What about coffee?"

"*Ja,* a little of that I have, too. The blockade runners get it through from time to time. Not to here, not since the Yankees came back, but in the Ten Thousand Islands they unload onto small boats, then bring their goods in overland, through the swamps."

I whistled softly. "That's a rough job."

"Very much so," he agreed. "But plenty they charge me for it, too."

"I'll take as much coffee as you've got, and five gallons of kerosene, if you can spare it."

"Sure, in two-gallon cans the kerosene ships. Six you will have to take, or four. For coffee, maybe five pounds I can let you have. What else do you need?"

"I reckon that's all I need if that's all you've got." I paused, then said: "How bad is Punch's arm?"

"Young Arthur's arm is going to be pretty bad, but maybe not so bad, you know?"

I shook my head. I said a minute ago that I could usually understand the things Müller said, but that wasn't always so. Usually it would be the way he strung his words together, more than his clabber-thick accent, that stumped me.

The elderly Dutchman, though, had long ago resigned himself to regularly having to restate a remark or opinion. Struggling to find the right words, he said: "Young Arthur, who you call Punch, I think all right he will be if the infection does not get any worse. I will give him some salve to put on it. It is for horses, this salve, but it is all I have. The rest, for humans, always it goes to where our boys are fighting. But the salve is good medicine, and it does not stink too bad. See that he keeps the wound clean, and the salve, at least once a day he should put it on. Don't forget always to wash the wound first."

"Tell him," I said, vaguely irritated that Müller seemed to be trying to dump the responsibility on me. I wasn't Punch's mama, after all.

"*Ja*, I will, but sometimes it is best also to tell a friend, no?" He hesitated. "You are his friend, *ja*?"

I sighed resolutely. "Yeah . . . *ja*. Don't worry, I'll remind him."

"Good." He was smiling now, grateful, I suppose, that I'd accepted at least part of the albatross' carcass to bear. [*Ed. Note:* Here McCallister is referring to Samuel Coleridge's poem, "The Rime of the Ancient Mariner" (1798), where a dead albatross becomes a metaphor for the carrying of a mental or emotional burden.]

"Now go," Müller told me, "but be careful. Troops I have not seen in town for almost a week, but there are sympathizers, even here in Punta Rassa, who feed them information . . . about our own soldiers, and the cow hunters, too. The Federals, they are always hungry for beef. Beef and information."

"I'll keep an eye out," I promised, picking up the Sharps where I'd left it leaning against the wall beside the door. I didn't tell Mister Müller good bye, and he didn't offer me an *adiós,* either. I waited in the shadows close to the outer wall until I heard the door's lock slide closed behind me, then strode purposely across the bare ground to where we'd left our horses, as if I had every right to be there. I led my marshtackie to the street, pausing at the alley's entrance only long enough to be sure there was no one loitering nearby, then swung a leg over the cantle and rode toward the Gulf.

My little marshtackie's hoofs didn't make much noise as we crossed the sandy loam toward the cattle pens. Night birds calling from the scrub, along with croaking of frogs and the cries of katydids, raised a bigger racket. As we drew near the shore, the gentle lapping of the Gulf's waves became more noticeable, a lulling melody I've always found comforting. The surf at Punta Rassa generally seemed tamer than other locations along the coast, its power tempered somewhat by the curving embrace of Sanibel Island, across the bay.

By 1864, cow pens covered most of the land south of town, with a wharf on the west side jutting into the bay. It was there that the cattle were loaded onto ships bound for various ports around the Caribbean. Cuba, mostly, but a lot of Florida beef went to other islands, too—Jamaica, Hispaniola, the Bahamas. Some even went as far south as the Yucatán Peninsula in Mexico.

My destination that evening was a small, shack-like building near the wharf, constructed of sun-scoured cypress and sand pine shingles. Despite the late hour—it was probably closing in on 10:00 p.m. by then—there was light glowing from the windows. I pulled up about fifty yards away, my gaze drifting cautiously over the surrounding pens. It lingered briefly on a sign hanging from a crossbar above the main entrance. The last time I'd been there, that sign had read: *Punta Rassa Wharf.* A lantern hanging from a post outside the small office revealed a new name that night—*Ashworth Shipping Company,* and in smaller print beneath that: *Lumber, Cattle, Hogs, Honey, Salt.*

My jaw tightened involuntarily as I studied the freshly painted sign, its owner's ambition set out there for everyone to see. Pa had dealt with W.B. Ashworth before, so I suppose my opinion of the man might have been more than a little colored by his assessment of Ashworth's character, as well as his cautionary warning on the holding grounds, just before pulling out for Georgia.

Get the gold, Boone. Don't let that slick-talkin' son-of-a-bitch con you into taking script. Bring the herd back if he tries.

Lightly tapping my mount's ribs with the sides of my stirrups, I rode on down to a smaller corral fronting the office. I kept my rifle with me as I climbed the long wooden ramp to the porch, my eyes darting swiftly, as if I expected to find a Yankee hiding inside every shadow. Although I tried to tread lightly, I guess the jingle of my spurs gave me away. I was still twenty feet shy of the front door when the light inside abruptly blinked out.

I jerked to a halt and half raised the Sharps, my heart thumping. Those damned Yankees had us all spooked.

"Who's out there?" a voice demanded from inside.

"It's Boone McCallister. I'm looking for W.B. Ashworth."

"McCallister? You kin to Jeff McCallister?"

"I'm his son. He sent me down here to talk to you about a note you sent him . . . assuming you're Ashworth."

There was a long pause, followed by what I swore was the sound of a door being quietly opened and closed. Although little pin-pricks of distrust were running up and down both arms, I held my ground. Finally the voice inside said: "Come on in, but have a care, friend. I have a gun that I'd gladly use if my hand is forced."

The cattle buyer's threat struck me the wrong way, and I strode swiftly across the porch and slammed the door open. Ashworth was relighting a squatty hurricane lamp on the wall behind his desk when I entered. He jerked around at my sudden appearance, the bang of the door's inner knob cracking as sharp as a drover's whip against the inside wall. Seeing the rifle in my left hand, he took an involuntary step backward. His match sputtered and went out—those early matches never did work well in Florida's humid climate—and he dropped the still glowing stick into a spittoon beside his desk.

W.B. Ashworth was a short, portly man in his mid-fifties, with a pasty complexion, thinning brown hair, and lips that always looked a little too wet and red. As if trying to regain some of the dignity he'd lost at my entrance, he pulled his chair around and reseated himself with a series of tiny huffs, as if my presence was more bother than opportunity. I didn't see the gun he'd threatened me with, although I didn't doubt that he had one stashed somewhere. Not many men went unarmed in those days, even if they didn't carry their firearms openly.

"I was expecting your father," Ashworth stated in a blustery tone.

"Pa sent me, instead." I glanced around the room. It was clean but sparsely furnished, just the desk and a couple of chairs, a coat rack on a cracked stand, and a single wooden filing cabinet in the corner. The floor was cypress—and I suppose by now you're starting to realize just how important that tree was to Florida's early pioneers—deeply gouged from the spurs of previous cow hunters, the walls plain and unpainted, without even a calendar to mark the seasons. My gaze lingered on a door in the rear wall, and the memory of that whisper of latch and hinges I thought I'd heard immediately after the light went out in Ashworth's office.

"Did you bring the agreed-upon merchandise?" Ashworth asked.

"I've got a shade over two hundred and fifty head of longhorns stashed out in the pines east of here, if that's what you're asking."

"Is that all?" He scowled magnificently. "I was hoping for closer to three hundred."

"You should've said three hundred, if that's what you wanted. I left the Flatiron with two hundred and sixty-four cows, but we lost a few along the way. I haven't done a final tally yet, but I'd guess we still have two hundred and fifty or fifty-five head."

"That's a lot of cattle to lose over such a short drive. What happened? Raiders?"

"The swamps."

Ashworth said—"Ahh."—and let it drop.

I've already mentioned we'd taken the long way into Punta Rassa because of the Yankees' return to the area, but I don't recall saying much about how dangerous that country just north of the Big Cypress could be. Although we'd stayed to high ground as much as possible, there hadn't been any way to avoid occasionally having to plunge straight into some of those deep marshes and sloughs that fringed the northern border of the swamp. It was in the middle of a half-mile-long slough, not too far west of Pete Dill's trading post on the upper Caloosahatchee, that we'd lost most of our cattle. At least a dozen big 'gators had appeared seemingly out of nowhere to converge on the rear of the herd as we drove through green-algae-blanketed water up to our horses' bellies. Even though Casey and I had ridden back as fast as our little marshtackies could carry us, opening fire on the big reptiles with our revolvers as soon as we got within range, we'd still lost five head. I think we probably lost a few years off the tail end of our lives, too.

A couple of days later, we lost another animal when it was bitten on the nose by a cottonmouth and had to be put down. Then later on, some Seminoles lifted several head out of the middle of our herd, slick as new boots on wet moss. We wouldn't have even known there were any Red Sticks around if I hadn't sent Ardell and Calvin back to look for the missing animals. [*Ed. Note:* Red Stick is an antiquated reference to the Creek Indian influence on the Seminoles of Southern Florida in the early 19th Century. Following the Indian defeat at the Battle of Horseshoe Bend in 1814, many Creek refugees from Alabama sought sanctuary among the Seminoles. Their influx aggrandized the Seminole nation, which in turn aided that tribe's resistance to white encroachment. The term Red Stick refers to the red-dyed war clubs and ceremonial branches used by Creek medicine men and warriors.]

After finding the Indians' trail, Ardell and Calvin had hightailed it back to where we'd stopped for the night to warn us of the Seminoles' presence. Some of the boys had wanted to go after the stolen cattle, but I put a stop to their plans before they got too fired up. After the Indian Wars, us McCallisters tried real hard to get along with the Seminoles. Pa said he'd rather feed them a few times a year than have to fight them again.

Let 'em have a cow every once in a while, he used to say whenever we found evidence that a party of Indians had crossed our range or driven off a few steers. *We've got enough.*

We did, too. At least up until the Civil War broke out. At one point Pa estimated the Flatiron brand was burned into the hides of at least fifteen thousand head of cattle, scattered along the upper Caloosahatchee and Pease Rivers, then on over the Highlands toward the Kissimmee. Of course, all that changed after the Northern invasion. If the South won, we figured to come out all right—Pa had several satchels filled with Southern script and promissory notes, received on herds already delivered to the Confederacy—but I think by '64, even the most die-hard Rebel had to know the war was turning against us. That was why Pa sent me to Punta Rassa with my own small gather, and warned me to accept only gold in return.

Ashworth sat there quietly for a moment. I suspect he was waiting for me to go on about what had happened to the cattle we'd lost along the trail, but I didn't see any need to fill him in on the matter. To be honest, I wasn't feeling overly charitable toward the man that night.

Sensing that I'd said all I meant to on the subject, Ashworth motioned toward a straight-back chair in front of his desk. "Might as well make yourself comfortable," he grumbled as he started rummaging through a desk drawer beside his knee. He came out a few seconds later with a sheet of paper covered with penciled notes and scratched-out sums. A solitary number near the bottom was circled several times, as if for emphasis. Reading it upside-down, I saw the figure—**$18 per**—and felt my muscles tighten.

"I don't know if your daddy had a chance to inform you of the agreed-upon price, but it is significantly more than what you've gotten in the past," Ashworth said.

"It was thirty-five dollars a head," I replied, wanting to establish that figure as quickly as possible. "And you're right, that's a lot more than we've ever gotten before."

Ashworth chuckled. "Well, thirty-five dollars a head was a starting point. I didn't have a firm commitment from my buyer at the time, so I was forced to make an offer based on several assumptions."

"It doesn't matter, Mister Ashworth. As long as I take home thirty-five dollars for every cow we leave in your corrals, Pa will be happy."

"Well, unfortunately, your pa's happiness doesn't factor into my final offer."

"The figure in that note you sent him does, though."

Ashworth paused to give me one of those glares weak men like to offer up when they're trying to feed you something they call steak, but comes closer to boiled pig's feet. "What did you say your name was?" he asked after a moment, when I just sat there staring back.

"It's Boone, Boone McCallister."

"Well . . . Boone, I am not opposed to dealing with one of your father's representatives, even someone as inexperienced in matters of business as yourself, but if there is going to be any difficulty in concluding this transaction, I may be forced to hold your cattle here while I send for your father to negotiate with him personally."

"My instructions from Pa was to bring you enough cattle to fill the hold and deck of a mid-sized ship bound for Cuba, and to collect thirty-five dollars in gold coin for every cow I delivered. He also said that if you tried to renege on your offer, I was to bring the herd back to the Flatiron, and we'd find another buyer."

Ashworth's face got real red at that. I imagine my face was also turning a faint shade of rust. Although Pa had warned me about this possibility, I'd hoped it wouldn't come to it. I was going to owe my crew a month's wages, whether I sold the herd or not, and I didn't relish the prospect of having to drive those cows back the same way we'd come, and risk losing even more of them to the swamps. But the ultimate decision would be

Ashworth's, because hell was going to freeze over before I backed down on either the price or the means of payment, which was still Spanish doubloons.

After an awkward silence, Ashworth stated: "See here, young man, I have obligations of my own to fulfill. I wrote your father in good faith, and won't allow a bull-headed youth to stand in the way of my completing this transaction."

I stood slowly, letting the muzzle of my rifle tip toward the floor. That was done more to draw attention to the Sharps than as any kind of threat, although I did want him to understand that I wouldn't be intimidated. "I'm pressed for time, Mister Ashworth, and won't waste too much of it sitting here in useless dickering. I did the math for two hundred and fifty head, and it comes out to eight thousand, seven hundred and fifty dollars . . . in gold. Do you have that kind of money on you?"

Ashworth's nostrils flared as he rose to his full height. It must have been disappointing to him to realize that, even stretched out as far as he could go, he was still several inches shorter than I was. "Get out, McCallister, and don't come back until you're willing to deal reasonably."

I swore and spun toward the door, yanking it open forcefully enough that it's a wonder I didn't pull the damned thing off its hinges. But before I could step outside, Ashworth called for me to wait. I turned back, glaring. The muscles in my legs were twitching with a desire to keep walking, but in the end I decided to hear him out.

"What do you want?" I managed to squeeze through a throat just about closed off with anger.

"I might . . . *might* . . . be able to raise my price a little," Ashworth said after a moment, and it was only then that it dawned on me that he'd been bluffing when he ordered me from the room, that he was actually hoping that I'd be the one to cave in first. I felt the rage flow out of me, and had to struggle not to laugh in his face.

"The price is thirty-five dollars a head, Mister Ashworth. If you're not interested at that price, there are other markets I can take them to."

He sneered. "And sell them for Confederate script?"

"No, sir," I said, and this time it was me laying it on thick as molasses. "Spanish doubloons, just like you offered."

Doubt flashed across the cattle buyer's face. He didn't believe me, but wasn't quite confident enough to call my bluff. Taking a deep breath, he said: "I don't have that kind of money with me, but I can get it."

"Thirty-five dollars?"

Ashworth's eyes narrowed. He looked hot enough to boil, but I guess he needed that herd more than he wanted to admit. Likely he already had a ship waiting down in the Ten Thousand Islands, its crew growing itchy to load up and get out of there before they were spotted by a Yankee gunboat. "I will pay you eight thousand, seven hundred and fifty dollars for whatever cattle you have, numbering at minimum two hundred and fifty head. If you want to take home any beeves above that amount, you may feel free to do so." A smirk crossed his face. "I'm sure the creatures of the swamps would appreciate your generosity."

"I'd probably just sell them to folks right here in Punta Rassa to butcher for their own table," I replied mildly, appreciating how quickly that smug expression melted off of Ashworth's mug. "Where do you want the herd delivered?"

"Right here, tomorrow morning after nine o'clock. I'll have the money by then, and men to help with the final tally."

I nodded and left the office, slamming the door closed behind me. Walking up the sandy alleyway to where I'd left my horse, I looked around for Punch, but he was nowhere to been seen, and I felt a twinge of concern as I stepped into my saddle and reined toward town. I'd gone maybe a hundred yards when a horseman nudged his pony out of the scrub on my left.

"Howdy, Boone," Punch called softly, jogging his marsh-tackie in my direction.

"What're you hiding from?" I asked, and I didn't mean it in a high-handed manner, either. Not in those uncertain times.

"I ain't sure," he admitted. "They's been some strange things going on that was making me kinda nervous. That's why I decided to stay up here."

"What kind of things?"

"I seen a man leave the corrals and make a run for the livery. A few minutes later, he scooted outta there like his britches were on fire."

Remember me mentioning that little prickly feeling earlier, when I thought I heard a door open and close in Ashworth's office? Well, it came back with a vengeance at Punch's words. "Which way'd he go?" I asked.

"Along the road."

I don't know what it's like today, but back then, there was only one road in and out of Punta Rassa, and about a dozen miles up that lay Fort Myers.

"Could you tell who it was?"

Punch shook his head. "It was too dark."

"But he came from the corrals?"

"That's what it looked like to me." When I didn't immediately reply, Punch said: "What do you think, Boone?"

"It might not be anything," I replied, although deep in my guts I knew that it was. "On the other hand, it might've been a Union sympathizer, heading for the fort."

"Why'd a Union man want to fetch the army for a couple of drifters like us? They wouldn't know we've got a herd stashed out in the scrub."

"Maybe, but I'm not sure I want to bet my neck in a noose on it."

"Maybe it was a Klee," Punch said out of the blue.

"A Klee? You mean one of Jacob's boys?"

"Mister Müller said Jacob Klee and his men rode into town yesterday. Said they was drinking real heavy last night at the Havana House, and that Jacob was telling people you fed his nephew to an alligator."

"What!"

Punch shrugged. "That's what Mister Müller told me."

"That son-of-a-bitch," I swore softly.

We sat there in silence for a few minutes, Punch waiting patiently as I tried to work it all out in my mind. To tell you the truth, my options were seeming mighty few and damned unpromising, but the one thing I couldn't ignore was my first responsibility, which was to get Pa's cattle into town and collect the gold from Ashworth so that we could rebuild the Flatiron after the war. As badly as I wanted to go after Jacob Klee and set him straight, I knew any thoughts of confronting the cattle rustler would have to wait.

"Head on back and tell Casey to get the herd started," I finally told Punch. "Tell him to go north, then follow the river in. It'll be faster than trying to make a drive through the swamps."

"Tonight?" Punch asked in surprise.

"Yeah, tonight. Ashworth said he wanted those cows delivered after nine o'clock tomorrow, but I'm not going to wait that long. Start riding, Punch, and tell Casey to hustle them cows along. I want to be out of here before first light if we can manage it."

Punch nodded and reined away, slapping the sides of his stirrups against his mount's ribs. My little marshtackie wanted to go with him, but I kept a tight rein and hung back until the young cow hunter had vanished into the darkness east of town. Then I twisted partway around in my saddle to stare at Ashworth's tiny office, sitting like a lump of squared-off mud at the edge of the corrals. He and I had some more business to take care of that night, but first I decided to ride up to the Havana House and find out what kind of lies Jacob Klee and his boys had been telling.

SESSION THREE

One of the things that always surprised me when I went to Texas in the fall of 1866 was how similar to Florida the Western cattle industry was. Sure, some of the terms were different—like Texans calling a motherless calf a maverick, instead of a heretic, or referring to drovers as cowboys instead of cow hunters—but there was so much you could have just picked up out of Florida and plopped down right in the middle of Texas and never known the difference.

The Havana House was like that. Named after the final destination of probably eighty percent of the beeves we shipped out of Punta Rassa, it was a combination saloon and meeting house, with rooms upstairs for sleeping, and cribs out back for whores. The Havana was a long, narrow building squeezed between a saddle shop on one side and an abandoned tannery on the other. It was constructed of cypress logs, hewn and fit so tightly together there was no need for chinking. The floor was rough puncheon, the ceiling low and smoke-stained, the furniture hard-used but serviceable. Except for the fact that the logs were cypress rather than cottonwood, the place would have looked right at home anywhere along the Chisholm Trail.

There was still no one in sight as I rode back into Punta Rassa. Judging from the position of the stars, I figured it had to be close to midnight. In a sleepy burg like Punta Rassa had become since the war siphoned off most of the state's able-bodied men, its remaining citizens had probably been in bed for hours. Only the Havana House seemed to be open. Dismounting out front, I climbed the steps to the boardwalk, loosening my six-gun in its holster as I peered in over the top of a pair of batwing doors.

The Havana's bar ran down the right-hand side of the room, its polished mahogany surface gleaming richly in the lamplight. A backbar made of the same warm wood stretched all the way to the ceiling. There was an oval mirror in its center, but the shelves along either side were nearly bare—no doubt another casualty of the Union blockade. A faro table, chuck-a-luck cage, and green felt poker table shared space against the rear wall, collecting dust and cobwebs. The half dozen other tables scattered around the room were plainly made, their surfaces scarred with initials or obscene images, carved into the wood with knives; stubby burn spots from neglected cigars rimmed each one like dark-furred woolly worms laid out in death—a dismal reflection of the town itself, I mused.

Except for Eric Burke, who owned the place, the big room was empty. Eric was sitting at a table near the front door, a pair of thick-lensed eyeglasses pushed up on his forehead, his feet crossed at the ankles atop a second chair, his head tipped so far back it looked painful. Soft snores wafted out over the batwings, along with the lingering odors of beer, whiskey, and tobacco, like memories of more prosperous days.

Pushing open the right-hand door, I stepped inside and moved to the bar. Somewhere deep within Eric's mind, the sound of my heels on the hardwood floor and the faint, musical jingle of spurs must have roused consciousness. He stirred, then jerked upright with a closing snap of his jaws. His eyes widened fearfully when he saw me standing alone at the bar, and he quickly fumbled his glasses down over the bridge of his nose.

"Dammit, Boone, why didn't you say something?" he grumbled when he realized who I was. Pushing to his feet, he moved around to the sober side of the establishment.

"To tell you the truth, Eric, you were looking so dang' peaceful, I wasn't sure I wanted to interrupt whatever it was you were dreaming about." I whistled softly, just to needle him. "Must've been pretty interesting, the way you were twitching."

He gave me a sour look and wiped the drool from a corner of his mouth with the back of his hand. "If I was twitching, it was because I was dreaming a bunch of randy cow hunters had come in wanting something to drink, and all I had was empty kegs."

I laughed and leaned into the bar, starting to relax for the first time that evening. I've always liked a saloon. There would be a time later on in life when that fondness grew into something of a problem, but that was long after I left Florida.

"Where is everyone?" I asked, more or less echoing Punch's earlier query, except that I was referring to Eric's usual bartender, and the girls who had once plied their trade at the Havana.

"Bob went to fight the Yankees, and the girls skated off not long after to follow the soldiers." He leaned forward on his elbows. "You alone, Boone, or did you come in with a herd?"

"I'm bringing in a small herd, but I wouldn't count on a long hooray."

"Them sum-bitchin' Yankees is the problem. Ain't nobody left no more except for little boys and old men. Little boys ain't got money, and old men ain't got hooray. If my eyes weren't so bad I couldn't see the end of a rifle barrel, I'd go off and shoot some bluebellies myself." He hesitated, then shook his head. "Hell with 'em. You want a beer, Boone, or something harder?"

"Maybe after we've got the herd delivered. Right now I'm looking for information."

"What kind?"

"Jacob Klee. I heard he brought his gang into town."

"Yeah," Eric replied warily. "They rode in yesterday about noon." He brought a glass mug out from under the counter. "You sure you don't want a beer?"

"I'm sure. Tell me about Jacob Klee."

"Aw, hell, you know that bunch. Troublemakers, every last one of 'em."

"You're working real hard at avoiding what we both know I'm talking about, Eric."

The barman sighed. "Yeah, they were here. Did some drinking, but mostly lost interest when they found out the whores had moved on. They brew their own rotgut down in the swamps, so I guess they didn't see much point in paying for what they could have for free back home."

"What about the 'gator?"

Eric stared at the top of the bar and didn't say anything for nearly a minute. Then he returned the mug to its place under the counter and brought out a shot glass and a half empty bottle. He poured to the rim, then nudged the glass across the bar. "You're gonna need a little medicine to make the rest of this go down, Boone."

"Just tell me what that skunk-kissing son-of-a-bitch said."

"All right. Jacob Klee was drinking heavy last night, like he had a real bad mad burning a hole in his gut. After a while he started making some claim that you and Casey Davis cornered his nephew out there on the prairie, wrapped him up in some rope, and tossed him in a 'gator hole." Eric was silent a moment, staring into the bar's reflection. Then he lifted his eyes to mine. "Is that true?"

"What do you think?"

"I don't know. There was a time not so long ago when I would have called Jake Klee a liar. Not to his face, mind you, but after he left. But things haven't been the same around here since the war, and it's common knowledge that your daddy's had his

69

share of trouble with Klees."

"Mostly with old Judah Klee, trying to run Pa off the range when we first came over the Highlands. Pa wasn't the only one that old man ran afoul of, either."

"The Klees say differently."

"Most thieves will tell you they're innocent."

"They say that Pease River country was rightfully theirs, and that it was your pa who horned in on land already claimed."

"To hear the Klees tell it, they once owned the entire state."

"Yeah, I reckon they do." Eric was staring at the bar again, deep in thought. After a bit, he said: "You McCallisters have always treated me fair, Boone, but I've never had any problems with Klees, either. I've got nothing against either of you."

"What about Dave Klee, Eric? Do you believe me, or Jacob?"

"I ain't heard your version of it yet."

I told him then, explaining how Jacob and his gang had been following us for several days, and how, after we'd confronted them south of the Caloosahatchee, Dave had apparently decided to try to flank our position. I described the cry we'd heard, and what Casey and I found when we went to investigate.

"You say he was armed?"

"We figure he was. We heard a shot that he said was at the 'gator."

Eric looked surprised at that. "You talked to him?"

"It was me and Casey who pulled him out of the water."

A scowl creased the bartender's forehead. "I'll be honest, Boone, I was having a hard time believing you'd go to all the trouble of tying up a man, then tossing him to a 'gator when you could have just as easily shot him."

"Hell's bells, Eric, are you telling me you believed that old windbag?"

"Look, you McCallisters are a hard bunch. I know you had to be, starting that ranch out there when those plains were filled with wolves and bears and bandits, not to mention Seminoles, but . . . yeah, it crossed my mind that maybe your daddy could've done something like that, and so maybe his sons could have, too."

"What's crossing your mind now?"

"I said I've never had any trouble with the Klees, and wasn't lying, but I know their reputation, too. I reckon I'd a lot sooner believe one of them could've done something like that than I could a McCallister. It's hard luck for ol' Davey, though. He was one of the good ones."

That is an opinion I've probably heard a thousand times over the years, even from men who'd never met David Klee, and it's always irritated me. I'll agree Dave seemed like a good sort, but you've got to remember that he was unemployed because of the war, dodging conscription by hiding out in the swamps with his uncle and cousins, and putting a sneak on our herd, so I've got to assume, since he wasn't an idiot and apparently had a loaded gun in his hand when that 'gator snagged him, that he was up to no good that night. Just like every other Klee I've ever had any dealings with. The fact is, when you ride with a bunch like old Judah's boys, you take your chances. Sometimes you'll reap the rewards, but as often as not, you'll pay a steep price for your lawlessness. I reckon that's what happened to Dave Klee that night below the Caloosahatchee, and that's why, to me, he wasn't one of the good ones.

"Where are they now?" I asked after a bit.

"Klees? They pulled out this afternoon."

"Which way were they headed?"

"I didn't see 'em leave, but there's only one way out of Punta Rassa unless you want to swim the bay or buck the swamps."

I nodded grimly. Jacob Klee had taken his men east, probably following the road at least as far as the lower crossing of the Caloosahatchee near Fort Myers. Where they'd gone from there would be anyone's guess.

Tossing a nickel on the bar, I said: "Thanks for the drink, Eric. And pass the word about what really happened to Dave Klee, will you?"

"Sure, although I don't know how much good it'll do. It makes a better story if people think you dangled him over a 'gator hole like bait on a hook."

Eric's words burned hot in my ears, but he was right. It's been more than seventy years now since that incident, and I still hear folks talking about how poor ol' David Klee got fed to an alligator.

Slipping outside and still watchful for Yankees or Klees—one being about as bad as the other, in my opinion—I gathered the reins to my marshtackie and stepped into the saddle. My skin started crawling again as soon as my butt hit leather, like someone was watching me from the shadows. I could see Ashworth's office from the upper end of the street, and was relieved to find the windows still lit from within, the door cracked open a few inches, as if hoping for a breeze. I rode slowly back to the corrals, only this time, instead of tying up out front, I led my pony deeper into the maze of pens, finally hitching him to a rail well back where he wouldn't be easily spotted. Leaving my Sharps on the saddle and hanging my spurs over the wide horn, I made my way quietly through the pens to Ashworth's front porch.

Without my spurs and by watching where I placed my feet, I managed to reach the front window without attracting any attention. I'm not sure what I was expecting, but if it was a fat man with his shirt pulled up to scratch his belly, then I'd hit pay dirt. I stood there for nearly a minute waiting for something to happen, but Ashworth seemed content to stay where he was, his fingers moving lazily over the bare mound of his stomach, ankles crossed atop his desk. I remember his eyes were closed in a look of total satisfaction. Then my gaze drifted to the floor beside his desk and I did a double-take. A small wooden chest sat there, its sides reinforced with strap iron, its hasp decoratively engraved; a heavy key protruded from the lock like a knife thrust into the back of a murder victim.

A smile twitched at the corners of my mouth as I eased over to the door and gently pushed it inward. Those hinges must have been recently oiled, because they didn't make a peep until nearly the halfway mark. Although a tiny sound, it caught Ashworth's attention immediately. His eyes flew open and his feet crashed to the floor. He yanked at the top drawer of his desk, but only rammed it solidly into his gut. When he did manage to fumble a stubby handgun from the drawer, he found that he'd grabbed it by the barrel instead of the grips, and ended up sitting there with the gun clenched uselessly in his right hand, his mouth flopped open with nothing coming out. I stepped into the room, my Navy leveled firmly on the cattle buyer's chest.

"Let it drop," I said.

"You!" Ashworth exclaimed, then returned the weapon to its drawer. "What the devil do you want?"

"I want to know who you sent out on a midnight ride earlier tonight, and I want to know where he went."

"I don't know what you're talking about."

"I'm talking about the man you sent out the back door when you heard me coming in the front."

Licking nervously at his lips, Ashworth said: "What were you doing, McCallister, spying on me?" Then he glanced at the iron-strapped box and chuckled. "Or is this what you came for?" He kicked the chest with the toe of his shoe, scooting it several inches to the side. "Go ahead, help yourself."

"It's empty," I said, puzzled. When I'd spotted it from the window, I'd been certain it held the gold doubloons for the cattle.

"You don't think I'd be foolish enough to keep that kind of money laying around my office, do you?"

I shook my head as if to clear it. "I don't care why you've got that chest sitting there, I just want to make sure you have the money on hand when my boys bring the herd in."

"I told you I would."

"You told me you'd have it after nine o'clock tomorrow. I've decided we're going to complete our transaction a little earlier."

"What do you mean, earlier?" Ashworth's brows were cocked with suspicion.

"I sent a man for the herd as soon as I found out you'd sent someone running off to . . . well, wherever it was you sent him. Was it to the Yankees at Fort Myers, or to fetch Jacob Klee and his boys? Are you the one behind that old man's attack in the palmettos?"

"You're crazy, McCallister. I wouldn't trust Jake Klee to unbutton his trousers before taking a piss, and I wouldn't deal with a Yankee for all the gold in Cuba."

"It doesn't matter. The herd should be on its way real soon. It'll be here before dawn, and you're going to have that gold ready as soon as we've got those cows penned."

Ashworth shook his head. "No."

"Yeah." I made a motion with the Colt's muzzle. "Let's go get it now."

"Now? Absolutely not! You'll have it by nine o'clock, but not a moment sooner."

Real soft, I said: "These are desperate times, Mister Ashworth. Ordinarily I wouldn't be so stubborn about it, but I'm in a hurry tonight, and don't intend to linger past dawn. Get your hind end out of that chair, and let's go fetch the gold."

"That's thievery, McCallister."

"No, sir, it's a precaution." I made that motion with the Colt again, and this time Ashworth edged warily out from behind his desk. "Don't worry," I assured him. "We'll still do a final count. If the numbers don't match, I'll make it right."

"You're taking what doesn't belong to you at gunpoint, young man. You can't justify that by . . . by the insane belief that the money is somehow already yours. Until those cattle are penned inside my corrals and I say the count is acceptable, you have no right to. . . ."

"Hush," I interrupted gently. "After the war, we can discuss other methods of payment, but tonight it's going to be my way. Now start walking, and I swear if you try to run or holler, I'll take one of your kneecaps off with a bullet."

I'm not going to repeat Ashworth's reply, other than to acknowledge that it was lengthy, spirited, and included a brief detour into my lineage. The important thing was that he started walking, taking me through the rear door into another crudely constructed room. I followed with my revolver in one hand, the cattle buyer's lamp, lifted from its bracket on the wall, in the other.

That back room actually had more furnishings than the office. There were stacks of cowhides along one side, a bundle of otter and raccoon pelts in a corner, two unmade cots—one with an honest-to-God Western buffalo robe for a mattress—a cedar wardrobe, a table littered with food scraps crawling with flies, and—pushed up against the wall behind Ashworth's office—a squatty floor safe on metal rollers.

There was a second door in this room, as well. Studying its location in the wall, I judged it would open near the long chute used to run cattle onto the wharf, where they could be loaded aboard waiting vessels. My eyes lingered on that door for a long moment, then I turned to Ashworth and told him to get moving. He wasted a few seconds glaring daggers in my direction, then got down on his knees in front of the safe. I set the lamp on the floor beside him so that he could see what he was doing, then stepped back where I could keep an eye on him and both doors. Hunching his shoulders to hide the combination, he started twirling the dial. The tumblers fell back with a trio of muffled clicks, then he pressed down on the main lever to release the catch. Stepping forward before he could open the door, I tapped his shoulder with the Navy's muzzle.

"Just so you understand, Mister Ashworth, if you bring anything out of that safe that ain't pure gold, I won't waste time shooting you in the knee."

Ashworth froze with his hand halfway inside the safe, honest fear showing in his eyes for the first time. After a moment's hesitation, he said: "I've got a pistol in there, McCallister. It's on top of the money."

"That seems like a good place to stash a pistol," I agreed. "That's why I spoke up when I did. I don't want to see any kind of misunderstanding foul our agreement."

"What do you want me to do about the gun?"

"I want you to bring it out real slow and set it on top of the safe. Real slow, Ashworth."

He did as instructed, and a lot slower than he needed to, too, although I appreciated the gesture. The weapon was one of those old single-shot horse pistols, a muzzleloader with a .72-caliber bore. I used my thumbnail to pry off the cap, and with the gun essentially disarmed, tossed it onto one of the bunks. "All right, bring it out."

Sweat was rolling freely down Ashworth's face as he began hauling heavy canvas sacks into the light, each one sagging with coins. I'd find out later that each bag contained exactly one hundred and ten gold doubloons, worth approximately $20 apiece. The total came to four solid bags, a slight overpayment, but nothing we couldn't work out after we'd tallied the herd. I also noticed, as the portly cattle buyer slammed the door shut and spun the dial, that he still had several sacks left. I didn't doubt that he had more cached elsewhere around town.

Hitching partway around on his knees, Ashworth said: "Satisfied?"

"I am if that's the whole amount."

"It's all there, plus a few dollars more."

"There'll be a few cows more, too. You'll still end up owing me before it's over."

All business now that his safe was securely locked, he said: "If the stock is in decent shape and the count warrants it, I'll make up the difference from my pocket."

"Gold or silver, Ashworth. I don't want script."

Struggling to his feet with a face as pink as a fresh-dug turnip, Ashworth snarled: "What kind of bandit are you, McCallister? All that gold sitting there, and you still won't take paper for a few measly bucks?"

"It ain't me that's made everyone around here distrust you," I replied mildly. "Come on, let's go fetch that trunk."

"No, you can go to hell. That trunk is worth five dollars. I was going to give it to you, but now, by God, you can pay for it. Gold or silver, kid. I won't take script."

Laughing, I said: "Fair enough. You can keep the trunk. I've got a good pack horse to haul that gold home." Picking up the lamp, I added: "Grab those sacks, W.B., and let's get out of here. I don't like a room without windows."

We returned to the front office, and Ashworth dumped the sacks on his desk with a solid clunk. Opening the top bag, I spilled its contents across the desk. It took only a moment to count out one hundred and twenty coins. Satisfied that it was all there, I returned the gold to the sack and tied off the drawstring.

"Happy?" Ashworth sneered.

"As a pig in mud," I replied cheerfully. Motioning toward the ladder-back chair in front of the desk, the one I'd sat in earlier,

I said: "Make yourself comfortable, W.B. It's going to be a while."

Moving around behind the desk, I opened the belly drawer and removed a stubby, four-barreled pepperbox pistol. After prying off the caps, I tossed the handgun back in the drawer and slid it closed. Then I seated myself in the cattle buyer's padded swivel chair and propped my heels on the corner of his desk, although I kept my Colt out where Ashworth could see it.

Punch must have really lit a fire under Casey's tail feathers, because it didn't seem like much time had passed at all before I heard the first plaintive bawl of a longhorn from the top of the street. Ashworth had moved his chair away from the desk and tipped it back against the wall. He was lightly dozing, but jerked instantly awake at the distant lowing.

"What was that?" he demanded.

"That's what you're buying tonight." I stood and motioned for him to follow me outside. "Let's go count your cows."

We walked down the long ramp to the main entrance to the pens, where the sign hanging from the crossbeam was creaking in a strengthening breeze off the Gulf. Dawn wouldn't be far off now, I knew.

Spying Casey and Negro Jim out in front of the herd, I felt a quick sense of relief. In those wild times, you just never knew.

Casey's whip cracked sharp as a pistol shot across the town as he and Jim bent the herd's leaders toward the corrals. Ashworth and I stood silently outside the gate. With the cattle lined out, Casey loped his marshtackie over to where we waited. "Howdy, boss," he said. "Everything all right?"

"So far," I replied, although I wasn't relaxing just yet.

"Where do you want these critters stacked?"

"Over here," Ashworth said, drawing the latch on the gate and walking it back to fasten to the corral rail. "Put them in here," he told Casey, then looked at me. "We'll rough count them as they go through."

Casey wheeled his marshtackie to return to the herd, while Ashworth lit a pair of lanterns hanging from iron spikes driven into the uprights on either side of the gate. While they were doing that, I went into the maze of corrals to fetch my horse, riding back through the gate just as the lead cows were coming up. Ashworth, I noticed, had already climbed onto the top rail of the outer corral with a ledger book and a couple of pencils. I took a position opposite him, folding both hands atop the broad horn of my Texas saddle and leaning forward for a better view. The cow hunters' whips were really popping now, forcing the rear of the herd forward even as the leaders balked at this new obstacle. Then the first of the longhorns darted through the gate, and I began to relax. Barring a lightning bolt or cannon fire, the rest would follow without resistance.

The cattle's incessant bawling must have awakened the town, because it wasn't long before a small crowd had gathered on the low rise above the pens. I guess it had been a while since they'd seen a herd as large as ours, and they were curious about who we were, and what we were up to.

I counted two hundred fifty-seven head. W.B. claimed two hundred fifty-five. Since neither of us wanted to do a recount, we agreed on two fifty-six. Ashworth grumbled some, but forked over an additional $210, and, as odd as it may sound, I believe I was more taken aback by what we got for those last six cows than I was the nearly $9,000 sitting in his office. Sacks of Spanish gold had grown kind of common around that part of Florida, especially when we were used to bringing in herds numbering closer to a thousand head. But getting over $200 for six scrawny beeves—and believe me, most of those scrub cows would be considered sacks of bones compared to the bulky Herefords and Angus you see on the ranges today—brought home the reality of just how much $35 was for a single animal.

While me and Casey went to fetch the gold from Ashworth's office, Jim and Ardell rode in among the cattle to cut out the two pack horses. We met back at the gate, and, after stashing the money inside one of the panniers, I ordered Jim to take the pack animals up to Müller's store and pick up the supplies the old German had promised to have waiting for us.

"You's gonna be comin' along real soon, ain't you, marse?" Jim asked.

"In a bit. Tell Müller I won't leave without settling up our account."

Jim looked relieved, and I was once again struck by how thin a line he had to walk sometimes. Out on the Flatiron range, Negro Jim was as equal as any man Pa had ever hired, and more so than most, due to his being a part of the McCallister crew for so long. It took coming into civilization every now and then to strike home how people really felt about colored folks. It had been the same way in Texas when I rode for some of those big outfits west of the Brazos. If there was a Negro on a crew, he'd be treated about as equal as any man there—until we got into a town where there were white women, lay-abouts, and troublemakers. Then it was "yes-suh" this and "no-suh" that, until I wanted to take an axe handle upside the skulls of some of those white-skinned sons-of-bitches who caused most of the trouble.

After Jim had ridden off with the pack horses, I turned to Ashworth and, after a moment's hesitation, stuck my hand out. He looked momentarily puzzled by the gesture, then grudgingly accepted the shake.

"No hard feelings, W.B.?"

The cattle buyer's mouth worked a few times, like he was wanting to get something off his chest. Then he spun on his heels and stalked back into his office without having uttered a word.

"I believe that ol' boy might be harboring a few ill feelings, after all, Boone," Casey observed.

"Well, I can't say that I blame him. I treated him pretty harsh."

"Punch told us about that rider he saw lighting a shuck outta town, and how Müller said them Yankees have got sympathizers right here in Punta Rassa, although I'm damned if I can figure their feelings."

"If I knew who they were, I'd hang 'em as traitors," Roy added, having ridden over with the rest of the crew.

"We ain't hanging anyone tonight, and we're a bunch of fools if we're still here when the sun comes up," I said. Although I'd already sent Jim up to the store with the pack horses and gold, I still had the $210 Ashworth had given for those last six cows. Digging the poke from my saddlebags, I tossed it to Casey with the instructions to take the boys up to the Havana House and buy them a drink.

"Just be ready to ride as soon as I get there with the supplies," I added.

Punch and Calvin hooted loudly at the prospect of free booze, but I noticed it was Pablo who was quickest to pivot his mount toward the saloon, driving his spurs into the animal's sides. I winced at the Cuban's casual brutality, but kept my feelings to myself.

With the boys gone, I reined my little marshtackie toward the beach-side trail I'd used when I left Müller's. Jim already had his mule and the extra horses tied up out front when I got there, with most of the supplies already stowed inside the panniers. He looked relieved when he saw me taking shape against the faint glow of the bay, and turned to call into the store.

"He's here now, Mistah Müller, like I said he'd be."

Werner Müller came out of the store with a lit pipe in one hand, an invoice sheet in the other. He stopped at the front edge of the verandah, the lamplight at his back stretching his shadow across the street. Although he'd pulled on a pair of britches and some shoes after treating Punch's wound, his hair was still tousled, stray wisps waving back and forth in the Gulf's breeze.

"Boone, the cattle you have finally brought back to Punta Rassa." He was grinning broadly, as if the sharp, green-manure scent of the herd had been sorely missed. "By dingy, I wasn't sure I would live long enough for another cow to see."

I laughed at the elderly German's elevated mood, and wondered how much of it came from his pleasure at seeing another herd, and how much stemmed from the merchandise he'd sold me that night. I'm not criticizing the man, mind you. No one has to tell me how a little extra coin jingling in a man's pocket can lift his spirits.

"You about got everything stowed away, Jim?" I asked as I hitched my horse to the front rail.

" 'Near 'bout, marse. Just a smidgen more of these grits and such, and we be ready to go home."

I reached inside the near-side pannier for one of the sacks of doubloons to pay Müller. It might seem kind of perplexing to you that, as poor as the rest of the South was, Florida always seemed to have a plentiful supply of gold. The fact is, most of that gold came from Cuba or one of the other Caribbean islands, almost all of it for the purchase of beef on the hoof.

Nowadays Florida lives on snowbirds and its citrus harvest, but, before that, cattle was king. I'm not saying we didn't have fruit trees, or that wealthy families from cities like New York, Philadelphia, and Boston hadn't been coming south for the winter long before the war. But it took the railroad to make those enterprises profitable enough to nudge the cattle industry off its throne, and the rails didn't start showing up in earnest until well into the 1880s. Before that, just about the whole state was an untamed frontier, with few towns of any significance, and even fewer banks.

Not that most of Florida's cattlemen would have trusted a bank, even if there had been one handy. It was a rough and tumble land, and we took care of our own. Later on, you'd hear about cattle barons such as Jake Summerlin and Judge Ziba King, woolly old coots who kept their gold in trunks in their bedrooms. Pa kept his buried in the hollowed-out section of an ancient oak tree about fifty yards behind the house. Worked just fine, too.

After settling up with Müller, I led my horse over to where Jim was checking the cinch on his mule. "The boys are up at the Havana House," I told him. "Do you want a drink before we head back?"

"I reckon I'd best not," he replied without much conviction.

"If you want one, Jim, we'll get you one."

"I don't wants to cause no trouble, marse." He hesitated as if weighing the pros and cons of his next words, then said: "I reckon if it weren't too much bother, I wouldn't mind havin' me a drink outside."

I nodded, and although it chapped my hind end that Jim felt too intimidated to stand at bar with the men he'd shared a hard trail with, I understood his reluctance. The injustice of a system that viewed a man as equal in one place but inferior in another might have angered me, but it would have been Jim who'd have to live with the consequences if someone took offense at the Negro's presence in a white man's saloon.

"How about a bottle?" I asked, swinging a leg over the cantle of my saddle.

"A bottle do sound mighty temptin'," Jim allowed. " 'Though I reckon Josie'd feel different about it."

"Well, hell, we just won't tell Josie."

Laughing happily, Jim mounted and we reined toward the

Havana, the pack horses lined out behind us. Jim's words brought Josie to my mind, and I knew she wouldn't have been too pleased to think of me going into a saloon, either.

Jim was Pa's first slave, but he'd bought Josie for him so many years before that their oldest boy, Joe-Jim, was only a couple of years younger than me. Joe-Jim was with Pa, helping him move that larger herd into Georgia, while Josie was back at the Flatiron with another colored woman Pa had only recently purchased to be Joe-Jim's wife—when that time came. Her name was Lena, and although she hadn't even been with us a year by then, everyone liked her. Joe-Jim was pulling at the traces to get married, but Pa said she was still too young, and had refused to grant permission to the union until she turned fifteen later that summer. Jim and Joe-Jim were already hard at work building a small home north of the main house for the newlyweds, close to the cabin where Jim and Josie lived.

We hauled up in front of the saloon and I dismounted at the rail. "Wait here and I'll grab you a bottle," I said, then climbed the steps to the boardwalk.

Earlier, while I was paying for our supplies, I'd heard the boys whooping and hollering in the distance, just like old times, but as I pushed through the swinging doors that night I could feel the tension in the room. It was like walking into a beard of Spanish moss, just after a heavy downpour.

"You know what that son-of-a-bitch Jacob Klee is sayin', Boone?" Roy demanded before the batwing doors had stopped flapping.

"I heard."

"He's saying it was you and Casey what throwed that half-witted nephew of his into a 'gator hole to get et."

I'll admit I felt oddly pleased that most of them seemed as outraged by Jake Klee's accusations as I'd been. Everyone was there except for Dick Langley, who Casey had sent out to keep an eye on the Fort Myers road. The others were gathered in a close group by the bar.

"It's a lie, and we all know it," I said, approaching the bar. "Word will spread soon enough."

Casey shook his head. "I ain't sure it will, Boone."

His reply caught me off guard. "I don't see how anyone who knows the McCallisters or Davises would believe a tale like that from a Klee," I said.

"Not everyone thinks as poorly of the Klees as you do," Ardell pointed out. "I'm not saying you're wrong, but a lot of people haven't had to deal with them the way your Pa did with old Judah."

"Ardell is making good sense, Boone," Eric interjected. "Stories like that can take on a life of their own after a while. It ain't just Dave Klee's death that'll fascinate people, it's the way it happened."

"The way they're *saying* it happened," I reminded him. "Besides, Dave Klee ain't the first man to get pulled under by a 'gator because he wasn't watching where he stepped."

Casey turned to the bar, leaning over it with his shoulders hunched like he was chilled. "I sure hope so," was all he said, but I could tell he didn't think it was likely, and that the others felt the same.

"What do you want to do about it?" I asked abruptly. "If anyone's got an idea, spill it out here where we can all see it."

"I'll tell you what we ought to do," Roy Turner growled. "We ought to go get that fat son-of-a-bitch, then drag him back here by his heels and make him confess. Make him do it where the whole town can hear, and know what a lying whore's son he really is."

But I was already shaking my head at that. "Jacob Klee isn't just one man. He's got nearly a dozen hardcases riding with him, and kin scattered all through these parts. Pull a stunt like that and we'd have a hundred men dogging us, screaming for our blood."

"So what are you going to do? Just let it slide?"

"Unless someone's got an idea that ain't likely to start a range war, I don't see where I've got much choice."

An uneasy silence greeted my words. When several of the boys exchanged furtive glances, I swore softly.

"What do you want me to do, dammit? Go after Jacob Klee with a gun?"

"What's wrong with that?" Roy demanded.

"I told Pa I'd look after the Flatiron until he got back, and that's what I intend to do."

Almost apologetically, Eric said: "I should have mentioned this earlier, Boone, but Klee was promising revenge when he rode out of here yesterday. He seemed pretty set on it."

"What kind of revenge?"

"The usual bullshit. How he was going to make you regret ever being born, and that you'd be howling like a baby and begging to die before he got through with you." Eric shrugged. "A lot of guys'll make threats like that when they're drunk or mad, but . . . well, Jake Klee ain't like a lot of guys, Boone. He didn't seem all that drunk, either."

I glanced at Casey, still leaning into the bar with his shoulders up to his ears. "What do you want to do, Case?"

"Much as I hate to admit it, I guess you're right. There's not much we can do right now."

"You're *both* gonna let this slide?" Roy burst out.

"I reckon we are," I replied softly. "At least for now."

Roy swore and spun toward the bar. Eric refilled his glass, then poured a shot for me. "On the house," he said.

I nodded my thanks and threw the whiskey against the back of my throat. It was kind of raw to be gulping, but I've had worse, and kept a straight face as I stared into the backbar mirror. The reflection was of the rear of the room—the empty gaming tables and dust-layered chuck-a-luck cage. No one spoke. Jacob Klee's threats had smothered the drovers' good humor like wet sand on a campfire. I had another whiskey out of the bottle the boys were passing around, then ordered a full one for Jim. Eric brought out a brown quart bottle stoppered with a chipped cork and sealed in beeswax.

"It ain't fancy from Kentucky, but it ain't bad, either. It'll cut varnish or wipe out a bad memory as quick as the good stuff."

I turned the bottle in my hand, smiling at the crude marks scratched into the glass—a pair of Xs separated by a short, crooked line, like this. [*Ed. Note:* A slip of paper, like that from the back of an envelope, was included in the McCallister file, containing a penciled inscription similar to the following: X∼X.]

That was Norm Wakley's mark, burned into the hides of his cattle, and carved into anything that wouldn't burn. Wakley was another Pease River settler, although he lived farther back in the scrub than most, where he spent more time making bush whiskey than he did popping cows out of the swamps. I liked Norman well enough, and would often ride up to his place on Whiskey Creek to visit, although I suspect my pa was right when he claimed I liked Norman's sixteen-year-old daughter, Trudy, a whole lot more than I did the old man.

"How much?" I asked, tapping the side of the bottle with a finger.

"Two bucks," Eric replied.

That was high for rotgut, but I had more money than options at that point, and forked it over without comment. Taking the bottle outside, I handed it to Jim. "You figure you can find your way back to those pines where we last stopped?"

Admiring the amber reflection of the saloon's light on the bottle's shoulder, it took a second for my question to sink in. Turning to me with a worried look, he said: "You wants me to go back that-away by my lonesome? That be a mighty long way for an old Negro like me, 'specially with a couple pack horses carrying so much good truck."

"You won't have to go all that way by yourself. We're going to stay here and wash out some problems, but that won't take long." I slapped his mule lightly on the hip, then stepped back out of the way. "Go on, Jim. You've got plenty of food and a good shotgun. You'll be fine."

Jim hesitated, glanced at the bottle like it was a friend about to embark on a long and dangerous journey, then twisted around in his saddle to shove it into his war bag.

I couldn't help grinning at his woebegone expression. "You don't have to wait until you get there to pull that cork," I said. "Just make sure you're sober enough when we catch up that you can still ride."

"I will, marse. I'll be there, and sober, too. Or leastways more sober than not."

He gave a tug on the lead rope to the first pack horse that set the whole string into motion, and started down that lonely stretch of road into the night. I watched him go for a minute, then turned back to the saloon with the smile sliding off my face. The drovers hadn't stirred in my absence, and I walked to the bar and ordered a fresh shot, not bothering to mask a quick, painful wince as I swallowed it down. Norm Wakley made good getting-drunk whiskey, but no one ever complained that it was too smooth.

Standing across the bar from me, Eric said: "This is the sorriest excuse for a hooray I've ever seen, Boone. I been to wakes that were more cheerful."

"I doubt if it's just Jacob Klee that's thrown water on everyone's spirits," I replied. "It's the whole damn' war that's got everyone feeling so glum. Last time I was here, you had a banjo picker sitting on the end of the bar playing his heart out, and whores enough for everyone. We could've gone down to Müller's and spent our hard earned cash on just about anything we wanted, too. Nowadays you've got to sneak in through the swamps just to come to town, and be careful you don't make too much noise doing it."

Eric shrugged and moved off. I guess the conversation was too close to the one we'd had earlier to warrant further effort. After a while, I took my whiskey and edged down the bar to where the rest of the crew were talking among themselves.

"It's time we did something," Roy was grumbling. "And I ain't talkin' about Jacob Klee, either."

"Then what are you talking about?" Ardell Hawes asked.

"I'm talkin' about going north and gettin' in some licks against those Yankee sons-of-bitches," Roy replied. "I'm tired of stayin' home nursin' cows while ever'one else is fightin'."

"Go on, then," Ardell said bluntly. "Nobody's stopping you."

"I intend to," Roy declared, his voice rising defiantly. "Maybe even form my own company. What about it, boys? Anyone here got the spine to do some good for the South?" His face fell when no one spoke up. "By God, are you tellin' me you're all a-scared to fight?"

"No one is afraid to fight," Ardell said sharply. "We wouldn't be here tonight if we were. But if I do decide to join, it won't be you I'll follow." He slewed partway around to peg me with a hard stare. "I'd follow you, Boone, if you wanted to put an outfit together."

"Boone!" Roy hooted. "Hell, Boone's too yellow to fight. You saw the way he led us here. It's a damned wonder we didn't all get et by 'gators."

"Boone took on a job and saw it through," Ardell said. "Didn't lose too many cows, and only one man hurt in a bushwhack. He'd suit me to lead."

"I'd join if Boone led," Punch affirmed.

"Hold on, boys," I interrupted. "I appreciate what y'all are saying, but I'm not going anywhere. I told Pa I'd stay home and look after the place, maybe start putting together another herd to run north. That's what I aim to do."

Ol' Roy, always one to start barking before he saw a squirrel, said: "Boone ain't got enough gumption to lead a honest-to-God fightin' outfit. He's only fit to stay home and keep outta the way, like his daddy told him to."

"Shut up, Roy," Ardell said, although he was still looking at me as he spoke. "You sure, Boone? I meant what I said about following you, if you put an outfit together."

"Yeah, I'm sure. Sorry, boys, but I gave Pa my word."

"All right, that's fair, but I still think Roy has a good idea. Not about forming his own company, but about those of us who want to go north where the real armies are fighting to start riding. Who's in?"

"I am," Calvin Oswald replied promptly.

"Count me in, too," Punch added.

Ardell looked at Roy and Pablo. "What about you two?"

"Not me," Pablo replied, shaking his head. "I go back to the Flatiron with Boone."

"Roy?"

Roy swore, then nodded. "Yeah, I'm in, dammit."

"Casey?"

"Naw, I'll go back to the Flatiron with Boone, but then I need to mosey on home and see what's doing. Pa put me in charge of the Cloverleaf, just like Boone's pa did him. I reckon that's what I'll do until he gets back from Georgia. I can decide then if I want to go fight Yankees." [*Ed. Note:* The Davis Ranch was known as the Cloverleaf in the 1860s; its brand was a four-leaf design said to represent Matthew Davis's four sons, of which Casey was the youngest.]

"Don't think on it too hard," Roy grumbled. "You wouldn't

want to tax your brain."

"Dang if you don't grow as irritating as a bog full of 'skeeters when you start drinking," I said to Roy.

"Don't worry about Turner," Ardell added with a grin. "A couple of months in a real cavalry'll take the starch out of him. Main thing is, there's four good Rebels about to join the fray. I say that ought to equal about two dozen Yankee shopkeepers."

"There'll be five of us, if Dick joins," Roy said.

"Dick needs to stay home with his wife and that new baby," Casey cut in.

"So should a lot of good men gettin' their butts shot off by Yankee snipers," Roy retorted.

"I'll ask, but Dick can do what he wants," Ardell said. "He doesn't have anything to prove, as far as I'm concerned." He looked at me. "You want some help getting back to the Flatiron, Boone?"

"No, we'll be fine." Stepping forward, I shook Ardell's hand enviously. "By God, I wish I was going with you, boy."

"You change your mind, we won't be hard to find."

Laughing, Punch said: "Look for where the fighting's thickest, Boone. That's where we'll be."

I smiled and shook Punch's hand, reminding him to take care of his arm. I wished the others luck, as well, then bought a final round for the house, Eric included. We were just finishing up when the sound of pounding hoofs interrupted our farewell celebration. Casey moved to the door to peer out over the top of the batwings. "Better douse those lights, Eric," he said. "That's Dick Langley, and he's coming in like he's got hounds snapping at his heels."

SESSION FOUR

I was the second one through the door that night, right behind Casey Davis. We stood on the boardwalk in front of the Havana House, staring nervously up the street in the direction of Fort Myers. Eric had taken Casey's advice to heart and was already quenching the saloon's lights, plunging the building into darkness. Glancing toward the Gulf, I realized that the whole town had gone dark while we'd been inside the Havana. Even Ashworth's office, down by the corrals, was as black as a chunk of coal, although I could still hear the cattle bawling nervously in their unfamiliar surroundings.

Dick didn't haul back on his reins until the last minute, bringing his mount to a plunging, head-shaking stop right in front of the saloon. "Riders coming!" he shouted. "A whole slew of 'em."

"How many?" I asked.

"Didn't see 'em, Boone, just heard 'em, but there's a passel. A lot more than what Jacob Klee's outfit could account for, that's certain sure. Maybe thirty or forty, coming along the road from Fort Myers at a good clip."

Several of the boys swore, and Ardell said: "It looks like you're going to get to fight some Yankees sooner than you thought, Roy."

"Bring on them dirty sons-of-bitches," Roy snarled, drawing his handgun to check its loads.

The rest of us were doing the same, running our thumbs

lightly over nipples to make sure the caps were all still snugly in place, checking that the cylinders were turning smoothly. Satisfied that my Navy was ready, I returned the gun to its holster, then started down the steps toward my horse. "Mount up, boys!" I called over my shoulder. "I don't want to fight them if we don't have to. Let's try slipping out through the swamps."

"The hell," Roy said in a startled manner. "I ain't runnin', Boone. I say we stand our ground right here, and let them cold-hearted bastards know what it's like to tangle with a bunch of he-'coons."

"No, not here," Ardell said, beating me to the punch. "Let's get out of town, where innocent people won't get hurt. Then we'll see. . . ." His words trailed off as a sound like the rumble of a distant stampede reached our ears. "Hell's fire, that's them, boys."

I glanced back to warn Eric to find a place to hide, but he'd already retreated inside the Havana, pulling the big outer doors closed behind him. Jerking my reins free, I swung into the saddle without using my stirrups. "Let's ride!" I shouted, pulling my mount toward the alley beside the saloon. Yet I'd barely moved away from the rail when a shot rang out from somewhere down the street, the bullet whistling so close past my ear that I instinctively jerked my head in the opposite direction. Two more shots came at us from the deeper shadows near the cow pens, and Ardell swore and yanked his right hand back, shaking it as if bee stung.

"This way!" I yelled, pulling my horse around and driving my heels into its ribs. My spurs, in case you're wondering, were still hanging off my saddle horn, where I'd left them the second time I approached Ashworth's office, although I doubt if they could have squeezed any more speed out of my little marsh-tackie. It was already streaking down Punta's Rassa's broad, dark street with a barn swallow's speed and agility.

The others fell in behind me, riding strung out and low over their ponies' necks, their revolvers and pistols drawn and ready to fire. To this day, I don't know who tried to ambush us from the corrals, although I'm fairly certain it wasn't Federals. They were still out in front of us, the thunder of their mounts' hoofs rising before us like a wall of flood water.

We met at the east end of the street, and Dick had been pretty close in his estimate—thirty-five to forty Union troopers, mounted astride their big Northern horses like they thought they could roll right over the top of us. We used our revolvers to explain to them the error of their thinking. Someone from the Yankee side of things kept yelling for us to halt, but we naturally didn't. The disjointed report of our pistols echoed along the wide street, drowning out the cries of the Federal commander as he tried to rally his men against our charge.

I don't think those bluebellies had any idea who was coming down the street toward them, and they quickly scattered before our guns. The Yankee in charge kept ordering his men to— "Hold firm."—in a shrill, ragged voice, but he might as well have been commanding a gaggle of geese for all the co-operation he was getting. I'd find out later that a lot of those boys had been new recruits out of New York, most of them as green as grass when it came to fighting, which was to our good fortune. I'll tell you what, we sure scattered their asses that night.

Likely, if we'd thought about it, we could have cornered the whole bunch and demanded their surrender, but we were more interested in flight at the time, and continued on into the scrub like so many fleeing rabbits. A few of those bluebellies managed to get off a shot or two, but I don't think most of them even got their revolvers out of those closed-flap holsters the army set so much store by.

I remember glancing behind me at one point and seeing Punch and Calvin racing their marshtackies side-by-side. No one else was in sight, but I wasn't worried. Those boys had been raised in the brush, and would survive just fine as long as they kept their wits about them.

I was starting to feel pretty good about the situation, until something happened that I didn't see coming at all. One minute we were racing east like a strong wind, and in the next, the air around us seemed to vibrate with the hum of spitting lead. Some years later I'd meet Eric Burke in Texas, where he'd gone after the Yankees burned down his saloon, and he told me it was a lieutenant named Hodges who ordered his men to dismount with their rifles, drop to one knee, then fire a concentrated volley toward the spot where us Flatiron riders had disappeared. Then he had his men reload and fire twice more, before he deemed we were probably out of range.

I ducked low over my saddle horn after the first volley, and was drumming a rapid beat against my horse's ribs when I heard Punch shouting for me to come back. I swore and pulled my mount to a stop.

"Boone, they shot Cal!" Punch yelled, and I swore again, before wheeling back to help.

I found Punch hovering fretfully over his buddy, his face pale in the starlight. Calvin's face looked even paler. There was a dark smear high and toward the center of the chest—an exit wound, I figured—and his breathing sounded wheezy and off-kilter.

"He's shot, Boone," Punch said needlessly.

That was when the third volley came, whistling overhead like a scythe. I ducked and swore, while my horse struggled to break free.

"Get back here!" I hollered, yanking hard on the reins. The horse ceased its fidgeting, but was still badly spooked by all the shouting and shooting.

"Cal," Punch said uncertainly, giving the younger man's

shoulder a quick shake. He looked up, his expression filled with dread. "He ain't breathing no more, Boone. Cal ain't breathing."

I laid a hand against the youngster's chest just to be certain, then rocked back on my heels, not sure what I should say or do. It was as if my world had been suddenly cut adrift, bouncing sideways down a boulder-strewn rapids with no one at the oars. Hell, you've got to remember that I was only a few years older than Cal myself, and he wasn't even shaving yet.

"What are we gonna do?" Punch whispered dully.

I shook my head, then grimly pushed to my feet. "Where's his horse?"

"It took off."

"All right." I hesitated, my thoughts a-whirl. "All right . . . we're . . . we're going to have to let someone else bury Cal. Someone from Punta Rassa. We can't wait, and it'd be too dangerous to take him with us."

"Leave him?" Punch asked incredulously.

"It's our only choice. Any minute now, them Yankees are going to come busting through here with their guns drawn. They won't give us a chance to fight or run or even surrender, they'll just shoot us where we stand, then leave us behind while they go after the others. Someone in Punta Rassa will find Cal, and see that he gets a proper burial. Come on, now. We can tell his folks when we get back. They can come fetch his body when things calm down."

I could tell Punch didn't care much for my plan, but he could definitely see the logic of getting out of there before thirty or forty Yankees showed up in a fighting mood. His face drawn nearly to tears, he stepped into his saddle and reined after me. We loped our marshtackies through the scrub, and I don't know about Punch, but my muscles were taut enough to play like a fiddle at the thought of catching a Union Minié ball in my back.

Although I really did expect those Yankees to follow us, they didn't. According to Eric, after that third volley, Hodges led his men down to the corrals and confiscated the herd that W.B. had bought from me just a few hours earlier. Eric said there was quite a bit of speculation afterward that maybe Ashworth had been behind the Federals' raid all along, maybe in hopes that he wouldn't have to shell out any hard coin for our herd, and that the buyer he'd lined up for our cattle hadn't been a Cuban ship's captain, after all, but those Fort Myers Yankees. The fact that Ashworth disappeared a couple of days later didn't help his position with the locals any.

As far as me and Punch, we continued on through the darkness with our imaginations filled with pursuing troops. We were still heading for the pines, but in a roundabout manner to avoid the swamps we'd nearly bogged down in only a few hours before. After a while I began to quit worrying about the Yankees behind us and started thinking about Negro Jim. I wondered if he was even aware of the Yankees' presence, especially if he hadn't heard the gunfire. That was a possibility. Out in the open, a firearm can be heard for a good long ways, but trees and brush can muffle a gunshot a lot more than most people realize.

Punch and I didn't get very far before we caught up with Roy, Ardell, and Dick Langley, sitting their heavily breathing mounts behind a screen of palmettos. Ardell perked up when he spotted us, but his expression fell when he saw the looks on our faces.

"You boys OK?" he asked tentatively.

I barely had a chance to nod before Punch blurted out the news about Cal. "We just left him there," the youth added miserably.

"It's for the best," Ardell replied after a moment of shocked silence. "Those woods are likely crawling with Yankees by now. They'll find Calvin and see he gets buried proper, or else let someone in town know where to find him." He looked at me. "We'd best ride, Boone, if we don't want to end up like Oswald."

I nodded toward his left hand, dripping blood from a wound above his thumb. "How bad?" I asked.

He shook his head dismissively. "It's just a burn. It'll heal quick enough."

"What about Casey and Pablo? Have you seen them?"

"I haven't, but if they're alive, they're likely heading for that pine grove, the same as the rest of us."

"Let's go see if they're there," I said, heeling my marshtackie to the head of the small column. It wasn't long afterward that I heard a whippoorwill's cry from a hammock on our right, and jerked back on my reins. Although my hand had dropped instinctively to the Navy's walnut grips, I didn't draw it. "Come on out, Casey."

A pair of horsemen emerged from the trees—Casey up front, Pablo close behind. Casey's eyes swept the group as he drew near, then settled on me with a questioning look. "Calvin took a bullet in the back," I explained. "He's dead."

Casey swore softly, but that was all. Pablo held his tongue, a stricken look on his face.

"Anybody seen Jim?" I asked.

There was a general round of noes, but nothing that concerned me yet. If Jim hadn't stumbled into a Yankee patrol, he was probably somewhere well ahead of us.

We moved out at a brisk walk, while the sky in the east finally began to lighten. I doubt if we'd gone more than a mile when a voice hailed us from a clump of rushes growing close to the banks of a tiny creek. Reining in that direction, we found Jim extracting himself from the tangle. There was a relieved smile on the Negro's lips, a worried cast to his eyes.

"Marse Boone, I surely am glad to see you!" Jim exclaimed, stepping forward to place a hand gently against my marshtackie's shoulder.

"Are you all right, Jim?"

"Yes'um, but they took the horses. Took old Molly, too."

Molly was Jim's mule, a leggy gray with more swamp savvy than your average marshtackie, although you'd never find a cow hunter who would admit it.

"Who took 'em?" Roy demanded, his face flushed with anger.

"Yankees, Mistah Roy. Was Yankees took them horses of Marse Boone's."

"What happened?" I asked, before Roy could work up any more fire.

"They come outta nowhere, had me surrounded 'fore I knew they was even about," Jim said. "Was a slew of 'em, too. They asked who I was and where I was goin' and where I was comin' from and a lot of other questions I didn't answer. Then they told me I was a free man and didn't have to be no slave no more. Said I should come with them to Fort Myers, only I told them I didn't want to go to Fort Myers. Told 'em I wanted to go home to my woman and family, but they said I couldn't. Said I was a free man now, and that I had to come with them to Fort Myers." He shook his head ruefully. "Maybe I don't rightly understand freedom, after all, marse."

Some of the boys laughed quietly. Roy swore and spat. I said: "No, I expect you understand what it means better than most. Sounds like it was the Federals who lost sight of its meaning."

"They surely did want me to come with them."

"Where are the horses now, Jim?" Casey asked.

"They took 'em, Mistah Casey. All them supplies Marse Boone bought from that German fella in Punta Rassa, they took those, too. They was gonna take me, but then that Yankee with all the fancy markings on his uniform said they had to get into town to stop those dirty Secesh, and that a sergeant named Moore was to stay behind and confiscate me and the horses." [*Ed. Note:* Secesh is a shortened form of Secessionist, usually used in a derogatory manner by pro-Union supporters to describe a person who endorsed the South's secession from the Union.]

"Why didn't they take you?" Casey asked.

"Well, when that fella with the fancy uniform took off with most of his men, those fellas that stayed behind started going through the packs like chicks under a corncrib. Once they found my bottle, they commenced to drinking, and while they was doing that, I skedaddled."

"Good for you," Casey said.

Jim was watching me closely. "I's powerful sorry, marse, but them Yankees had me outnumbered by a good bit."

"It ain't your fault, Jim," I told him, then kicked a boot free of its stirrup and lowered my arm. "Grab on. You can ride behind me until we catch up with that sergeant and our packs."

"We goin' after 'em, Boone?" Roy asked.

"I am. You boys don't have to if you don't want to."

"The hell," Roy growled. "Let's go get them Yankee sons-of-bitches."

Looking relieved that I wasn't angry, Jim grabbed my arm near the elbow and I pulled him up behind me. My marshtackie lowered its rump like it wanted to buck at the added weight, but settled down with a firm hand and sharp scolding.

We moved out at a jog, keeping our eyes peeled in every direction for Yankees, but the flat plain between us and the Caloosahatchee seemed deserted until we reached the main trail between Fort Myers and Punta Rassa. It was there that we spotted the tracks of the sergeant and his men, along with those of our pack horses. They were heading east, toward the fort.

"That's them," Jim said excitedly. "I been followin' ol' Molly so many years, I'd rec'nize her tracks at the bottom of an ocean."

We kept riding as the light grew stronger, and may not have caught up at all if those Yankees hadn't stopped beside the road to finish off Jim's bottle of sour mash whiskey. We reined into the scrub as soon as we spotted them, and me and Casey dismounted, then crept forward on foot. At about eighty yards, we settled down to study the tiny detail in the misty gray light. There were four of them, gathered around a smoldering fire under the sprawling limbs of a solitary oak. At first glance you would have thought they were preparing breakfast, but, with a second, you would have noticed how inactive they seemed, not to mention the lack of kettles and skillets. Only one man was on his feet, and he was leaning against the trunk of the tree with his legs braced stiffly in front of him. The others were slumped in front of their fire with their chins dragging their chests, arms slack in a pose I'd seen many times after an end-of-drive spree. Shoot, I'd suffered through more than a few early-bird hangovers myself since my first encounter with a bottle on my sixteenth birthday.

"How many jugs of bug juice did you give Jim?" Casey asked.

"Just the one, but I also bought a bottle of blackberry wine from Müller to take home. Looks like they might've found that, too."

"Well, blackberry wine ain't got the same kick as a couple of swallows of Norman Wakley's popskull, but I reckon it'll help. It looks like them four are about as pickled as they're going to get, and plum for the plucking."

"Well, hell, let's go pluck 'em."

We scooted back to where the others were waiting, and I told Jim to crawl down. "Stay out of sight until we've got those Yankees corralled," I told him.

Jim dropped to the ground and handed me the reins. I left

the Sharps hitched to my rig, but palmed my Navy Colt. The way those ol' boys in blue wool were acting, I didn't expect them to take much notice of us until we knocked at their door, and that's pretty much how it happened. I led my men around to come at them from behind that big ol' oak tree, then split them apart and spread them out so that we came on our prey from both sides. Me and Casey and Ardell quickly dismounted, but we needn't have hurried. I think I was as surprised as those Yankees were when we were able to walk into camp undetected.

"Here now," said the man leaning against oak's broad trunk. He started fumbling for the Springfield rifle leaning against the tree at his side, but couldn't seem to get his fingers to work properly.

"Leave it," Ardell snapped, while Casey and I threw down on the three soldiers hunched over the sputtering flames of their fire. Two of them spotted us immediately, but the last one, a sandy-haired kid who couldn't have been much older than Calvin's fifteen-plus years, didn't notice anything amiss until I poked him with the Colt's muzzle. He looked up, grunting in surprise when he saw all the revolvers pointed at him, but when he tried to stand up, he lost his balance and started stumbling backward until he fell on his butt in the dew-wet grass. He rolled over on his stomach and started to heave. We waited until he was finished, then Ardell grabbed him by his shirt collar and hauled him back to the fire. The man standing under the oak tree wore sergeant's stripes. I figured him for Moore.

"You boys drop your guns, then move on over beside your sergeant," I ordered the trio at the fire.

"You kids don't know who you're messing with," the sergeant growled at me with a whiskey slur. Judging that he was still on his feet, I suspect he might have been the soberest Yankee there.

"I think we do," I countered. "You're Sergeant Moore, from Fort Myers, sent down here to harass innocent civilians and steal people's property."

Moore spat in disdain. "Like hell, you Rebel trash. We're down here to kick your Secesh asses up above your ears, then send that coward Jeff Davis to the gallows."

I glanced at Casey and whistled. "He must be one tough son-of-a-gun if he thinks he's going to accomplish all of that on his own."

"I got plenty of men to help me," the sergeant replied, but I noticed he was starting to look around, maybe taking stock of his situation, which wasn't as solid as it had been when he left Fort Myers the night before with close to forty troopers at his back and a lieutenant up front. "What do you scum plan to do with us?" he demanded with noticeably less vigor.

"We're going to hang you," Casey replied.

"Hold on, Case," I said quickly. "That ain't been decided yet."

"The hell it ain't," Roy shot back. "They killed Calvin, didn't they?"

"Not this bunch."

"It's the same thing, Boone," Ardell replied evenly. He was staring at me, his eyes narrowed in determination. "You know what they're doing up north, places like Chattanooga and Vicksburg. You know what they'll do down here, too, once they get a foothold."

Well, I didn't like it, but I knew Ardell was right. This was war, and it was ugly. I was about to find out just how much uglier it could get. The Yankees had their horses picketed nearby. Reluctantly I told Pablo and Punch to bring them in.

"Roy," I said with an edge to my voice, "you claim there ain't a knot you can't tie. Does that include a hangman's noose?"

Growling low in his throat, Roy slid from his saddle. "It sure as hell does," he said, heading for the Yankees' horses. "Gimme that," he snapped to Pablo, yanking the picket rope from the

Cuban's hand. He started forming a noose even as he circled the giant oak, looking for a handy limb.

Moore was glaring at me, not unlike the way Ashworth had the night before, trying to intimidate me into accepting a lower offer for Pa's herd. "If you go through with this, kid, you might as well put your own neck in there along with mine, because Lieutenant Hodges'll hound you all the way to the Atlantic."

"Maybe you ought to start putting things in order with your Maker, instead of blabbering about what your buddies will do," Ardell advised.

"Sarge," one of the men spoke up, as if not quite sure he believed what was taking shape around him.

"That goes for the rest of you, too," Ardell said. "If you got prayers to send, get 'em off."

"You can't hang us," Moore protested. "We're regulars. You've got to treat us like prisoners of war."

Casey hesitated, glancing at Ardell, then me. "Is that true?"

"We aren't soldiers yet," Ardell replied. "If they'd captured us last night in Punta Rassa, they'd have hanged us on the spot as traitors."

"That's because you ain't soldiers," Moore argued. "Hell, look it up, or find some Reb officer and ask him. You boys can't hang us. It's against the law."

"So is stealing pack horses and scaring Negros that ain't your property," I said, my anger flaring. I nodded to Roy. "Get those ropes strung, before the rest of Hodges's bluebellies show up."

I spotted Jim from the corner of my eye. He was standing next to the spilled packs, silently watching our preparations. I wanted to walk over and see what he thought, maybe feel him out about how Pa might have handled the situation, like I had that night at Chestnut Thumb. Then, inexplicably, I turned my back on the old colored man. I didn't want to hear what he had to say, or what he thought Pa might think. This was my decision. For better or worse, there was no backing out now.

Well, we couldn't find a limb long enough or straight enough to hang all four men side-by-side, but we did locate four branches stout enough to hang them individually. That's what we did, stringing up the sergeant first, then the men under his command. We did it one at a time, with the sandy-haired kid last, still too drunk to fully realize what was going on, which was probably for the best. When it was done, I told Jim to pack up what the Yankees had scattered. Only later would it occur to me that they must have found the whiskey and wine before they did the gold. I wondered what their response would have been if they'd known of the fortune that lay so close to their pilfering fingers. I doubt they would have been sitting around a dying fire like turkeys at a rifle frolic if they had.

With the packs in place, I told Jim to start riding. "Keep those horses moving until we catch up," I added, then turned back to where the others were standing solemnly around the gray ashes of the fire. The Yankees were still swinging gently, although I don't recall there being any breeze that morning. Not after we got away from the coast.

I'll admit I felt about half sick by what we'd done, racked with all kinds of guilt and doubt. I think the others felt that way, too. Even ol' Roy was sporting a hound-dog expression that morning. But I have to say, even after all these years, I think we did the right thing. I would show leniency only once before this was all over, and regret that far more than I ever have hanging those Fort Myers Yankees.

After setting Jim on his way to Pete Dill's trading post on the Upper Caloosahatchee, I told the boys to turn the Yankee horses loose, then toss their saddles and tack into the scrub. After the war, a lot of cow hunters would grow real fond of those McClellan rigs the Union favored. They offered more solid seating for the drover, and better ventilation for both horse and rider, what with the open frame down the middle, but, at the time, I was more worried about being caught with them in our possession.

I was the last one in the saddle that morning, and, after reining around to face the others, I said: "You boys still set on riding north to join the fight?"

Clearing his throat, Ardell replied: "We were talking about that while you were helping Jim reload the pack horses, Boone, and we've decided we'd like to tag along with you for a spell, if you don't mind."

"I'm just going back to the Flatiron."

"You're going through Dill's place first, though, right?"

"Always do."

In 1864, Pete Dill's trading post was about the only hub of information in that part of Florida's interior. Pete traded mostly with the Seminoles, exchanging supplies for hides, furs, and plumes, although he'd sell to anyone with hard cash in their poke. Pete always kept a good supply of liquor on the premises, and served whiskey to all manner of men on their way through that part of the country, be they white, black, or red. I would have swung past Pete's place under any circumstance, but I was especially curious about what he'd heard regarding Dave Klee's demise, and Jacob Klee's intentions. I didn't have any doubts that he'd know something.

"We'll ride with you as far as Dill's," Ardell said. "I'd like to hear what he has to say."

Meaning, I took it, that he was also wondering about the Klees.

"Let's make tracks," I said, heeling my marshtackie into a lope.

I don't mind admitting that I was grateful for the company. I figured when those Union boys of Hodges's found out what we'd done, they'd be swarming after us like wasps for retribution. I wanted to be as far away from that oak tree as possible when it happened.

We caught up with Jim less than a mile down the road. Not wanting another run-in with Federal troops, I led the boys south, back into the northern fringe of the Big Cypress. I think we all breathed a sigh of relief when the jungle finally closed in behind us.

It had taken us two weeks to reach Punta Rassa after crossing the Caloosahatchee River at its upper ford. It took us four days going back, and that largely on account of the difficult route we followed. Before the war, you could have made that trip in two, staying to open country.

Pete Dill's place sat north of the river, just below the upper ford, near the falls at Lake Flirt. It was a large, cypress-log cabin with a verandah across the front and pine shingles on the roof. The trading room, living quarters, and storeroom were all under one roof, so as you can imagine, it was a fairly large structure.

Even though the building stood a good hundred yards from the river's edge, Pete had built it on six-foot pilings to keep the floor above flood stage during the rainy hurricane season. Set beside the main trading post was a corral with a lean-to tack shed, and a larger pasture out back surrounded by a split-rail pine fence.

Still leery after our encounter with the Yankees at Punta Rassa, we hung back in the scrub while Ardell rode ahead to scout the place. He returned thirty minutes later to announce that the way was clear.

"Not a piece of blue uniform in sight," was how he put it.

It was late afternoon when we finally rode up to the trading post. There were only a few horses in the pasture out back, all of them Pete's, and all for sale or trade. A kettle hanging from an iron tripod above a low fire in front of the post smelled of simmering cabbage soup, raising an anticipatory rumble from my stomach.

Pete's Seminole woman stood bent at the waist in the shallows along the river, washing clothes. She straightened when she saw us, the hem of her brightly colored skirt—vivid reds and yellows and greens over a black background—tucked into the waistband, exposing dimpled, copper-brown knees. She met our hungry gazes stoically, until I finally told the boys to keep their minds on the business at hand. Pete's wife was as pretty as a freshly minted nickel, but it was common knowledge that she'd killed a man with a knife when he tried to take advantage of her one night. Knowing her even the little that I did, it was a story I didn't doubt.

Standing at the far end of the trade counter as we trooped inside, Pete Dill greeted most of us by name, although I don't think he knew Dick Langley, who hailed from farther north. Jim was the last one through, and Pete greeted him as warmly as any of us. Removing his hat as he stepped to one side, Jim said: "Afternoon, Mistah Pete."

Dill was a beefy man with a quick laugh and a fiery temper. Already well into middle age when I first met him, he wore his steel-gray hair long, despite the slick baldness it fringed. He had a bushy beard but no mustache, and a corncob pipe thrust into a corner of his mouth like it was hammered there. Tobacco smoke curled lazily past one squinted blue eye. I remember once asking Pa, back when I was a little squirt, if old man Dill slept with that pipe between his lips, and Pa had chuckled and said: "Likely he does, boy."

Pete had always been friendly with the McCallisters and the Davises, largely, I think, because he'd served with my pa and Negro Jim and Matt and Big Ed during the Indian Wars. He was watching us charily that day, though, which put me instantly on guard.

"You boys looking to wet your whistlers?" Pete asked.

"I wouldn't turn down something with a little kick," I replied. "Might pay a few cents more if it wasn't some of Norm Wakley's rotgut."

Pete chuckled from deep in his chest, and the atmosphere in the room grew a smidge lighter. "Wakley's stuff is all I've got since the blockade. Ol' Norm'd make a fortune if there was anyone left down here to buy his stuff." He set a bottle and six glasses on the counter in front of us and started pouring. Glancing at Jim, still hanging back by the door, he added: "It's all right with me if you want a drink, Jim, as long as it's OK with your master."

I swung around on one elbow. "You want a snort, Jim?"

"If it ain't too much trouble, a snort would go down mighty fine," Jim said.

"Come on up and grab one, then."

I could see Roy Turner's expression darken at my invitation, but he wisely kept his tongue in check. I figured that of everyone there, only Roy, and maybe Pablo, would object to drinking with a black man. Pete sure never seemed to have a problem with it.

The trader fished two more glasses from under the counter and poured rounds for himself and Jim. Roy grumbled a little when Jim bellied up to the bar, which I know Jim heard because he quickly backed away when Pete handed him his whiskey. I felt like punching Roy Turner in the nose right there, but instead gritted my teeth and remained silent. Sometimes you've just got to swallow back the ire that rises in your throat, even if it does taste like bile at times.

"To the Confederacy," Ardell said loudly, and we all cheered and threw back our drinks. Punch choked a little on the whiskey's fire, but kept it down all right. The rest of us, having had more experience with hard spirits, never batted an eye, and

Jim's smile broadened as the whiskey's warmth spread through his system.

"That's mighty fine sippin' whiskey, Mistah Pete!" Jim exclaimed, and several of us laughed at the absurdity of calling anything out of Norman Wakley's copper still fine.

Pete refilled everyone's glasses, but we took our time with that second round. I could still feel the first one knocking around my gullet like a madman with a sledge-hammer. Casual like, as he topped off the last glass, Pete said: "Which way you heading, Boone?"

"I'm bound for home. We sold a small herd to a buyer in Punta Rassa, is why we're so far south." Pete studied me quietly for a moment, until I started to grow uneasy. "You got something you want to say?"

"Mostly just thinking. That and wondering if you knew what Jacob Klee's been saying."

Me and Casey swore in unison, and Roy growled: "If he's tryin' to lay blame on Casey and Boone for Dave Klee gettin' pulled under by a 'gator, that's pure hog shit."

"That a fact?" Pete asked mildly.

"You damn' right that's a fact," Roy answered. "You can ask any of us. We was all there." He turned to Pablo, standing at his side. "Ain't that right, Torres?"

Pablo ducked his head in order to avoid Turner's gaze. After a terse moment, he muttered: "I did not see it."

"You didn't have to see it!" Roy exclaimed. "You was there, boy. We all were."

"It's a lie, Pete," Casey said, interrupting the conversation between Roy and Pablo. In a quiet voice, he outlined what had happened at Chestnut Thumb, then told the trader about what the Klees had said about us in Punta Rassa. "It ain't nothing but a lie, though," he finished. "You know me 'n' Boone."

"I know your daddies, too," Pete replied soberly. "Things got bloody during the Seminole Wars, but neither man shied away from what had to be done."

"We wouldn't, either," I said with a trace of heat in my words. "But I wouldn't feed a man to an alligator, no matter how I felt about him. Neither would Casey. You've got to know that."

"Jacob said a couple of Flatiron riders shot Davey first, just to make him bleed, then threw him in that 'gator hole." After an uncomfortable pause, he added: "Said he heard you boys laughing about it afterward."

"Laughing!" I exclaimed, but Pete held up a hand before I could take off.

"Don't go blowing out a tooth, Boone. I've been dealing with old Judah's kith and kin ever since I came to the 'glades. I know which ones I trust, and which ones I wouldn't turn my back on for a wagonload of gold. Jacob Klee's a bad one. He's a double-crossing, mean-hearted old codger, but he does tend to believe his own lies after a while. That's why . . . well, I thought maybe you boys had already been home, and now you were headed south."

My spine stiffened at the trader's words. "What's that mean, Pete?" I asked tonelessly.

"It means Jacob came through here with ten men about three days ago, but only four went south with him, into the swamps. The other six went north."

"Toward the Flatiron?"

"Maybe. The Flatiron or a hundred other places they could've been headed for, but something the old man said struck me as odd. As them six were walking out to get their 'tackies, Jacob said . . . 'Let 'em know you were there, boys.' "

I swore softly and pushed away from the bar. In my mind I was picturing the Flatiron's buildings, the two lone colored women left at home to keep the place in order. "You said three days ago?"

"Late in the day. Jacob and the four that stayed with him spent the night down by the river, but those six that he sent north took off that same evening." He looked down, started to reach for his drink, then pulled his hand back. "About how far is it to the Flatiron, Boone?"

"Two days, pushing hard."

"So if they were heading for your daddy's place. . . ."

"Seems like," I said heavily, setting my glass on the counter, its contents untouched. Casey and the others did the same. Only Pablo swallowed his, downing it quick, then stepping away from the bar.

"We riding, Boone?" Casey asked.

"You damn' right we're riding," I replied grimly. "Hard."

Excerpted from
Journal of a Military Physician:
A New Yorker's Experiences in Florida During the
Late Hostilities
by
Capt. Robert Winterton, 110th NY Inf., Ret.
The Potomac Press, 1950

Chapter Eight

A Hanging On the Caloosahatchee

[*Ed. Note:* Captain James Doyle, of the 110th New York Infantry, was Garrison Commander at Fort Myers during its occupancy of 1863-1865. Captain Robert Winterton was chief surgeon there under Doyle's command; the son of Dr. William B. Winterton, of Mexico, New York, Robert Winterton was commissioned a captain upon his enlistment at Oswego, in July, 1862. Lieutenant Oliver Hodges was commissioned a 2nd Lieutenant at Oswego by then state Senator Cheney Ames that same month.

The 110th was mustered into service on August 25, 1862. By March of 1864, Fort Myers, Florida, was home to a detached company of the 110th New York, a detached company of the 2nd United States Colored Infantry, and the 2nd Florida Cavalry, made up primarily of local Union sympathizers and Confederate deserters.]

. . . the garrison was rendered quite livid as news of the treatment suffered by Sergeant Moore and his men spread throughout the post and its surrounding colony of refugees. Captain Doyle took immediate steps to launch a punitive expedition against the perpetrators of this act of cowardice, and at once ordered Lieutenant Hodges into the field with a force of eight mounted Infantry to apprehend and "settle the mettle" of the

113

guilty party. Identification was made possible by certain col-laborators sympathetic to the preservation of the Grand Union.

The traitors were identified as Bone(sic) McCallister, Casey Hawes (sic), Roy Turner, Arthur Hawes (sic), Richard Langley, Calvin Oswald, a dark-skinned accomplice of either Spanish or Indian blood, and a notorious killer known only as "Punch," so named for his prowess with a revolver.

[Lieutenant] Hodges was given explicit orders, overheard by myself, to apprehend these men and see to their immediate execution by either rope or firing squad, the method to be at the discretion of the lieutenant and as circumstances dictated.

SESSION FIVE

I was thinking at breakfast this morning about how I kind of started this story with Dave Klee's death, and then just kept going from there without filling you in on the whens and whys and what-fors. Maybe I ought to do that now, so that you have a better understanding of how this all came about.

My daddy's name was Jefferson Thomas McCallister. He was born in Wilkes County, Georgia, on July 5th, 1798, but moved to the Lower St. Johns River in Florida with his parents in 1807 or 1808, as best he could remember. Pa had two brothers, Franklin Benjamin and Adam Samuel, and if you think you're seeing a trend there, you ain't mistaken.

Neither Frank nor Adam saw any need to continue the tradition begun with Grandpappy McCallister, but our pa thought it was a fine idea. My full name, in case you haven't guessed by now, is Boone Daniel, the second youngest of the six surviving sons of Jefferson and Julia McCallister.

Pa wasn't as much a fan of the Revolution as he was the old-time frontiersmen, and named his boys accordingly. The oldest was Lewis Meriwether, followed by Clark William, then Crockett David, Kenton Simon—who we called Bud for some reason I was never made privy to—then me, and lastly, Stone Michael, named after Michael Stoner, who probably isn't as well-known as those others, but was still a rip-roarer from the Allegheny country.

Maybe it was Pa's fascination with those early explorers that put such a lust for wandering in his soul. Or else it was the other way around. Whatever the cause, Pa had it bad, that bug to see what lay beyond the next bend in the river, or behind that distant hammock of cypress trees. By the time he was fourteen, he'd explored most of that country along the lower St. Johns River, and was a right fair hunter and trapper, too, although I guess there wasn't a lot of money in it in those days, what with the war with England pulling the rug out from under the fur trade. [*Ed. Note:* McCallister is referring to the War of 1812 here, with Great Britain.]

When he was sixteen, Pa finally set out on his own, traveling all the way up the St. Johns in a dug-out he'd hollowed and shaped himself. I guess he was gone for more than a year, and my grandparents had pretty well given him up for dead when he finally came back with his dug-out nearly overflowing with hides, pelts, and plumes. He had him a sturdy raft in tow, as well, carrying even more pelts, along with several hollow-log casks filled with honey.

Pa made a chunk of money off that trip, and kept on doing well for himself with his hunting and trapping and trading, until Grandpappy finally conceded the boy wasn't lazy, as he'd originally thought, but just not cut out for farming, like most of the McCallister men before him.

Over the next decade, Pa explored just about every crook and cranny northern and central Florida had to offer, and there are some who said, not even that many years ago, that Jeff McCallister was the first white man to see those vast, cattle-rich prairies along the upper Pease and Caloosahatchee Rivers, although it was a claim Pa always dismissed.

"Every time I thought I was the first to do something or see something, I'd bump into someone who had been there before me or done it earlier," he once remarked to us boys.

But if he wasn't the first—not counting the Spaniards and

Indians, of course—then he sure as heck was *one* of the first. Even Pa will admit to that.

"It was like Eden in those days," he'd reminisce, then go on to tell us about how fine the hunting and trapping was, about how he sometimes got along just fine with the local tribes, but at other times had to shoot quick to keep his scalp intact.

"It was a damn' fine life," he'd usually finish with a faraway look in his eyes.

Then, when Pa was twenty-eight, he met Ma, and his wandering days were over. Well, not altogether, but as far as taking off on his lonesome for months or even years at a time, those days were behind him.

My ma was born Julia Silkhart in 1811, the only daughter of Joshua Silkhart, of Jacksonville. Joshua was a merchant in that port city until his death in 1836. Ma's mother died in childbirth, leaving me without much kin to speak of on that side of the family, but with cousins aplenty on my paternal side.

I mentioned six surviving sons, but didn't say anything about those siblings who didn't live. There were six of those, too—four sisters and two brothers, all of whom passed away before their fifth birthday of one ailment or another. That Florida frontier was hard on women and kids, and it finally took Ma when she was barely forty. I was six at the time; Stone was just two.

Ma and Pa lived in Jacksonville for nearly a year after they were married, then moved upriver, where Pa opened a trading post south of St. George Lake, a place not unlike Pete Dill's, he said. Pa mostly traded with the Seminoles, taking in pelts and hides from raccoons, otters, bear, deer, bobcat, and wolves, plus all kinds of plumes, from egrets to ibis. In exchange he carried just about anything a son or daughter of the wilderness might want—flint and steel, muskets, traps, blankets and cloth, silver and copper gee-gaws, jewelry, knives, tomahawks, beads—you name it. Pa's business went under for good during the Second Seminole War, which is when he gave up trading to become a rancher.

He settled in the Kissimmee area first, which was prime cattle range in those days, but moved his operation over to the west side of the Highlands in 1848, when cattle ranged free for the taking and the market was barely one hundred miles away in a little hick cow town outside of Fort Brooke called Tampa. Back in those days, smaller ports like Punta Rassa and Punta Gorda didn't get much cattle trade at all, but of course that changed with the North's invasion of the Confederacy.

If Pa wasn't the first white man to lay eyes on that Upper Pease River country, I think it's safe to say he was the first to settle on it permanently. It was Ma's idea to set up camp on the banks of the Pease until Pa located a likely spot for a home. I think she was hoping it would be the last time we ever had to move, and, for her, it was.

The place they settled on was about two miles back from the main river, atop a little hammock of live oaks with a good spring not fifty feet from the main house. They built their own cabin first, then a shack for the slaves. They had three by then, Jim and Josie and Joe-Jim, tottering around on his chubby little bowed legs, while Stone followed him everywhere our ma would allow. Then Pa set about putting his mark on any unbranded cow, hog, or horse he could wrestle to the ground long enough to slap an iron to.

People sometimes ask where Pa got the idea for the Flatiron brand, since it's a difficult one for cattle rustlers to alter, but he'd be the first to admit it wasn't born from foresight so much as necessity. They needed something to identify their stock, and didn't have enough unused iron on the place to forge their own, nor time to ride all the way into Kissimmee or Tampa to buy one. What they did have was a part of Ma's dowry, a trio of flatirons in varying sizes for pressing shirts and such. There not being a whole lot of call for fancy out in the scrub, Pa confiscated the largest of those irons for his own needs, and the Flatiron ranch was born. It was made official when Pa finally got to Tampa to register his brand and marks at the courthouse there. [*Ed. Note:* The marks McCallister is referring to are the notches cut into the ears and dewlaps of livestock to further identify ownership; the McCallister marks were a notch in the lower right ear with a moon-shaped cut in the outer ear of cattle, and two notches, one in the upper right ear and the other in the lower right ear, on hogs; horses carried just the brand.]

You don't have enough recording disks in your satchel for me to relate what it was like to start a ranch in those days, all the back-breaking labor, the successes that only barely outnumbered the failures, until Pa had the Flatiron rooted firmly enough to believe it was real. Then the War of Northern Aggression broke out, throwing a kink in everyone's plans before the dust at Fort Sumter had even settled in Charleston Harbor.

By the time Pa started driving herds north to supply the Confederacy, the Flatiron was pretty well established. We'd long since moved out of the original cabin, building a bigger house near it, a long log structure with eight rooms—every two-room section separated by its own dogtrot—and a wide verandah across the front. Pa turned the old cabin over to Jim and Josie, and warned us boys to stay out of it unless we were invited inside.

By '64 we also had a twelve-stall barn with a melding of corrals and small pastures out back, a limestone milk house where we kept the dairy products from a pair of Guernseys Pa had brought back from Tampa some years before, a chicken coop, smokehouse, summer kitchen, a small blacksmith shop, sheds for wagons and tack, and a four-bed bunkhouse for the hired men—when we had any. With six grown sons and a pair of slaves at his beck and call, Pa generally had more than enough hands to run an outfit even as large and far-flung as the Flatiron. Yet it seemed like there were always a few men staying on for one reason or another, either drifters on their way through to some place else or temporary hands like Casey and Pablo.

Pa's pride and joy, though—and Ma's, too—was the pitch-sealed water tower he and Jim had built just north of the kitchen, made of cypress planks hauled in from a mill in Kissimmee, then put together on-site. It stood about twelve feet above the ground, with the water pumped in by a windmill standing over the spring about fifteen yards away. A pipe from the tank ran fresh, cool water into a galvanized sink under the kitchen's north window with just a twist of a valve.

I'll tell you what, Ma loved that tower, and she loved Pa all the more for building it for her. They'd had a rough life, those two, raising a family out in the wilderness, creating a small kingdom of sorts where only palmetto and cabbage palm had grown before. I think for Ma, that water flowing straight into the house was a reward beyond measure for all the grief and sacrifices she'd endured while following her husband into the heart of a lonely frontier.

For Pa, it was a means to show his appreciation for the woman who had stood at his side through all those rough years. The fact that she loved it so much made it extra special to him. To all us boys, for that matter. For its time, the Flatiron was a pretty prosperous ranch, although there would be larger ones before the heyday of the cattle industry was smothered out by citrus groves and tourism.

It was that water tower that first caught my attention when the seven of us rode in on badly jaded horses. Pete Dill's words, repeating Jacob Klee's admonition to his kin to—*Let 'em know you were there, boys.*—still rings in my mind to this day.

They'd let us know, all right, and my heart sank at the breadth of the destruction. The stables, summer kitchen, and bunkhouse had been burned to the ground, the Guernseys and their calves killed in their pasture. The chicken house had been pulled over in a crumbled heap. I could see several crushed hens from the ranch entrance, and figured those that hadn't been killed outright had scattered into the forest behind the house, where they wouldn't last long in that wild thicket filled with foxes, large snakes, and wildcats.

But what hit me hardest was that they'd pulled down the water tower. It lay on its side, splintered beyond redemption, the ground still muddy from where the cool spring water had splashed across the ranch yard. Staring dully at the wreckage, I felt tears brim at my eyes, and angrily knuckled them away.

Negro Jim jumped off his horse as soon as we entered the yard and raced toward the cabin he shared with Josie. He was shouting as he ran, but she wasn't answering, and any feelings I'd had for a stack of lumber and pine pitch that could be replaced with a week's worth of labor vanished in an instant. Jim darted inside the cabin, only to reappear a few seconds later, his eyes wide with dread.

With my own gut-numbing terror growing, I leaped from the back of my lathered mount. "Spread out and find them," I snapped to the others.

Casey took charge of the crew—ordering some of the boys into the trees, the others to start searching the outbuildings—while I headed for the main house. My pulse thundered as I paused outside the kicked-in kitchen door. Then gingerly I stepped inside.

Klee's boys had been there, too, and torn the place apart in their search for . . . well, at first I couldn't fathom what they might have been looking for. Then it occurred to me. I've already mentioned how in those days we dealt mainly in Span-ish gold—doubloons, *reales,* even *pesos*—money that Pa kept in a metal chest buried inside a hollow tree at the edge of the forest. It was our gold Klee's men had been grubbing for, and they must have thought we'd hidden it in the house. The kitchen was a shambles, and I'd soon learn the rest of the place hadn't fared any better, although at that moment it was neither gold nor mossy water towers or broken dinnerware that was nearly crushing me under its weight. Licking at lips gone as dry as a long-dead mouse, I advanced on the big bedroom next to the kitchen, where Pa slept. I hadn't quite reached the door when I heard a shout from the trees behind the house.

Drawing my revolver, I ran through the dogtrot to the rear of the house, my knees turning kind of mushy at the sight of Josie running out of the woods. Jim was laughing and crying at the same time as he swept her up in his arms and spun her in circles. Holstering the Navy, I jumped off the porch and ran out to where they stood hugging one another with fat tears spilling across their black cheeks. It wasn't long before the others showed up, everyone grinning from ear-to-ear and making silly jokes to vent off some of the tension. They were still jabbering when it dawned on me that Josie was alone.

Jim must have realized it at the same instant, because he eased her back a step and said: "Where's Lena, honey? Where's our little Lena?"

Josie turned to me, her expression collapsing. "Oh, Marse Boone, they took her. They took Lena."

"Who took her?" Jim demanded, shaking her gently until her eyes came back to his.

"Them men," she sobbed. "Them ones what come here and set fire to the buildin's and kicked ever'thin' to pieces."

"What men, Josie?" I interrupted, my voice harsher than I meant for it to be. "Did you get a look at them?"

"I did, marse, I surely did, but I didn't recognize them a bit. Not none of 'em."

"Did you see which way they came from?" Casey asked. "Or which way they went when they left?"

"Yes, suh. They come from the south, but went off to the east."

"How many were there, Josie?" I asked more gently.

She held up six fingers. "Was this many, marse, all of 'em big, mean-lookin' men, too. Like they could eat little baby children for breakfast, was they hungry enough."

"Klee's men," Casey said.

"The ol' devil, Judah Klee?" Josie asked.

"His son, most like," Jim replied. "We had us a tangle with them on our way to Punta Rassa, and they's plenty mad about it still."

Taking Josie's arm, I led her toward the main house. "Are you all right?" I asked. "Did they hurt you?"

"No, suh, they didn't, though they sure enough threatened to. Said they'd peel the hide offen my back with whips if I didn't tell 'em where Marse Jeff keeps his gold."

"Did you tell them?"

"No, suh, I didn't. They sent me out to the summer kitchen to fix up some food, but I didn't go to the summer kitchen. I took off for the woods, but. . . ." She stopped and her voice began to tremble. "Poor little Lena, they took her with them, marse. They called and called for me to come in, and made all kinds of threats when I wouldn't. Then they took some meat and grits and hoecake, and set fire to ever'thin' before they rode out. Said they'd be back, though. I heard 'em callin' for me to tell you and your daddy, when he got home, that they'd be back for what was still owed them."

"Dave," Casey stated flatly.

"Dave's just an excuse," I replied bitterly. "Jacob's mad about his nephew, but wants someone else to pay for it. I doubt if he's ever considered his own blame. If they hadn't been following us, scheming to steal our herd, Dave wouldn't have been anywhere near that 'gator hole."

We reached the main house and entered the kitchen. Casey righted a chair, and Jim helped Josie into it. Then I shooed everyone but Jim outside, so we could look her over. Except for briar scratches and her concern for Lena, the woman seemed fine.

I think I mentioned Lena earlier, the gal Pa brought home for Joe-Jim to marry. Lena wasn't pure-spear African—not many Negros were by then—but she was unusual in that her mixed heritage was of Indian blood, rather than white.

Not many folks realize that a lot of Indians kept slaves. Some of the Eastern tribes, the Seminoles among them, bought and sold Africans in the same manner as whites, while more Western tribes like the Sioux and Comanches just took whoever they could snatch, white, black, or Mexican. [*Ed. Note:* When Billy Bowlegs surrendered in 1858, officially ending the Third Seminole War, he was sent to the Indian Nations in what is now Eastern Oklahoma; in his procession at the time of his exile were fifty Negro slaves, two wives, several children, and $100,000 in "hard cash".]

Despite her Indian blood, Lena was chocolate-hued and as pretty as a newborn colt on green pasture. Pa had purchased her from a good family in Tampa, paying $1,200 for her and a trunk full of clothes and kitchen stuff for her new home. I think Pa expected Joe-Jim to marry her right off, but Josie'd put her foot down when she discovered the girl was barely fourteen. Pa hadn't argued. Since Ma's death to the Yellow Jack, he'd pretty much turned all the household duties over to Josie, and her word was law on most matters—never forgetting, of course, that she was as much Pa's property as the kettle she cooked her cabbage in.

I've heard slavery referred to as a "peculiar institution", but for those of us who lived during those times, who remember the reality of it, "peculiar" doesn't hardly do it justice.

After sending Jim to fetch his wife a tall mug of cold spring water, I pulled a chair around and sat down in front of her. "When did they leave?" was my first question.

"Yesterday morning. They took that gray filly your daddy set such store by, and those two bays you was breakin' to saddle, and the sorrel you'd sometimes ride."

"What else did they take? Could you see?"

"Some, I could. They took the kitchen shotgun and some blankets and your daddy's fancy suit, the one he was married in, and that your mama wanted him to be buried in, and that jug of moonshine what Mistah Wakley makes in his still. They took some foodstuff, too, hams and such from the smokehouse, but that was near 'bout all I could see from the woods. I was afraid to come back too soon, marse. 'Fraid they was hidin' somewheres, waitin' to catch me soon as I showed myself."

"You were smart to stay hidden," I assured her, although I doubted if Klee's men had hung around too long. They'd be worried about me coming back with my trail crew, and want to be long gone before I did.

Patting the top of Josie's shoulder with relief, I went to the door. Jim met me as he was coming in, and I assured him that I'd stay away from the kitchen to give them some privacy. Casey and the others were waiting for me in the dogtrot. Tipping my head for them to follow, I walked down the verandah until we were out of Josie's hearing. Roy was the first to ask what we were all thinking.

"You reckon they'll abuse that girl?"

"They might," I admitted. "I'd hate to count on Jacob Klee for any kind of mercy, or his men, either. On the other hand, if he's got plans for her, he might keep his boys away."

"What kind of plans?" Punch asked.

"Maybe some kind of trade. Jacob might claim he's hurting over that wayward nephew of his, but I wager his grief could be eased for the right price."

"You think he's keeping her for ransom?" Ardell asked.

"I don't know. Maybe he is, maybe he ain't. Maybe he figures a good slave is compensation enough. Either way, we'll set him straight."

Silence greeted my words.

"What are you talking about, Boone?" Casey asked after a pause.

I remember giving him a funny look, not quite sure I understood what *he* was talking about. Then I said: "I'm going after Lena, and when she's safe, I'm going to set things right for what they done here."

"You're . . . going into the swamps?" Punch asked with an odd hitch to his voice.

"Yeah, I am, but nobody's saying you have to go with me."

"No," Punch hurriedly amended. "I'll go. I just . . . it took me by surprise, is all."

"We're all goin'," Roy growled, and when I glanced at him, I noticed that his fingers were still wrapped tightly around his holstered revolver. "We're gonna root that cow thief out once and for all," he added.

"We're going after Lena first," I reminded him. "After that, we'll do what we can to put an end to their lawlessness." My gaze traveled the knot of cow hunters standing before me. "What about it, boys? Are you still riding for the Flatiron, or are you anxious to get up north and fight Yankees?"

"I'm going south with you," Casey said firmly, and the others quickly nodded their assent. All except Pablo, who stared broodingly across the vast plain to the east.

"What about it, Torres?" I asked. "Are you going with us?"

"I hired on to hunt cattle," he replied. "Not to fight your

papa's enemies."

"The hell," Roy grunted in surprise, then added heatedly: "By damn, this ain't Cuba, Torres. We ride for the brand around here, or go back where we came from."

Pablo brought his gaze around to stare me in the eye, but I couldn't tell a thing from his expression. "*Sí*," he said after a lengthy pause. "I will ride after the *chica negra,* if that is what *el pequeño jefe* wishes."

I didn't speak Spanish at the time, but Ardell did. I looked to him for a translation, but he gave me a quick shake of his head, instead. "It's settled," he said, and I exhaled loudly, in relief. I'd assumed at first that they would all ride with me, but Punch's startled reaction and Pablo's surly response had given me cause for doubt. Of course, had I known then what *el pequeño jefe* actually meant, I might not have been so quick with my gratitude. [*Ed. Note: El pequeño jefe* is Spanish for "the little boss"—a derogatory term as used in this instance.]

"We'll need fresh horses, and a night's rest won't hurt," I said. "We'll need to put together some supplies, too." I nodded toward the open range stretching away to the east, the dusty prairie and distant curve of the horizon. "Ardell, take Punch and Roy and Pablo and see if you can round up some fresh mounts. Casey, take Dick along with you and try to find a trail for us to follow tomorrow. I'll start sifting through the rubble here and see what I can find that we might be able to use."

"Let's go, boys," Ardell said briskly, dropping off the verandah and stalking toward his lathered marshtackie. The others followed silently, mounting their weary animals and turning toward the prairies. When they were gone, I pulled the panniers from the pack horses and set them on the verandah to be taken care of later, then went exploring.

I started for the smokehouse, hoping the raiders had left behind some food, but they hadn't. Nothing we could use, at any rate. To show you what kind of men we were dealing with, what they hadn't taken, they'd urinated and defecated on. My stomach did a quick flip when I saw the stinking remains, and my temper started bubbling like a pot left too long on a hot stove. Returning to the house, I began working through the various rooms, starting at the far end and making my way toward the kitchen.

Those boys had been thorough in their destruction, although erratic. What they could break or ruin easily, they'd done, but if it was something that was going to require effort, they'd passed on by. For instance, there wasn't a mirror or water pitcher left unshattered in the entire house, but the mattresses and linens and extra clothes, which would have burned fairly quickly if they'd taken time to haul them outside, had been left untouched.

I'll confess I was puzzled by their seemingly hit-or-miss approach. They'd burned the bunkhouse, the summer kitchen, and the barn, for cripes sake, so why hadn't they also set fire to the house, or to Jim and Josie's cabin? Roy would swear afterward that it was just plain laziness on their part, and point to the slovenly shacks they'd left behind when they abandoned their Lake Okeechobee compound. Who knows, maybe he's right. If anyone listening to these recordings can offer a better explanation, I'd admire to hear it.

My anger had settled into a cold, hard resolve by the time I worked my way back to the winter kitchen. I walked inside to find the room empty. Glancing through a window, I saw Jim's mule tied out in front of their cabin, and figured he and Josie had returned to their own home, where they'd feel more comfortable. I couldn't blame them, and was actually kind of glad to be able to continue my exploration without having to monitor my vocabulary around Josie, who didn't normally tolerate our cursing.

If you're not familiar with winter kitchens and summer

kitchens, then maybe I ought to explain. A winter kitchen is a part of the main house where a family did its cooking during the cooler months. We seldom used ours because of the unbearable heat it generated in that mostly hot, humid landscape, and had built a summer kitchen out back of the main house where Ma and Josie—then Josie and Lena, after Ma's passing—would cook, preserve, and put up garden truck in glass jars and clay crocks.

Not anticipating much luck as I started rummaging through what the Klees hadn't destroyed, I was pleasantly surprised when I came across a three-gallon crock of pork chops stashed under the spice table, and a half-sack of coontie on one of the higher shelves. [*Ed. Note:* Coontie (*zamia pumila*) is a fern-like plant whose pounded and heavily-washed stem is used to produce a starchy type of flour; although toxic if consumed raw, processed coontie was an important trade and food source for Florida's native tribes and early Euro-American explorers and settlers; during the Union blockade, it was a common substitute for wheat flour.]

After kindling a blaze outside, I fished the pork chops out of the crock, scooping away the layers of heavy white lard that kept the meat fresh and protected from insects and spoilage. Then I fetched the only remaining sack of coffee beans I'd gotten from Müller and set a pot on to boil while I ground the beans with a scorched grinder that had survived the worst of the summer kitchen's flames. Josie came out before I could start the biscuits and told me to shoo.

"Ain't no reason I can't fix up some good eats for a crew of hungry cow hunters," she scolded, but I noticed her eyes were red from crying, and that she was still sniffling as she set about heating her griddle and slapping coontie into biscuit patties.

Jim fetched my horse and his mule and led them over. "You want me to unsaddle your 'tackie, marse?"

"Not until Ardell and the others get back, and I know we've got fresh mounts."

"Mistah Ardell and them others is already comin' in. Looks like they's got eight, nine 'tackies with 'em, too."

I looked up in relief from where I had been staring moodily at the flames. "Then I reckon I can take care of my own horse, Jim. Molly, too. You stay here with Josie, in case she needs any more wood or water."

"Yes'um," Jim replied gratefully.

I led the horse and mule around front and hitched them to a middle rail of the small corral behind what remained of the barn, then swung a gate wide as Ardell and his crew trotted into the yard, driving nine good mounts before them. A grin—my first since returning to the Flatiron—tugged at the corners of my mouth when I recognized those horses. They were part of the stock Pa had used on his last drive to Georgia, including a tall bay gelding with a wide blaze down its face that I liked to ride. While neither as quick nor as agile as my swamp-bred marshtackie, that bay was a good horse, with a long stride and a lot of staying power. I was really glad to see it.

Ardell swung down while I latched the gate and stripped the saddle from his mount's back. He nodded toward the main house, not knowing that Josie was around back putting together a meal. "She OK?"

"She will be. She's worried about Lena, now that she knows Jim is safe."

"Makes sense. When do we go after them?"

I swung my saddle over the top rail of the corral, then pulled up a clump of gama and started wiping down my marshtackie's sweaty back. The gama was a substitute for the brushes and currycombs we'd lost in the fire, but better than nothing. I took my time answering Ardell's question, trying to sort it all out in my mind while avoiding my first inclination, which was to mount up immediately and take off at a gallop. Finally I said: "I reckon tomorrow will be soon enough. We'll get a decent night's sleep and a good breakfast in the morning. I'm going to have Jim stay behind this time, look after the place while we're gone."

Ardell looked surprised by my decision. "Those Klees are burrowed down in those swamps like ticks in a dog's ear, Boone. We'll likely need every man we can bring along."

"We can't go in there like a troop of bluebellies, all shiny brass and blowing bugles. We'll have to slip in quiet-like, and try to ghost Lena out of there before they know we're around."

"What's Jim going to do here if some of Klee's men show up? Or a pack of deserters?"

"He's got that shotgun Pa gave him."

Ardell snorted. "A black man pulls a gun on a white man in these parts, he'll hang before the powder smoke clears."

"Not if there's just one of them, or not if his master backs him up."

"It's damn' risky for Jim, is my opinion."

"If there's too many, he and Josie can slope for tall timber. He can use the shotgun for meat, if he has to."

"I think you're just worried about Josie."

Something about Ardell's words struck me wrong, and I stopped rubbing on my mount's flank. "That's right," I said. "Josie ain't just a Negro to me, nor to any of us McCallisters. She was my mother after Ma died, or as close to a ma as I'm ever likely to get. And Jim's been more like an uncle than any of my real uncles ever were. They're my family, Ardell. Joe-Jim and Lena, too."

Ardell didn't reply right away, or meet my gaze. After a couple of minutes, he said: "I guess I hadn't thought of it that way."

Embarrassed by my flare-up, I said: "Jim can start putting the place back together while we're gone. I don't reckon one man will make that much of a difference."

"It's your call, Boone. You know I'll back whatever decision you make."

"Thanks, Ardell." I turned away self-consciously and resumed rubbing down my marshtackie. When I was done, I turned the little horse loose to find its own way out to pasture, knowing we'd round him up again before the next drive.

I started on Jim's mule next. Ardell and the others had already taken care of their own mounts and the pack horses, and wandered off, but I wasn't in any hurry. I wanted to think a while, and puttering with livestock was a way for me to do that—mindless, relaxing labor. It was just about full dark when I finally turned Molly loose and headed for the house.

The boys were gathered on the verandah, smoking pipes and talking quietly among themselves. Ignoring them, I walked around to the far side of the house where Jim and Josie were putting the finishing touches on the evening's meal. Firelight danced across the ebony planes of their faces, emphasizing the deep lines that feathered outward from their eyes and corrugated their foreheads. I paused in the darkness next to the house to watch, caught off guard by the unexpected emotions that swirled through me. I guess it was the blindness of youth that had prevented me from realizing how much Jim and Josie had aged in recent years, and that there would come a time when neither would be a part of my life any more. It had taken the Klees' raid, including the abduction of Lena, to bring home the mortality of those two stalwart figures of the Flatiron, and the knowledge was like a fist planted so deep in my chest that for a moment I found it difficult to breathe.

Numbly I started forward. The soft jingle of my spurs alerted them that someone was approaching, and it tore at my heart to see the quick alarm that came over their faces.

"It's me!" I called, just before entering the firelight.

"Marse Boone, you surely did give me a start," Josie chided.

"You sing out, next time."

I grinned weakly and nodded. "All right," I replied, as if properly chastised.

Jim remained silent until Josie turned back to her fire, then started peppering me with questions.

"What we gonna do, marse?"

"About Lena?" I shook my head. "I don't rightly know. We've got to get her out of there somehow, but first we've got to find her, and those swamps are man-killers. I ain't keen on going in without a guide."

"They say that Mistah Jacob has got hisself an island not even the devil hisself can find."

"An island would be about the only way they could survive down there," I agreed.

"Can't even find it, is what them Klee boys said."

I hesitated. "How do you know that?"

Jim nodded toward Josie, bent over a griddle sizzling with pork chops. "My Josie come sneaking in after dark to listen to them boys talkin'. She heard 'em say so."

"Is that right, Josie? You heard them?"

"Yes, suh, I did." She set a long iron fork across the edge of the griddle and straightened with a faint popping of joints in her back and knees. "It was after night come on full. I sneaked in to see could I help Lena, but they was keepin' her close. Had a rope tied loose around her neck. I heard 'em talkin', though."

"What did they say?"

"Said they was gonna go find that old man, the daddy."

"Judah?"

"Didn't say no names, just they was afraid to try findin' that island without no one to guide 'em, so they was gonna go find the old man and wait for the others there."

"Where?"

"Way off down south, marse. Near Fort Dallas."

133

"Dallas?" I whistled softly, envisioning that route to Fort Dallas, way down on the Miami River. "Is that where they said the old man was, near Fort Dallas?"

"Yes, suh. Said leastwise they figured he was. Said they was gonna wait there for the others, like they was expectin' them real soon."

"What else did they say?"

"I reckon that's all, marse. Just that they was gonna take Lena to Fort Dallas, 'stead of into those swamps."

Josie's words had my thoughts spinning. Going into the swamps to look for a kidnapped slave was one thing, and probably would have been impossible to accomplish without a guide, but Fort Dallas was a whole different bird. In my mind I started putting together what little I knew of the abandoned army post, hidden inside the sheltering cove of Biscayne Bay.

My knowledge of the place was skimpy. Fort Dallas had been used by the United States Army during the Seminole Wars, then abandoned about the time of Billy Bowlegs's surrender. Although officially still in Union hands, from what I'd heard, the place hadn't been permanently reoccupied like the forts at Tampa and Myers. It was probably Dallas' remote location—a jumping-off point to just about nowhere unless you were looking for Indians in the 'glades—that kept the post outside the sphere of military relevance. Although folks said the Federal Navy sometimes used Dallas to maintain a Yankee presence in the region, and would sometimes dock at the wharf that jutted into the river just inside the mouth of the Miami, I don't think there were ever any real plans to use it against the Confederacy.

I'd heard there was a town of sorts down there, too, although at the time I didn't know its name. Of course I'm talking about what would eventually become the city of Miami, and the seat of Dade County. They say Miami has turned into a pretty good-sized little burg since Henry Flagler extended his railroad down there in the 1890s—maybe thirty or forty thousand people living in that mosquito-ridden jungle is what I've read—but back in '64 you couldn't really call it a town at all. Nor was it a place most folks would want to visit. Not unless they were hiding from the law.

"That where we're goin', marse?" Jim asked, drawing my thoughts back to the Flatiron.

"Yeah, maybe," I replied absently, then quickly corrected myself. "No, I am. I want you to stay here and start cleaning up."

Jim got a real funny look on his face at that. "You wantin' me to stay behind, marse?"

"I'm afraid so, Jim. I don't want what happened here to ever happen again because I pulled all the men off the place."

"Marse, I gots to go," Jim said in a small, anguished tone I'd never heard him use before. "I got to help bring Lena home. I promised Joe-Jim I'd take care of her like she was my own daughter. Like I would you or any of your brothers."

"Don't worry about Lena. We'll get her back." I started to walk away, my thoughts already turning to that long journey before us, when Jim's voice thundered across the darkness.

"Boone!"

I spun around, my mouth agape at the Negro's impertinence. Jim had taken a dragging half step forward, his face twisted in suffering made all the worse by the fluctuating light of the fire. "Please, marse, please don't make me stay to home."

There was fear in the black man's eyes—as well they should have been for such presumptiveness, some would say—but I knew Jim's apprehension wasn't for himself.

"Please, marse," he nearly whispered.

"Jim, you know what's going to happen down there."

"Yes'um."

"There could be shooting, maybe men getting shot, even dying."

"Yes'um, but I ain't afraid to die, marse. Not if it brings Lena home."

"That's not what I'm talking about. You . . . do you think you can do what you might have to, if it comes to a fight?"

"Yes'um. Be just like I did with your daddy, during the Indian Wars."

My resolve was weakening to the point that I think I was starting to plead more than Jim. "You know what'll happen if you're caught with a gun, Jim. Or if I'm hurt or killed and can't speak up for you?"

"Yes'um, I know. Them white men down there, they'd hang me real quick."

"Can you face that, turning a gun on a white man?"

"I can if it's them Klees what took Lena, and chased my Josie into the woods to live like a wild animal. I could kill those men real easy, if you give me the say-so."

"Let him go," a voice said, so gentle it might have been the soughing of the evening breeze. I looked at Josie, standing over her griddle with her eyes cast toward the fire, and wondered if I'd really heard someone speak, or if it had just been my imagination. Then Josie raised her eyes to mine, and I knew the words had been hers.

I looked at Jim. "All right," I said quietly. "You can come."

Jim's smile was like a flash of yellow ivory in the firelight. I wanted to tell him to wipe it off, to remind him that he'd be lucky if he lived to see his wife or son again, let alone find Lena, but I didn't. Gritting my teeth in helpless frustration, I started to walk away. I hadn't gone more than a few paces when Jim called to me.

"Marse Boone."

I stopped and turned. "Yeah?"

"I . . . I's sorry about the uppity way I talked. I didn't mean no disrespect. I was just . . . worried. Worried for Lena."

I nodded stiffly, my face turning warm with an overwhelming sense of shame. "Jim," I said raggedly, "I reckon you're about the last man I know who needs to apologize to me for anything." Then I spun on my heel and swiftly walked away.

Michael Zimmer

Excerpted from:
Florida Reminiscences:
Personal Recollections from the Highlands
Edited by
Wilbur Collinsworth
Self-Published, 1892
Host First Edition, June, 1976

Chapter Seven
Jack Chandler
1834-1901

. . . [P]eople say those Yankees from Fort Myers never came inland, but I know for a fact that is a lie, because I seen them up by Stearn's Lake once, toward the end of the war. [*Ed. Note:* Chandler is probably referring here to either Lake Placid or Lake June, south of Sebring, Florida.] I was trapping otter and such, and keeping my nose to my own fire, and not traipsing off to fight people I didn't know, when I seen eight or ten of them Yankees riding hell bent to the north. Later on I was told by a Indian trader named Dill that they were after some cow hunters that hung some Yankees on the road between Fort Myers and Punta Rassa. Lucky I seen them coming before they seen me, and ducked out of sight before they got too close. I seen their faces, though, and they were a mean-looking bunch, them Yankees. I never did see the cow hunters they was chasing, but I'll bet it was a bloody battle when they finally caught up. . . .

SESSION SIX

That machine does make a racket when it reaches the end of a disk, doesn't it? It didn't bother me, but I can see how it might startle some. Thanks for the warning, though. It might have been more jarring if I hadn't known it was getting close.

Before your recorder started clattering like it was coming apart, we were talking about our pulling out for Fort Dallas the next day, and how we took along an extra mount for Lena. I packed some grub in the saddlebags, then tied a ten-foot square of oilcloth behind the flat English seat as shelter in case of rain. Although it was the dry season, Florida sometimes forgets there is such a thing, and I wanted to be prepared.

I'll admit I was worried about leaving Josie behind. I gave her the loan of Dick Langley's shotgun, then told her to bury the gold I'd gotten for the herd in the hollow tree after we were gone. I didn't want to do it while the boys were around, even though I trusted everyone there. That gold was just for the family to know about, not friends.

"When you've got it hidden, take some food and blankets and go hide in the woods until we get back," I told her. "Or until Pa does."

"Shoo, I don't need to hide in no woods like some scared bunny. I be just fine in my own home, 'specially now that I got this fine shotgun of Mistah Dick's."

"Do what I say, Josie."

She smiled and patted my cheek affectionately. "You is a

139

good boy, Marse Boone. Your mama would have been real proud of you. We all are."

Well, hell! How do you argue with someone like that?

"Just keep an eye on the horizon," I finally said, accepting my defeat. "If you see anyone coming, hightail it into the trees until you know who it is."

"Yes, suh," she replied, so that I knew I'd at least made a little progress.

Stepping into my saddle, I glanced at Casey, who just shrugged. He and Dick had returned well after dark the night before without having found any sign of the men who'd ransacked the Flatiron.

"We rode a big arc to the south and east, but didn't turn up anything I could say for sure was them," he'd told me as he pulled the saddle from the back of his sweating mount.

I knew it was chancy, taking the idle chatter of a bunch of hardcases as gospel, but maybe not as bad as plunging into those swamps south of the Caloosahatchee in a blind attempt to locate Jacob Klee's alleged island hide-away. I'd never been to Fort Dallas, and neither had any of the men riding with me, but I had a general idea of how to get there. Ride due east into the rising sun, then turn south at the Atlantic. It would be more difficult than that, of course, but it was a start. Roy said he knew a cow hunter who had been as far south as Fort Lauderdale without too much trouble, although he claimed the route below there would be hell to get through.

"Mangrove forests in every direction, 'skeeters big enough to suck the blood out of a 'gator, water moccasins and rattlesnakes under every bush," was the way Roy described it, and, as it turned out, he wasn't too far off the mark. That's why I have such a difficult time picturing Miami as being anything more today than the corner of hell it had been in 1864.

By taking a roundabout course to avoid the swamps below

Lake Istokpoga, it was going to be roughly a two-hundred-mile journey from the Flatiron to the Miami River, but, even in as much of a hurry as we were, I wanted our first stop to be Dick Langley's cabin, just west of Istokpoga.

Like most of us—myself included in those carefree days— Dick had grand visions of the future. He'd talked about some of them on the drive to Punta Rassa, all of us but the night guard sitting around an early evening fire, drinking chicory for coffee and shooting the bull. Dick wanted five thousand head of longhorns carrying his as-yet unregistered brand by the time he turned thirty, and a better home for his wife and son than the tiny cabin they were currently living in.

"Something like what your daddy's got, Boone," he'd said one night not long after we crossed the Caloosahatchee.

I didn't point out that Pa had been long past thirty before he got to where he was. Dick would find out how tough it was to build a ranch soon enough, unless he actually pulled it off, in which case I intended to be the first among us to offer up a toast to his success.

It was a hard day's ride from the Flatiron to Dick's cabin, but we were anxious to make up for lost time, and pushed our horses more than we probably should have, what with the distance yet to cover. We crossed the Highlands near Jack Creek, and came in sight of our destination late that afternoon.

Dick's wife was a pretty, dark-haired gal of sixteen at most, though Cracker tough, as only that scrub breed can be. Her name was Emma May, and she was standing next to a washtub of boiling water as we approached. Freshly washed laundry hung from a rope stretched from the cabin to a nearby tripod made of palmetto stalks.

Emma May was shading her eyes from the westering sun with her palm flat above her brows when she recognized her husband, who had galloped ahead in his eagerness to be home.

Dick jumped from his saddle before his mount could come to a complete stop, and strode quickly over to where Emma May was standing beside her fire-blackened tub. Then he halted a couple of feet away, the two of them standing there gawking at one another like fools as the rest of us rode into the yard.

"Well, go ahead and hug her, ya damn' numbskull!" Ardell called, and the rest of us hooted laughter to see them so happy. Dick took Emma May in his arms like she was made of clay, then glanced over his shoulder to see if we were still watching. We were, of course, until Ardell said: "Come on, boys, let's give them some privacy."

We rode around the north side of the cabin where we were out of sight, and dismounted to rest our sweaty shanks. I could see Lake Istokpoga off in the distance, its deep blue waters looking griddle-flat beneath a haze of humidity.

"We gonna stay the night, Boone?" Punch asked.

I already knew the answer, but glanced off to the west anyway. We still had a good two hours of daylight left. Three if we wanted to push on into the smoky dusk. "No," I replied, "but Dick is." My gaze fell on Langley's mount that Ardell had brought around back with us. "Pull that saddle and bridle and turn it loose," I instructed.

"What for?" Roy demanded, but Ardell was already tugging at the cinch.

"Because Dick's got something more important to do here," I replied.

After stripping the tack, Ardell led the horse out a ways, then slapped its hip with the loose ends of the reins. The horse snorted and took off, and although it didn't go far, I hoped it would be enough to hinder Dick's efforts to catch it again, should he prove too stubborn to stay behind.

Roy hadn't replied to my answer, and I could tell he was having trouble deciphering what it meant. I left him to ponder it alone as I walked back around the front of the house. Emma May was just entering the cabin. Dick came over to meet me, a grin like a 4th of July banner plastered across his face.

"Emma May's got a 'possum she ketched last night she was fixing to perloo," he said. "She's got a little leftover raccoon she can add to the pot, too. It won't take long. You boys are in for a treat. Ain't nobody makes 'possum perloo like my Emma May." [*Ed. Note:* Perloo is the Cracker pronunciation of pileau, a rice dish of varying meats.]

"Sounds like she's been eating good," I said.

"She knows how to take care of herself, for a fact," Dick replied proudly.

I could hear the baby fussing inside, above the rattle of cast iron and tin utensils. "I reckon he misses his daddy," I said gently.

"Well, his daddy sure as heck missed him."

Taking a deep breath, I said: "I want you to stay here, Dick. Me and the boys'll go on and take care of this business with Jacob Klee. If we can, we'll stop by on the way home and let you know how it went."

Dick was scowling and shaking his head before I'd finished speaking. "Naw, I'm coming along."

"No, you're staying here . . . taking care of your family."

"Emma May done just fine while we drove that herd to Punta Rassa."

"That was different. You were making money then, and we didn't know if we'd have to fight or not. What we're going to do down on the Miami is pure dangerous, and there's a fair chance somebody'll get killed. Do you want to make Emma May a widow before your son is six months old?"

I could tell my words were having an effect on him, but Dick Langley was loyal to the core. The Flatiron was going after a stolen slave and four pirated horses. Abandoning pursuit now must have felt traitorous to him, yet the more that baby cried, the more determined I became.

"Boone, one more gun. . . ." He let his words trail off. "That's why you wanted me to leave my shotgun with Josie, ain't it?"

"You've got a good rifle you left here for Emma May, so you and Josie are both armed now. Stay here, Dick." I nodded toward the cabin door. "Go on in there and take care of that young one. We'll see you when we get back."

"What . . . what about the others?" He was staring toward the corner of the cabin like a butt-kicked hound.

"We've already talked it out," I lied. "No one's going to think you're a coward. Hell, we all saw how you stood your ground at Chestnut Thumb, and then again when those Yankees jumped us in Punta Rassa." I hesitated a moment, then thrust a hand toward him. He took it reluctantly, but at least he took it.

"You boys ride safe, Boone, and if you need me, you shout real loud, and I'll be there."

"I know you will." My grip tightened unexpectedly, and I turned away before I said something stupid. "Take care of your family," I added over my shoulder. "And tell Emma May we'll share a kettle of perloo some other time. Right now we've got to ride."

Walking back around the corner, I grabbed the bay's reins and swung a leg over that Texas rig's tall cantle. "Let's go," I said brusquely, and we kicked our horses into a lope, riding north to skirt the lake on drier ground rather than risk that marshy country to the south. No one spoke or asked about Dick. Not even Roy.

We camped that first night not far from Lake Istokpoga, then got another early start the next morning. It was two more days to the Indian River, a lot of it through some really swampy country, so our progress was slow. My only consolation was that I figured it would be just as difficult for Klee's men.

It was somewhere in that country between Istokpoga and the Indian that I began to get an itchy feeling between my shoulder blades. I'm not talking about a mosquito bite kind of discomfort, but a sense that something wasn't quite right—don't ask me what. It was the way I'd felt the previous week, just before discovering Jacob Klee and his boys were following us. As far as I could tell at that point, though, nobody else was showing any signs of unease, so I decided to keep my mouth shut and my eyes open, and see what developed.

At the Indian River, we finally turned south toward the ruins of old Fort Pierce. [*Ed. Note:* Like Fort Dallas on the Miami River, Forts Pierce, Capron, Jupiter, and Lauderdale were constructed during the Seminole Wars in an effort to confine the tribe to the unpopulated southern reaches of the state.] There was a settlement of sorts near where the old fort had stood, consisting of a trading post, a saloon, and a blacksmith shop, scattered among the huts and shacks. We made our cautious way down what passed as the main thoroughfare to the saloon and tied up out front. Our eyes were darting every which way as we climbed the steps to the verandah, watching not only for Jacob Klee's men, but also for Federal troops. We were pretty close to the coast by then, and more than a little concerned that Yankees might have slipped inland along the old military road that ran parallel to the Atlantic.

I told Ardell to stay outside and keep an eye on the street, and he grabbed Punch as the youngster started inside, hauling him out of line to help watch. After entering, Jim moved off to one side like he always did, while Casey made his way down the length of the room to a rear door. He shoved it open and peered outside for a few seconds, then closed it and shook his head. With that, me and Roy and Pablo moved up center to the bar, while Casey took a position at its far end. There was no one else in the room save for the bartender, a lanky, sallow-faced individual well into his fifties, with a bald head, a poorly trimmed mustache, and crossed eyes that seemed to follow everyone at once.

"You boys bounty hunters, looking for deserters?" he asked, to which Casey replied: "Nope."

"Bounty dodgers?" he persisted, then chuckled to make sure we understood that it didn't matter to him one way or the other.

"We're cow hunters," Roy said irritably. "Do we look like cowards?"

The bartender shook his head. "No, now that you mention it, you look like cow hunters."

"You got any whiskey?" I asked. That might seem like a foolish question today, but you've got to remember that we were still dealing with the Union blockade in those years, not to mention the settlement's isolation. If a port town like Punta Rassa ran consistently low on supplies, I'd hate to think what life was like at Fort Pierce. [*Ed. Note:* Although McCallister refers to the tiny community outside the ruins of the old military post as Fort Pierce, the actual city of that name wasn't incorporated until 1901.]

"I got brush lightning," the bartender said. "It ain't too bad to drink, just don't spill any on your clothes, as it has a tendency to eat right through cotton or wool." He paused to chuckle at his own joke, but sobered up when he didn't get a reaction from us. Dipping his fingers inside several glasses at once, he toted them over, along with a half-gallon jug of liquor. His eyes drifted to where Jim was standing silently beside the door. "Your Negro can stay there if he don't cause no trouble, but I don't serve 'em in my establishment."

I guess I was feeling edgy that day, because my temper flared like kerosene spilled on hot coals at the bar-dog's words. He noticed it, too, and took a swift step back before he could even get those glasses set down.

"It's my damned place," he snarled defensively, "and it'll be me that decides who drinks and who don't."

"Mister . . . ," I started to say, but Jim spoke up before I could get a good roll on.

"It's OK, marse," he said quietly. "I'll go stand outside with Mistah Ardell and Mistah Punch, if that be all right by you."

It took a moment for me to nod stiffly. I was still mad as hell, but reminded myself that I wasn't there to start a brawl. I needed information, and in a settlement as tiny as Fort Pierce, I wasn't going to have a lot of options. "Take Ardell's place, and tell him to have a look around the trading post," I told Jim.

"Yes'um, I will."

I fixed my gaze on the bartender, my mood still bristly. "Pour," I told him, jutting my chin toward the jug cradled in his left arm.

Licking nervously at his lips, the bartender stepped forward and began filling glasses. I saw him hesitate briefly in front of Pablo, but I guess he decided he'd pushed his luck far enough for one day, and tipped the chipped jug over the Cuban's glass.

"That'll be six bits, in coin," he said, stoppering the jug with a short length of corncob.

I tossed the money across the bar, then pulled my drink closer. It smelled raw and tasted a whole lot worse. I don't know where that ol' boy was getting his liquor, but it didn't hold a candle to Norm Wakley's stuff, and that ain't saying much. Steeling myself to the task, I managed to get it all down without choking.

"Sweet . . . Jesus," Roy gasped, slapping his empty glass down on the counter. Turning to me, he managed a hoarse, whispery laugh. "Get Punch in here, Boone. I want to see the look on his face after downin' a shot of this 'gator piss."

Well, hell, that was Roy for you.

"Punch is doing just fine where he's at," I replied, thinking the younger man had enough on his mind without a jackass like Roy Turner digging spurs into him.

I don't believe I've mentioned this yet, but Punch had taken Calvin's death pretty hard. Being about the same age, those two had naturally buddied up, and even though we were all saddened by Cal's passing, you could tell it was nagging at Punch a lot more than the rest of us.

Nodding to the barman, I said: "Splash a little more whiskey in our glasses, friend. I barely tasted that last one."

The barkeep laughed at my cockiness, and I forced a smile, the ruffle between us kind of smoothing out. I drank the next glass slowly, and I swear my lips were starting to go numb by the time I got it all down, but I figured we owed the man that much—for the information I wanted.

"Where you boys from?" the bartender asked, growing more congenial with the prospect of increasing the number of coins in his pockets.

"West of here," Casey replied. He'd eased down the bar to collect his second whiskey, and was standing next to Pablo now.

"If east is your destination, you've just about reached the end of the line. The Atlantic ain't but a good long spit to the other side of town, and there ain't no cows that way that I've ever heard of. Not unless they've sprouted gills."

"We're heading south," I said, and noticed the change that came into his eyes.

"Ain't many cows south of here, either."

"We ain't lookin' for cows," Roy said belligerently, the raw lightning in his belly already having its usual effect on him. "We're lookin' for some trash that came this way a few days ago."

"I ain't seen no one to fit that description," the bartender replied pointedly. He started to move off, and I reached out and grabbed his arm.

"Six men and a colored gal of about fifteen," I said.

Shrugging, he said: "That don't ring no bell, mister." He tried to pull free, but I tightened my grip, while Roy drew his revolver and set it on the counter in front of him. The bartender eyed that pistol for a long minute, then said: "Day before yesterday."

I couldn't help a relieved sigh, having been half scared ever since we left the Flatiron that I'd guessed wrong, and that Klee's men had gone south, after all.

"Was the girl hurt?" Casey asked.

"She looked all right to me, but it was dark." He paused with a smug grin, until I realized his reply was just a dig at the color of Lena's skin.

Letting go of his arm, I said: "When did they leave?"

"Pulled out that same night, heading south to . . . well, wherever south takes 'em, I guess. They didn't say."

Doing the math in my head, I realized that despite our detour to Dick Langley's cabin, we'd still managed to shave a little time off their lead. "Did they say who they were?" I asked. "Any names?"

"It ain't my job to ask a man his name. I just pour the drinks. They had a couple at that table yonder, then bought a jug for the trail and left. I got no idea what they did after they walked out my door." He paused, his gaze sweeping the business side of the bar. "Any of you boys want another drink?"

"I reckon we're done," I replied, and tipped my head toward the door for the others to follow me outside.

Jim was standing at the edge of the verandah as we exited, one shoulder propped casually against the post. I noticed there wasn't much for him to keep an eye on—a pair of shoats rooting in the weeds at the edge of town, and the steady puffing of smoke from a bellows in the blacksmith shop as the smithy cherried his coals. Ardell and Punch were nowhere in sight.

"They's over to the tradin' post," Jim said as if reading my mind. "Went to talk to the smithy first, but didn't stay even a minute. They been at the post ever since."

Not wanting to interrupt, I had us wait in front of the saloon until Ardell and Punch emerged from the trading post some twenty minutes later. They sauntered over to where we were standing. Punch was toting a slab of cured ham over one shoulder, and Ardell had the neck of a burlap sack twisted around his fist. He didn't offer any kind of explanation as to its contents, and no one asked.

"The smithy saw them, but didn't talk to them," Ardell reported. "Said they spent a couple of hours in the saloon, then rode on. He said Lena was with them, and that she didn't look like she'd been hurt, but he thought she was scared. Said it bothered him, but not enough to risk getting his head shot off for interfering in what wasn't any of his business. The clerk at the trading post said about the same thing. He didn't talk to them, either." Tipping his head toward the post, Ardell added: "They're not much better provisioned than Müller was, as far as guns and ammunition, but they had a few things Punch and I took an interest in."

Punch got a big smile on his face, but refused to elaborate when Roy asked him why he was grinning like an idiot.

"You learn anything in there?" Ardell asked, nodding toward the saloon.

"Just another Negro hater," Casey replied stonily.

We mounted our horses and rode back to the west until we were clear of town, then veered off to the south, ducking and dodging the tattered sheets of Spanish moss that hung from the oaks and magnolias like long-forgotten linens. There were trails all through here, made by local townspeople and feral hogs, but a lot of them seemed to wander without purpose. We pushed on doggedly until we came to a piney ridge running north and south along the coast. I didn't say anything to the boys, but I was glad to find it. That ridge was about the only way there was to reach a lot of those old forts and trading posts and settlements along Florida's southeast coast. It was a strip of pine woods maybe five or six miles wide in spots, but crammed in between deep swamps on one side and the Atlantic on the other. From what I'd heard, it ran almost all the way to Fort Dallas.

Once we reached the pines, our journey became a lot easier. Things improved even more when we came to a well-marked trail, its moist soil marred by the prints of shod horses. I wasn't much of a tracker, then or now, but no one lives on the frontier without picking up a little knowledge, and I was betting those tracks couldn't have been more than forty-eight hours old.

"I'll be damned," Casey said softly, eyeing the hoof marks gouged into the layers of pine needles. "We've found 'em."

I was inclined to agree, but dismounted anyway to run my fingers along the edges of the tracks, moving from one set of prints to the next. I could feel my excitement growing as the story left in the sod took shape before my eyes. Although not positive, I estimated at least ten horses had passed this way, but it was the tracks of a smaller animal that convinced me we were on the right trail—the gray filly Pa had been so proud of because of her long, clean lines. My mood was sailing high as I walked back to my horse, but it fell like a rock when I spotted a detachment of Yankee soldiers coming up behind us. Dick Langley rode with them, hands tied tight to his saddle, his face a mass of bruises and dried blood.

SESSION SEVEN

Years later, I would find out from Eric Burke, who I met again in Texas, that the officer sent out from Fort Myers to capture us was the same Lieutenant Hodges who'd tried to corral us there in Punta Rassa. That day outside of Fort Pierce, Hodges halted his command about sixty yards away, then ordered his men to spread out as much as the narrow trail would allow. Although he had eight troopers with him, they didn't look especially dangerous. In fact, they looked more like a bunch of spindly-legged kids sitting nervously astride their big cavalry mounts, sporting long Springfield rifles and apprehensive expressions. I'll give them credit, though. As frightened as they appeared, they didn't hesitate when Hodges told them to ready their weapons.

I put my hand on my revolver but didn't draw it. Real quiet, I said: "Spread out, boys. Let's see what they want before we start shooting."

They did as instructed, and a couple of them—Pablo and Ardell—actually rode into the trees where they would be harder to hit, yet would have a clear field of fire down the middle of the trail. Hodges barked a command over his shoulder, and a skinny little corporal rode forward, dragging Dick Langley's marshtackie behind him on a lead rope. I recognized Dick's horse right off as one of the Flatiron mounts we'd switched our saddles to after that hard ride in from Pete Dill's trading post.

"Which one of you is Bone McCallister?" Hodges called.

Roy shook his head in disgust. "It's Boone McCallister, you pecker-headed Yankee fool!" he shouted back.

"Hold your tongue," Casey said sharply. "This is still Boone's outfit."

I appreciated the admonition. The truth is, I would have been real happy if those Yankees hadn't known my name at all, but since they obviously did, there wasn't any point in my denying it. Not with the muzzle of that corporal's revolver pressed against the side of Dick's chest.

"I'm McCallister," I replied, raising my voice to be heard.

"McCallister, you may consider yourself and your men under arrest. Surrender your weapons immediately, then ride forward with your hands in the air."

Roy snorted in derision. "Is that boy daft, Boone? There ain't a one of us here that don't know what they'd do if we gave up our pistols."

"They'd hang us," I responded bluntly, then lifted my voice to the watching Yankees. "We won't surrender, bluebelly, but, if you turn our man loose, we'll let you live. You can ride on back to wherever you came from and tell your commanding officer how you tried to catch us, but couldn't."

I'll admit I was surprised by the fire in Hodges's reply. "I will see you sent to hell, McCallister," the lieutenant bellowed, leaning so far forward in his saddle I thought he might fall off, "and send your Secesh gang with you! Now throw down your arms and come forward with your hands raised."

Casey whistled softly. "That ol' boy is primed for blood, Boone."

"He's got us roasting over a slow fire, too," I acknowledged. "We've got to mind our mettle as long as they've got Dick."

"Why do we worry about Langley?" Pablo asked suddenly, catching me off guard with his question. "He is not a Flatiron rider."

"What the hell, Torres!" Roy exclaimed. "He's as much a Flatiron rider as any of us."

Pablo's face drew down in a scowl, but he didn't say anything else. I stared at him a moment longer, then turned away, faced with more pressing concerns. "Let's ease forward a bit," I told the boys. "We're pushing our range from here."

A Colt Navy like the one I carried in those days was fairly accurate out to about a hundred yards if you used a large enough target, like the four-foot-tall oak stump Pa had left standing behind our house. Before the Union blockade made ammunition so precious, us McCallisters would stand on the back porch and fire away at that stump three or four evenings a week, until we nearly had the thing blown away. Sometimes Pa would shoot with us, just to keep his hand in, as he liked to say, although I suspect it was also to remind us who the he-'coon was on the Flatiron, and that it sure as heck wasn't any of us boys. Pa was the best shot with rifle or handgun that I ever knew, although toward the end, my older brother Lew started to make him work a little harder to retain the title.

There's a big difference between shooting at a stump and firing at a living, breathing target, though. Particularly from the back of a frightened horse, and especially when the target in question is shooting back—even at only sixty yards. Wanting to get closer, where our revolvers would be an advantage over the Federals' single-shot muzzleloaders, I lightly tapped the bay's ribs with the sides of my stirrups. The boys eased out behind me, but we didn't cover more than a few feet when Hodges yelled at us to stop where we were and throw down our guns.

"Do it now," the lieutenant warned. "If you don't comply immediately, I'll order your man shot on the spot."

We quickly pulled up, our horses starting to fidget as the tension along the trail increased. It was like an electrical charge from a thunderstorm, tickling the hair along my arms. So far, no one in our bunch had drawn a gun, and the Yankees were keeping their muzzles pointed skyward, as well—all except for that skinny little corporal holding his pistol on Dick—but we were all like kegs of gunpowder, ready to go off at the slightest spark.

"Boone!" Dick shouted unexpectedly. "Don't do it."

The corporal flinched, and I could see the lieutenant's shoulders stiffen. For a moment I was sure one of them would tell Langley to shut up, but then Hodges made a small motion with his hand, and the corporal lowered the hammer on his weapon.

"A deal, McCallister," Hodges proposed. "If you and your men surrender without incident, I shall allow young Langley to return to his home unharmed."

"It's a trick," Casey said tersely, looking at me. "You can't trust a damned Yankee, Boone. They'll say whatever it takes to win, then turn around and shove a knife through your guts the second they've got what they want."

I don't know, maybe that's not being fair to Northerners, but it was the way we felt at the time, the way a lot of us still do when it comes to the North. But I couldn't let Hodges or one of his men just shoot Dick down in cold blood, either. Not if there was something I could do to prevent it.

"Make your offer, Yankee!" I called.

Casey and Roy cursed softly but with venom, and Pablo said: "I will not do it."

"Hold on, dammit," I said. "Hearing what he's got to say doesn't mean we'll do it, and it might give us a little time."

"Time ain't going to work in our favor here, Boone," Casey argued.

I guess Hodges didn't intend to let that happen, either. "I've made my offer, McCallister. You have ten seconds to reply."

"Boone!" Dick shouted, and this time Hodges gave him a

sharp look and said something to the skinny corporal I couldn't hear. The corporal lowered his revolver and reached for Langley's collar, and Dick said—"Let 'em have it."—and threw himself from the saddle.

Dick's move caught everyone by surprise. Then all hell broke loose. I drove my spurs into the bay's ribs even as I drew my Navy, pounding forward with the revolver thrust before me because I didn't know what else to do. Several of the boys—Casey and Punch and Roy—rode beside me, while Jim and Ardell swung down from their saddles and started firing from the ground.

It was all wildly crazy for maybe forty-five seconds. Dick's horse bolted with the young cow hunter still lashed firmly to the open pommel of his flat saddle. He was hanging on, though, and trying to get a foot back in the stirrup even as his horse swerved wide to avoid my bay. Meanwhile, Minié balls were thumping past our ears, and men yelled in both fury and fear. I heard Roy scream a curse behind me, but didn't look around to see why. I was firing as fast as I could thumb the hammer back and pull the trigger, although not doing much damage for all my effort. Like I said a minute ago, shooting is a lot different in the heat of battle, and I lacked the experience at that time to keep a cool head. Only two of my shots hit their mark, but that turned out to be enough when it was lumped in with the others. Especially Negro Jim cutting loose with his shotgun.

Rifles and revolvers are nice, but never underestimate the influence of a shotgun in a close-up gunfight. I'm not just talking about the swath of destruction it can cut, either. I was near enough to those Yankees by the time Jim let go of his first round that I could see the way the expressions changed on the faces of those green-as-grass New Yorkers. Jim's buckshot tore through them like the reaper's scythe, spilling two men from their seats with the first blast, and two more with the second—half of

Hodges's command unhorsed within the space of ten seconds. The others scattered like flushed quail as the smoke from our guns rolled toward them. Those who were still mounted raced their horses back toward the settlement at Fort Pierce, while others fled on foot. I saw the corporal plunging unarmed into the trees west of the trail; running mindlessly in his terror, he was soon swallowed by Florida's thick, low-growth flora.

Three Union soldiers remained on the trail, the lieutenant among them. Stepping down, I let go of the bay's reins and the horse immediately scampered into the pines. It didn't go far before stopping and staring back over its shoulder, its nostrils flared like velvety trumpets, flanks quivering. With my jaw set like granite in concrete, I walked over to where Hodges lay on his back. His eyes were open, but already glazed in death. I was shocked when I looked into his face. He seemed young, surely no more than twenty or twenty-one. It would be a while before it dawned on me that, as young as he might have been, the lieutenant was still a couple of years older than I was. It was a sobering realization, and it haunted me for some days afterward. I think that was the first time I truly understood that I was no longer just Jeff McCallister's son. I was Boone McCallister, a man grown—even if I didn't yet feel that way.

"Marse?"

I turned and holstered my empty revolver. Jim stood a few yards away, his hand on the shoulder of Dick Langley's marsh-tackie. Dick looked drawn and pale and was covered in filth, no small amount of it being his own dried blood, but he seemed otherwise intact.

"If I could afford it, I'd buy this darkie from you," Dick said quietly.

"Shoo," Jim replied, grinning. "Ol' Mistah Jeff, he'd never sell Negro Jim."

"He'd better not," Dick said emphatically. He slid from his

saddle to the ground, where Jim caught him and held him firm until he had his balance. "He likely saved my life back there," Dick added, tipping his head toward the trail behind him.

"His 'tackie was fair spooked," Jim agreed. "I seen Mistah Dick's hands was tied, so I went after him. Don't know about savin' his life, though."

"You did good, Jim. Thanks," I said, and the older man got a funny, flustered look on his face.

" 'Tweren't nothin', marse," he insisted, then abruptly handed me the reins to Dick's mount and walked away.

Casey and Roy came over, nodding their pleasure at seeing their friend still alive and in one piece. Glancing at Roy, I said: "I heard you holler."

He held up his hand. It was empty and the forefinger slightly swollen, but otherwise it appeared unharmed.

"One of them damned Yankees shot my pistol outta my hand," he said. "Like to took my trigger finger off with it. Ruined the gun, too."

"Take the lieutenant's," I said distractedly, already turning away to take stock of our situation.

The first thing I noticed was that Ardell and Pablo were gone. I asked the boys if they knew what had happened, and Punch said: "Pablo went after them soldiers that were running away. Ardell went after him."

"After Pablo?"

"Looked so," Punch agreed. "He was shouting for Torres to let 'em go, but ol' Torres wasn't payin' him no attention."

Although Punch's words brought a quick scowl to my face, I didn't say anything. We went back to where the dead Yankees were sprawled across the trail, and I'll tell you what, that was a solid lesson learned about bunching up when someone is shooting at you. I figured Jim had dropped at least three of them, but I didn't say anything on account of Jim being black. I figured the others probably knew it as well as I did, but felt confident that they wouldn't bring it up outside of our own circle. Negro Jim had saved our hides that day, no two ways about it. If he hadn't cut loose with his shotgun when he did, and kept his head while doing it, we'd have likely lost a man or two ourselves, if not the whole battle.

All but one of the Yankees' horses had fled. The one that remained had a wound in its side that looked like it had come from one of its own. Those Minié balls punched a deep hole into the toughest hide. Leading the horse off the trail, I used my Sharps to put it out of its misery, while the others hauled the dead Yankees into the trees on the opposite side and laid them out side-by-side. We stood around a while, wondering if we should bury them, or at least say some words over their bodies, but I finally said the bluebellies could do their own praying when they came back for the bodies.

"What about that corporal?" Casey asked, jutting his chin toward the deep forest west of the trail.

"Shoo, let the 'gators have him," Roy said, to which I was inclined to agree.

"He can find his own way out," I replied. "Time's wasting, and Klee's men are getting farther away." I turned to Dick Langley, sitting his horse nearby. He'd cleaned up as best he could in a nearby slough, but still looked rough-used. "You coming with us?"

Dick hesitated, then shook his head. "No. They burned our cabin, Boone. Emma May got a chance and ducked into the scrub with our boy, but she's out there unarmed and with no shelter. She's a tough ol' gal, but that's too much to ask of anyone. I'm going back, though I feel bad for doing so."

"You've no reason to feel bad."

"In case you're wondering, it was me that told 'em which way y'all were heading. That corporal had Emma May's arm twisted up behind her back so that it like to snapped."

"I figured it had to be something like that," I said, although I'll confess that until that moment, I hadn't even considered how they'd found us. Still, I knew I eventually would have started wondering, so I appreciated Dick telling me. And I never did blame him for it. Truthfully I probably would have thought less of him if he hadn't done everything he could to protect his family. "Go on back to your wife and that little boy," I said. "When we get this thing with the Klees settled, we'll come by and help you raise another cabin."

Dick nodded appreciatively and reined away, the Springfield musket he'd confiscated from the field carried across his saddle. And that was that, as far as Dick Langley is concerned. If you're interested, he and his family did prosper in the years that followed, and that youngster of his grew up to be a DeSoto County commissioner, a man of some influence, is what I've heard, although I can't say from personal knowledge. By the time Homer Langley won his first election, I'd been a Texas cowboy for better than twenty years.

I walked into the trees to retrieve my bay, and when I came back, the others were already mounted and waiting for me. Roy was wearing the lieutenant's Army model Colt revolver at his waist, and Casey had tied a trio of Springfield rifles and their ammunition pouches to the spare mount we'd brought along for Lena. Although Roy had wanted to go through the pockets of the dead soldiers to see if they had anything of value, I'd told him to leave them be. Roy had naturally balked, but Casey and Punch quickly jumped in to back me up, and even Jim had ventured to say he thought it was a bad idea to rob from the dead. Faced with so much opposition, Roy had grudgingly abandoned his search. The guns were a different matter, though. This was war, and even if we decided not to use the Springfields ourselves, we'd either see that they got into proper

Southern hands, or toss them into the swamps where the Yankees would never find them.

"Which way we going, Boone?" Punch asked.

"We're going after Lena and our horses."

"What about Ardell and Pablo?"

"They'll have to catch up as best they can," I said, then reined away from the scene of the battle with the others falling in silently behind me.

We continued on through the shady pines until we came to the remains of a campfire at the edge of a grassy vale, several miles south of where we'd fought the Yankees. Dismounting and handing the bay's reins to Punch, I told the others to stay back, then motioned for Casey to follow me into the abandoned camp. It was Casey who discovered the rope-slick bark of a pine, set back from the fire and tied low, like you'd do for either a dog or a human, instead of a horse. His shout brought everyone over.

"This be the place?" Jim asked bitterly, dropping to one knee to rub the backs of his fingers softly over the crushed grass where the prisoner had lain. "This where them skunks kept her trussed like a hog for market?"

"That's what it looks like," I replied gently.

He looked up, a fire burning in his dark eyes like nothing I'd ever seen before. He didn't say anything, though. He couldn't, being colored and all, but I recognized the anger that boiled just below the surface, and silently nodded my acknowledgement of it.

"We'll get her back," I promised.

"Yes'um," Jim replied icily. "We surely will."

"Hey, here's something!" Roy called. He'd moved on past the tree where Lena had been tied and was lifting something hard and brown out of the tall grass. He swung it on his finger as he brought it back, a whiskey jug of the same style, but about twice the size as the one the Fort Pierce bartender had poured our drinks from.

"Looks like they might've been here a while," Casey observed.

Sniffing the uncorked mouth, Roy winced dramatically. "This is the same rotgut we had this mornin', all right. If they drank this whole jug in one settin', I'll bet they was passed out here for a good long spell."

Kneeling at the fire, Casey cautiously pushed his fingers into the ashes. "These are still kind of warm," he announced. "I'd say Roy is right."

"About time you figured that out," Roy replied with feigned indignation.

Standing and brushing off his fingers, Casey said: "We're closing the gap, Boone."

I nodded solemnly, then walked over to where Punch had left his marshtackie and my long-legged bay ground-tied. I swung a tired leg over the cantle, then glanced at Casey, who was staring back up the trail with furrowed brows. "They'll be along," I said, knowing he was starting to fret over Ardell and Pablo's long absence. Hell, I was, too.

"You notice how that Cuban's been acting funny ever since we left Punta Rassa," Casey asked, still watching our back trail.

"What do you mean?"

"Think about it. I doubt he's said a dozen words to any of us since Rassa."

"Since that night Dave Klee got et by a 'gator, is more like," Roy amended. "I been noticin' it, too, although I got to admit I appreciated him stayin' quiet for a change."

"He's seemed real moody to me, too," Punch added.

"Like he's got a bad bellyache or something," said Roy.

"Something's sure been eating at him," Casey declared. "That remark he made about Dick not being a Flatiron hand, I nearly dropped my pistol."

I didn't reply, but instead let my thoughts drift back over the preceding week. Although normally pretty gregarious, Torres had become strangely silent and withdrawn since . . . when? Was Roy right, claiming his mood had turned dark that night at Chestnut Thumb, when Dave Klee had been pulled under by an alligator?

"He's probably just . . . ," I started, then let my words trail off. The fact is, I'd been so caught up in my own problems ever since the Thumb that I'd barely registered the change in Pablo's character, and hadn't cared when I did notice it. Shaking my head as if to clear it of cobwebs, I said: "Let's mount up. We can worry about Torres later. Right now I want to keep dogging Klee's men."

We rode on, pushing our mounts a little harder, but resisting the urge to throw them into a run. You might be wondering why, what with our prey being just a few hours ahead of us by then. Actually there's a good reason.

Have you ever noticed how those movie cowboys are always riding here and about at a full-out gallop, their horses' manes and tails flying in the wind, their coats shining like they've been recently oiled? Not a speck of dust on horse or tack, and those movie actors just about as clean, unless they're some scruffy sidekick like Gabby Hayes or Fuzzy St. John.

But that's not how it was in Florida, or anywhere out West that I've ever been to. Horseback travel in those days was dirty, and it was hard on both you and your mount. You ride a horse at even a fast lope under those conditions, and more than likely that horse'll drop out from under you before you've covered fifty miles. It just can't be done, unless you don't mind killing your mount to do it. That's why, even in as much of a hurry as we were in, we mostly kept our pace to a walk—maybe three to five miles an hour, depending on the terrain. Oh, we'd jog our marshtackies along from time to time, and would even lope them once in a while, when we had solid, open ground under us. But for the most part we walked, knowing they were going to have to carry us all the way to Fort Dallas and, more importantly, back out again.

As the miles dropped away and the sun slid down through the pines, I began to notice my own mood starting to dip. Judging from the increasingly somber expressions of the others, I'd guess they were feeling the same. I couldn't say what was eating at the others, but I know that for me, my anger had started to dull in the days since we'd ridden out of the Flatiron like knights-errant. Our time since then had been filled with travel, with new sights and fresh discoveries. But now, with our encounter with the Yankees still fresh in our minds and the knowledge that we were drawing near the end of our pursuit of the Klees, the reality of what might lie ahead was beginning to sharpen its focus.

I'd said all along that freeing Lena was our primary goal, and that recovering our stolen horses or exacting revenge for what Jacob's boys had done to the ranch would happen only after she was safe. But if the entire Klee clan had taken up residence along the Lower Miami, rescuing anyone was going to be almighty chancy. When you're two hundred miles away and mad as a 'gator with a toothache, it's pretty easy to believe that you and your friends are invincible, but the closer we got to tossing the fat into the fire, the more I realized how vulnerable we really were. Those Klees were a hard bunch, every one of them. Rustlers and murderers and highwaymen, and a whole lot more dangerous than a detachment of New York farm boys. As far as us, well, when you got right down to it, except for Jim, we were all just boys ourselves. Maybe a little rougher around the edges than Hodges's men, but nothing near like what we'd be going up against there on the Miami. We'd be outnumbered and outgunned, and that was a sobering assessment for a young buck like myself. I expect it was for the others, too.

Along about dark we peeled off into the trees and found a little vale with enough grass to satisfy our horses. After seeing to our stock and gathering enough wood for a quick fire, we settled down for a supper of lukewarm grits and salty ham. When Roy started to add more wood to the blaze after we'd eaten, I told him to let it die.

"We're getting too close to Klee's men to take any chances," I said. "I don't want them catching sight of our fire."

Normally Roy would have argued the point, but that night he just tossed his stick aside and leaned back against his saddle to stare into the lowering flames. We sat in silence for a good long time that evening, lost in our own melancholy as the fire shrank into a pulsating red blob. I don't know how far down we might have sunk if Jim hadn't perked up when he did.

"Listen, marse. You hear that?"

Jack-knifing into a sitting position, I quickly pulled the Sharps across my lap. "No, what was it?"

" 'Tackies, sounds like."

"I hear it," Punch said excitedly.

Casey stood, scowling into the night. We could all hear it by then, the steady clopping of hoofs from the north. "You reckon it's them?" he asked.

I knew who he meant, and probably so do you. Pushing to my feet, I told the others to step back into the trees. Then I strode toward the trail, maybe twenty yards away. As dark as it was, it didn't take long before I stepped on a twig and announced my presence to the world. Dropping to a crouch, I waited tensely, but the horses had drawn up at the loud crack of a pine limb under my heel, and silence drifted through the forest like fog. Then I heard a voice, little more than a hiss coming through the forest, and my shoulders slumped in relief.

"Boone," the voice repeated, a little louder this time.

I stood and said: "Come on in, boys."

Well, it was Ardell, all right, and Pablo right behind him. They rode into the vale where the light was better and quietly dismounted.

"Glad to see you, Boone," Ardell said. "I was beginning to think we'd passed you in the dark."

"Where've you been?" Punch asked.

The question brought a sharp look from Ardell. Glancing briefly at Pablo, he said: "We can talk about it later. You boys got any grub left?"

"Some." I nodded to Punch, then Jim. "Take care of their horses. Casey, kick that flame up a mite. Just enough to warm up some ham and grits and a couple of coontie biscuits."

We returned to the fire and settled down on our blankets. Although curious about where the two men had been, I maintained a strained silence until Punch and Jim returned from seeing to the horses. I wanted to cover this just once, and not have to bring it up again.

Jim and Punch got back about the same time Casey set a billy of ham-fried grits on the ground between Ardell and Pablo. Ardell filled his plate first, taking about half. Pablo eyed the tin utensil suspiciously, then pulled it onto his lap and began wolfing grub straight from the billy, as if taking his pent-up rage out on the food instead of whatever it was that was eating at him. At Pablo's side, Ardell began speaking between mouthfuls.

"We ended up all the way back at Fort Pierce," he said, then nodded toward Pablo. "Chasing this one."

Without looking up, Pablo growled: "It was foolish to let the Yankee *niños* escape."

"He was dead set on killing every last one of them, and seemed put out that I wouldn't let him."

I looked at Pablo, seeing him in a way I never had before. It made me wonder what had changed in the man over the preceding week. Or had he been that way all along, his animus un-

166

noticed in the day-to-day operations of running a ranch the size of the Flatiron?

"Those *soldados,* they will return to the fort. Then others will come after us," Pablo stated darkly.

"Not as bad wounded as that boy was," Ardell said in a disgruntled tone.

Pablo glowered, but held his tongue. Casey and I exchanged puzzled glances. Jim looked wary, but Roy and Punch, I noticed, were staring in fascination as the story unfolded.

"Any of them soldiers, did they get away?" Jim asked softly.

"All but one," Ardell confirmed bitterly. "I didn't know what Torres had in mind until we came to a wounded Yankee laid up along the road with his arm shredded by buckshot. I figured as long as he didn't fight, we'd see to his wounds as best we could, then send him on his way, but Pablo had a different notion. When we got up to him, Pablo drew one of his revolvers and shot that Yankee dead before I could stop him."

"Sweet Jesus," Roy said softly.

"You hanged those Yankee *soldados* on the road from Punta Rassa," Pablo replied in an accusatory voice. "Is this road different?"

Well, he had a point there, but if the road wasn't all that much different, our situation surely was. We'd been dealing with a larger bunch back at Punta Rassa, for one thing. And for another, those Rassa Yankees had just killed Calvin Oswald. That might not be much of an excuse in your eyes, but it's the way it was. I said the other day that I didn't regret our hanging those boys, and I don't. But I'll also tell you now that I'm not sad those bluebellies who jumped us below Fort Pierce got away, either. Or at least the three who did.

I didn't have a reply for Pablo's accusation, so I didn't try to make one. Surprisingly none of the others did, either, and a tense hush fell over the camp. [*Ed. Note:* No mention of the three surviving soldiers, or of the corporal who reportedly fled into the swamps, could be found, although oral tradition suggests a party of Fort Pierce residents went out during this period to bury a detachment of Union troopers, killed in battle along the road south of the settlement; whether this is the same detachment of Federals that McCallister mentions could not be determined.]

With the bone-dry wood we were using, it didn't take long for the fire to die and darkness to close in. When the two cow hunters finished eating, Ardell took all the utensils, including Pablo's tin billy, into the trees and scrubbed them out with sand and leaves. Although not as thorough as a pan of hot, soapy water, sand makes a handy substitute when nothing else is available. You might be wondering about liquid in that southeastern location, and I'll admit there were streams and ponds nearby, but we didn't like to wander too far off after nightfall, on account of water moccasins, copperheads, rattlesnakes, and alligators.

When Ardell came back, he told Punch to fetch the burlap bag from his saddle. With everything that had taken place that day, I'd plumb forgotten about the coarsely woven sack Ardell had brought with him from the Fort Pierce trading post that morning, but I could tell from the eager way Punch scampered to do the older man's bidding that he hadn't.

"What have you got in there, Ardell?" Casey asked, roused from his melancholy.

"Probably a dead cat he forgot to fry up for supper," Roy predicted gloomily.

We'd been eating poorly since leaving the Flatiron, and I don't think any of us felt especially satisfied when it came to our bellies. Even a little chicory would have helped, but we were traveling fast and light, and had left our coffee pot at home.

"It's not a dead cat, but I can buy you one when we get to

Fort Jupiter," Ardell replied, accepting the bag Punch swung across the blinking embers. "The rest of you might prefer something a little tastier."

With a flourish, he dumped the contents of the bag onto a saddle blanket he'd spread out in front of him like a tablecloth, although decorated with horse hair and horse sweat rather than a bright gingham print—not that any of us cared a hoot. We leaned forward to see what kind of prize Ardell was springing on us, and several of the boys shouted in delight as a loaf of bread and a squat container of jam rolled into the dim light from the stars.

"Holy hell," Roy breathed, grabbing the little crock. "What have you got in here, Ardell?"

"Pineapple jam and bread made from honest-to-God wheat flour, instead of that coontie crap we've been eating since the blockade."

I'll tell you what, my mouth started watering fit to float a small boat as Ardell held the first loaf of real bread any of us had seen in years over the coals where the light was brightest, displaying it like a nugget of fresh-dug gold.

"What about it, Roy?" Ardell grinned. "You still got your mouth set on dead cat?"

Laughing, Roy said: "I reckon bread and jam'll do." He whipped out a short-bladed skinning knife and handed it across the fire. "Start carvin' on that thing, boy. I'm half froze for something sweet."

"I'd just about trade my horse for that loaf of bread," Punch said almost reverently, and I had to laugh at the hungry way he was hanging over Ardell's shoulder, watching him slice the wheel-shaped loaf into six even wedges.

That bread and jam was a real treat, but as you might expect among five half-starved lads of such tender teenage years, it didn't last nearly long enough. We cleaned it up to the last crumb and the last smidgen of jam, wiped from the bottom of the crock with dirty fingers, then leaned back against our saddles afterward to savor the lingering taste of pineapple and baked dough. With our moods lightened, it didn't take long before our conversation picked up. Even Punch seemed to be having a fine old time that evening, his first since Calvin's death.

Only Pablo held himself aloof from the general camaraderie. As soon as Ardell's treat was gone, he heaved to his feet and lumbered off into the trees. I didn't think much of it at first—shoot, snakes or not, we all have to slip off into the darkness from time to time—but when he didn't come back after a reasonable amount of time, I stood and told the boys I needed to see a man about a horse. Then I stepped off into the trees in the same general direction as Pablo.

I found him leaning against a slender pine about thirty yards away. Even in the ink-like darkness under the trees, it wasn't difficult to find him, guided as I was by the heady aroma of liquor.

"Hey, *amigo*," I greeted while still several yards away, not wanting to startle a man when he'd been drinking. From the smell floating out from under that tree, I figured Pablo must have been hitting that bottle pretty hard.

Pablo jumped, then quickly turned his head this way and that until he spotted me against the lighter background of the clearing. I could see his scowl even in the dimness under his sombrero. "Why do you follow me?" he demanded.

"Who said I was following you? I was just taking a walk."

"Walk somewhere else. I got this place."

I eased forward, ignoring the veiled threat in his words. "Where'd you get the whiskey?"

"None of your business," he replied curtly, then tipped the bottle to his lips and took a long pull.

"You didn't get it in Fort Pierce, or the Havana House," I

said. "All they had was popskull in a jug."

Pablo growled something unintelligible, then confessed that he'd bought it from Müller. "Why?" he asked then. "Do the McCallisters got a rule against drinking whiskey?"

As a matter of fact, we did, at least during roundups and on cattle drives, and I figured this was a damned sight more important than a cattle drive. I wasn't sure how Pablo would react if I told him to put it away, though. Especially in his current mood. Deciding on a roundabout tack, I said: "You got much left?"

"It is mine," he retorted defensively. "If them *gilipollas* want to give away what is theirs, then I will eat it or drink it, but I don't give up none of what is my own."

"I'm not asking for a drink, I just asked how much you had left." I could feel my voice hardening, the warmth of blood rushing to my face. "You need to put that bottle away, Pablo," I said, trying to keep the annoyance out of my voice. "You know the rules."

"*Me cago en reglas,*" he snapped, and if I'd known then what he was saying, I'd have probably reacted differently—the asshole. "I will make my own rules from now on," he finished sulkily.

"Not while you're drawing McCallister pay."

Pablo's head jerked toward me, and I eased a hand up to cover the Navy's grips. Animosity shimmered between us like heat off a branding iron. I half expected him to take a swing at me, if not reach for his own gun, so I was caught off guard when he shoved the cork back in the bottle and whacked it tight with the palm of his hand.

"You are happy now, McCallister?"

"Not too damn' much," I replied. "You keep that bottle corked, or go find another outfit to ride for."

"One where I do not have to take orders from a *muchacho*?"

171

"That's your choice, Torres," I replied flatly, then spun and stalked back to the clearing.

I could tell the others knew something was up as soon as I got back. They watched curiously as I flopped down in front of the ash-covered embers of the fire. It was Casey who broke the uneasy silence.

"You find him?"

I stared into the graying coals a moment, debating my reply. Then I rose and lifted my saddle by its horn. "From here on, we'll post a guard at night. Casey, you take the first watch. Roll Roy out of his blankets at midnight." I glanced at Turner. "You wake me at three, and I'll take the last watch."

Roy nodded. "Will do, boss."

Lugging my saddle in my left hand and the Sharps in my right, I went to the far side of the clearing and spread my bedroll. I was aware of the others watching my every move, and realized, as I pried my boots off, that I'd taken a lot of my anger at Pablo out on them, instead of where it belonged. Still too ticked off to care, I laid back with my saddle for a pillow and arranged my guns around me, where they'd be handy to reach in case of trouble.

I guess I was more exhausted than mad, because it didn't take long to drop off. I came up groggily when Roy shook me awake, pinching the sleep from my eyes with a thumb and forefinger as I glanced around the tiny meadow. It took a second or two to realize how late it was, the sky already turning pale with the coming dawn, birds stirring the woods with their songs.

"Dammit, Roy," I started to flare, then stopped when I saw the condition of his face. "What happened to you?"

"That son-of-a-bitchin' fat Cuban is what happened," Roy replied, although not as heatedly as I might have expected. There was a purpling bruise visible through the mop of hair over his forehead, a thread of dried blood across one cheek. I stood with my rifle in hand, but there was nothing to see. Over by the fire, Ardell and Jim were just pulling on their boots, as yet unaware that anything was amiss.

"When?" I asked tersely.

"I don't know." He eased down at the foot of my bed, looking oddly frail in the gray light.

"Are you going to puke, Roy?"

"I don't know that, either," he admitted, then gave me a black look. "Don't worry, I won't get anything on your blankets if I do." Then he dropped his head to the palm of his right hand, the elbow propped on his knee. "Besides, I've just about puked my guts out already."

"When?" I persisted.

"After I woke up. It felt like my stomach was tied in knots for a while."

"I mean when did Pablo jump you?"

There was that glower again, kind of reassuring, to tell you the truth. Without it I might have been more worried about his health. "I already told you I don't know. I was standin' out in the trees between us and the trail when I heard him come up. I asked what he was doin', but the son-of-a-bitch didn't even answer. I guess he already had his pistol out, because as soon as he got close, he belted me over the head with it."

I was pulling on my boots as Roy spoke, my eyes going to where the horses were picketed in the tall grass at the far end of the little vale. I swore softly when my count came up two short.

"He took that extra horse you brought along for Lena," Roy confirmed. "I saw that when I came back. It looked like he took some supplies, too."

Jim was standing now, his gaze sweeping the clearing. Worry furrowed his brows when he realized what was going on. "Pablo?" he called to me.

I nodded as Ardell began looking around, and Casey and

Punch sat up in their quilts and oilcloth. "What's going on?" Casey asked.

"That son-of-a-bitch Torres hit me over the head and stole our horses is what's going on," Roy snapped, as if the prospect of having to repeat everything he'd already told me was too overwhelming to contemplate.

"How long's he been gone?" Ardell asked.

"Long enough," I cut in, before Roy could work up any more ire. "Jim, take a look along the trail, see if you can find his tracks."

Rearing up from where he'd been sitting hunched at the foot of my bed, Roy said: "You ain't thinkin' of goin' after him, are you? I say let the bastard run. I never did trust him."

"He's got our food, and he's got Lena's horse," I reminded him.

"He doesn't have all our food!" Ardell called. He was squatted beside the saddlebags, tied behind the English rig we'd brought along for Lena. "Looks like he might have taken some pork and grits, but nothing we can't live without." He looked across the fire to where I was standing. "I've got to side with Roy on this one, Boone. Wherever Torres went, we don't need him. Not as much as we need to get down to Fort Dallas and find that girl. The longer she's there, the more likely it is something bad will happen to her."

I was nodding grudging acceptance even as Jim returned to camp.

"I followed his tracks as far as the main trail, marse, but couldn't tell which way he went from there. Ground's all churned up, and it ain't quite light enough yet to 'cipher."

"It doesn't matter. We're going on to Fort Dallas and get Lena."

Looking relieved, Jim said: "I'll go fetch our horses, if that be all right with you?"

I waved him away, my thoughts awhirl at this unexpected calamity. Yet I knew Ardell was right. We had enough grub in our saddlebags to make it to Fort Dallas, and we could put Lena on one of the horses Klee's boys had lifted out of our pasture.

Roy came over to the fire and I had him brush the hair off his forehead so I could have a look. There was a shallow cut just inside the hairline that hadn't bled overly much, and a walnut-sized knot under that. The flesh around the wound was mottled in angry blues and deep yellows.

"That ol' boy gave you a wallop, didn't he?" I probed gently at the swollen flesh, and Roy jerked away with an outburst of obscenities.

"If I ever run across that fat Cuban again, I'll give him a dose of what-for, and see how he likes it," he vowed.

"I doubt if he comes back," Ardell said. "It ain't just clubbing you with a pistol barrel he's got to worry about. He stole a horse, and that's fifty lashes with a bullwhip in any man's camp."

"We ought to string him up," Roy muttered darkly. "That's what they'd do in Texas."

"We ain't in Texas," I reminded him, then glanced at Punch, who was standing back out of the way. "You still got some of that salve Müller gave you?"

"Yeah, near about the whole tin."

I winced inwardly at his reply, recalling the old German's admonitions for me to look after my young friend's wound. I'd done a poor job of it, I reflected, remembering Punch's hang-dog expression in the days following Calvin's death, not to mention the danger I'd put him in by bringing him along after Klee's brigands. Shaking my head as if to banish any regrets, I said: "Go fetch it."

"Just keep your damned salve," Roy grumbled. "The day I can't take a rap from a gun barrel and keep on ridin' is the day

I'll throw myself in a 'gator hole and call it quits." Then he flashed me and Casey a guilty look, but neither of us took it the wrong way. It was just an expression in those parts, like "that's how the cow ate the cabbage," or "it's hotter than nickel night in a whorehouse."

"Let's get mounted," I said as Jim appeared with my bay and his little marshtackie. "We can eat in the saddle."

It took only minutes to ready our mounts, then ride out of that clearing with its mixed bowl of memories—real bread and pineapple jam, alongside an act of treason that burned in my craw like lit kerosene. I don't think anyone looked back as the trees closed in behind us.

We kept riding south, following the same trail we'd held to the day before. I could see fresh tracks in front of us, but didn't bother to examine them. That sandy ridge was only a few miles wide, according to the information Ardell had picked up in Fort Pierce. There wasn't anywhere for Klee's men to go unless they wanted to sneak off into the brush and double back, which none of us expected.

I put Roy up front where I could keep an eye on him. His color improved as the day went on, which I took as a good sign, but it was his steady complaining about allowing an asshole like Pablo Torres to ride along on such an important mission when everyone knew he couldn't be counted on that gave me the most reassurance. A blow to the head can be tricky, but Roy seemed to be recovering just fine.

We reached the remains of Fort Jupiter early the next morning, guided the last half mile or so by the crown of the Jupiter Lighthouse, glimpsed through the trees. The lighthouse had been disabled early in the war by Confederate sympathizers who'd feared the structure might be used to aid the enemy, but it remained a towering landmark for a motley bunch of bone-weary cow hunters. The fort itself had been abandoned years before, and was already being overrun by jungle. Florida never did waste time reclaiming what man discarded.

There was a settlement of sorts at Jupiter, too, maybe a dozen homes looking as fragile as toadstools in a cow pen. There was no saloon and not much of a trading post, just a sign nailed to the verandah of a squatty log cabin that announced hides and plumes bought and sold. A *Whiskey Available* addition had been scratched out with a knife, then shaded with charcoal.

A lanky man with a thick gray stubble came onto the porch as we drew up. He was carrying a fine Kentucky long rifle—the fancy kind, with rococo carving on the stock and wire inlay running throughout its tightly curled maple stock—like he knew how to use it, and I didn't doubt that he could.

"What do you want?" the storekeeper asked.

"What have you got?" was Roy's bristly response, even though the rest of us could tell it was the wrong approach to take with a man like that.

Swinging the rifle around to cover Roy's belly, the trader said: "Nothing I won't give up dear."

"Easy, friend, we mean no harm," I remarked. "We'd buy some bread or jam, if you've got it. Gunpowder and caps for our pistols, too."

"Ain't got no powder nor lead nor caps to spare. No bread, either, but I got some blackberry jam I could let you have . . . assuming you can pay for it."

"We've developed a sweet tooth after sampling some Fort Pierce pineapple jam last night," I replied. "I'd buy a small crock of whatever you've got if the price is fair."

The trader's gaze narrowed shrewdly. "Ten cents. It's a pint jar."

"Done," Ardell said swiftly. He reached into a pocket for a dime that he tossed to the trader.

"Jilly," the storekeeper called over his shoulder, after checking the coin for purity, but the woman was already there, a dark glass jar in hand. "Toss it to that young fella over there," he ordered, "but don't get 'twix them and my rifle. Then get on back in the house."

She did as instructed, and Ardell snagged the jar deftly out of the air, then tucked it inside his saddlebag. By the time he looked up again, the woman was gone.

Scowling, Roy said: "It strikes me that you've got a prickly manner for someone who what wants to sell his wares."

"Mister, I don't much care if I sell anything or not. It's bushwhackers and thieves I worry about. Which are you?"

"Neither," Casey and I said simultaneously, and Ardell added: "We're just cow hunters, friend, looking for some stolen horses and a Negro girl that was taken off our friend's ranch."

The trader looked at me when the others did. "She was your gal, then?"

"My pa's, rightly," I answered, "but he's off north with a herd. I was left in charge. We intend to get her back. The horses, too."

"No offense, mister, but you don't hardly look tough enough to go up against that Miami bunch."

"We'll hold our own, and then some," Roy fired back.

The trader shrugged. "You'll have to do better than holding your own, but it don't make me no never mind." As if finally satisfied that we were not a threat to home or family, he allowed the muzzle of his long rifle to swing toward the porch ceiling, the butt thumped solidly between his feet. "They was through here yesterday afternoon, extra horses on a lead and a pretty little colored gal that looked like she'd fetch a fair reward."

"What kind of reward?" I asked suspiciously.

"Don't go jumping the gun, mister. I ain't got her, and wouldn't want her if she was offered to me. I just said she looked like she'd bring a good price on market, if somebody took a notion to sell her."

"She ain't for sale," Jim blurted, and I think he surprised himself as much as anyone else with his boldness. He looked at me like he was going to apologize, but I gave him a small wave of my hand to let him know that it was all right.

"Your daughter?" the trader asked Jim.

"She was promised to his son," I explained.

"Well, for what it's worth, she didn't look none too hurt when I saw her, although I can't speak for what's in store for her down south. That's a rough crowd around Fort Dallas. Didn't use to be that way, but things have changed since the war."

"How do you know they were taking her to Dallas?" Ardell asked, voicing a question that had been on my mind ever since the trader mentioned Miami.

"That's where all the vermin ends up any more."

"Have you ever been there?" Casey asked.

"Not personally, but I see the kind of men who pass through on their way. I wouldn't want to tangle with any of them if I didn't have to." He slew a glance toward Roy. "Reckon that's why I'm so touchy around strangers, friend."

Roy just shook his head and looked away, not quite ready to let go of his anger. Ardell said: "You reckon we ought to ride, Boone? We've got a lot of country to cover before sundown."

"Likely we should," I agreed, gathering the bay's reins. "Obliged for the information, friend," I told the storekeeper, then started to rein away.

"That your brand?" the trader asked suddenly, nodding toward the bay's hip.

Hauling back on my reins, I allowed that it was.

"It's the Flatiron brand," Casey elaborated. "From over on the Pease River."

"It does look kind of like the bottom of a flatiron," the man admitted. "Reason I asked was because I saw that brand again this morning."

"This morning?" I echoed, frowning. "Where?" But even as the query exited my lips, the answer came back like a sack filled with rocks.

"Was a Spaniard, looked like. He passed on by without stopping. I noticed the mark, though. It's a hard one to miss."

"A Cuban," I corrected quietly.

The trader shrugged. "Both about the same in my eyes. This guy had a flighty look about him, though. I doubt I would have lowered my rifle, had he come over."

"That'd be smart thinkin'," Roy growled. He turned to me, his eyes ablaze. "He's headin' south, Boone, headin' for Fort Dallas."

I nodded almost sadly, the knife's plunge complete now—to the hilt. It was Casey who put my feelings into words.

"That damn' turncoat is going to join up with the Klees."

SESSION EIGHT

We left Jupiter settlement in a swirl of emotions, although I think it's safe to say we were sharing similar feelings in regard to Pablo's betrayal. We didn't talk about it, but you could tell from the grim expressions on everyone's face that it was heavy on their minds. It sure was on mine.

There was no longer a ferry over the Loxahatchee River, not even a dug-out moored to the bank, so we had to construct a makeshift raft out of palmetto, lashed together with vines, to float our gear across the river. Then, stripped down to bare butts atop the bony spines of our horses, we swam to the south bank, towing the raft with us. That would have been a hell of an adventure and a wagonload of fun under normal circumstances, what with the river's powerful current sweeping us steadily toward the Atlantic inlet barely a hundred yards away, but we clambered out the far side just as doleful as when we went in.

The old military road below the river wasn't hard to find. Like so much of the development along Florida's southeast coast in those early years, the road was a remnant of the Seminole Wars, a jungle passage for troops and supplies between Fort Jupiter and the New River Settlement at old Fort Lauderdale, a two-day ride to the south. [*Ed. Note:* Florida's Military Trail was constructed under the command of Major William Lauderdale's Tennessee Volunteers in 1838, following the Battle of Loxahatchee during the Second Seminole War; the original fort and current city are named after him.]

181

Nightfall caught us on a narrow strip of land squeezed down between a long fresh-water lake on one side and the Atlantic on the other. Being so near the coast, we decided to camp on the beach. Ardell found some turtle eggs buried in the sand, and we kindled a fire of driftwood from who-knew-where and had eggs and ham for supper. Afterward we finally began to air our feelings about Pablo. I don't guess there's much point in relating everything that was said that night, other than that we were all pretty burned about it, and didn't get to sleep until late.

We set off the next day under a mantle of clouds as gray and dismal as our mood. The wind blew brisk out of the northwest, and the temperatures dropped rapidly. Around noon a series of rain squalls swept across the coast, making travel miserable, although no one suggested stopping. We reached Lauderdale just before dusk on the second day after crossing the Loxahatchee, and reined up at the edge of what was then known as New River Settlement. There wasn't much left of the old town, and what looked like it might have been recently inhabited was deserted when we came through. We briefly explored the place, and finally found an old Negro man in a hut along the river, but when he saw us coming, he scrambled down the bank into a cypress dug-out and swiftly set paddle to water. Roy, being Roy, started to reach for his rifle, but Ardell told him to put it away and not be so stupid, a suggestion Casey and I both seconded.

"I don't know what he was so afraid of," Roy grumbled, sliding his rifle back through the leather loop that hung off the side of his saddle.

"Maybe some crazy-eyed cow hunter with a rifle," Ardell told him. Glancing around the rain-soddened community, he added: "Let's get out of here, Boone. This place is giving me the cold jitters."

"Suits me," I agreed, reining my horse around.

I left Fort Lauderdale with the same impressions I'd had of
Forts Pierce and Jupiter, not an especially nice place to visit,
and I'd sure as hell never want to live there, although I've heard
that since the land boom of the 1920s, it's not nearly as desolate
as it used to be.

We were in our saddles before dawn the next morning, the
landscape still damp and chilly from the previous day, but at
least the skies were clear. I remember us startling a flock of
egrets out of a slough shortly after setting off, and how amazed
I'd been by the brilliance of their feathers against the deep blue
of the sky, like shards of broken china tossed into the air. The
vividness of the colors nearly took my breath away.

That was happening a lot the farther south we traveled. Like
I was really noticing the world—its scents and sights and
sounds—for the first time. Even the feel of the breeze against
my flesh triggered odd sensations throughout my body. I figured
then it was because of the newness of the country we were
traveling through, but I think now it might have been more the
uncertainty of what we were riding into, and the possibility that
some of us might not ride out again.

I was hoping the ridge we'd followed south from Fort Pierce
would take us all the way to Fort Dallas, but it didn't. We were
still well north of the Miami when the pines finally gave way to
more traditional terrain. It wasn't long afterward that we found
ourselves once again following a narrow track through dense
foliage, surrounded on both sides by swamps. The cooler
temperatures of the day before gave way to a damp, oppressive
heat, and mosquitoes, midges, and greenhead flies swarmed us
in thick clouds that nearly drove our horses crazy with their
incessant biting.

Despite these rough conditions, we pushed on with a dogged
determination. As the sun edged nearer the horizon, I began to
fear that we wouldn't find a suitable spot to make camp before

nightfall closed the trail. Sure as hell, we weren't going to cover much ground after dark. In that thick jungle of mangrove, cypress, Spanish moss, and wrist-thick vines that created a tunnel-like canopy above us, we'd be like blind men in a maze, only this one baited with poisonous snakes and deadly alligators. It was just about dusk when I heard Jim's soft call from the rear. I reined up hock-deep in still water as the old Negro rode up beside me, his eyes darting anxiously.

"Marse Boone," he said quietly. "You know I rode with your daddy in the Indian Wars."

"Yeah, I know it." Jim's participation in the Seminole Wars had never been a secret, so I was wondering why he was bringing it up then.

"Thing is, Marse, after a few months down in those swamps below the Caloosahatchee, a lot of us what was scoutin' for General Harney and them, we got to where we could feel trouble a-comin'." Jim's gaze had been probing the shadows, but then he turned to me with a look in his eyes that sent a chill down my spine. "I gots that feelin' now, Marse. Real bad."

"What do we do?"

"Well, I's thinkin' was your daddy around, he'd maybe want. . . ."

"Jim," I cut in, although careful to keep my voice low, in case someone was close by, listening and watching. "Just tell us what to do."

"Yes'um, well, I gots me a powerful urge to get off this here trail, and I think we'd all. . . ."

"Jim," I interrupted again.

"Yes'um?"

"Lead the way."

Jim nodded briskly and said—"Follow me."—and reined off the trail, plunging his mount into the deeper waters to the west. Twisting in my saddle, I ordered the others to stay close and not make any more noise than they had to. Then I heeled my bay after Jim's tough little marshtackie.

I'll tell you what, that's spooky country down there around Miami. At least it was when I was there in '64. The cypress trees grew close and tall as we wound deeper into the swamp, and the exposed roots of mangroves hugged the edges of the wetlands like arthritic knees. We covered maybe half a mile—no small feat in that watery terrain—before Jim began angling south again. We were belly-deep to my bay horse at the time, crossing an algae-green pool, and movement off my shoulder caught my eye.

My heart just about shot past my tonsils when I spotted a four-foot water moccasin cutting a serpentine path through the green scum toward us. I started to call to Jim, but he'd already spotted it. He looked at me and shook his head, a warning for me not to shoot, but I'd be damned if I'd let that moccasin drive its deadly fangs into my horse.

That snake was heading toward me like it was being reeled in on a fishing line. I waited until it was about ten feet away, then kicked out with my boot to splash water and algae in front of it. The snake immediately drew up, kind of coiling right there on the water, and reared its head several inches out of the slime, it's mouth opening wide and threatening.

I've heard people call water moccasins cottonmouths, and if you've ever stared down the throat of one, you'll know real quick where that description comes from. In the dusky twilight, the inside of that snake's mouth—even its tongue—looked as white as a freshly washed cotton boll. It made a kind of hissing sound, and I swear the aroma of cucumbers nearly choked me in my saddle. I don't know why it is that I smell cukes when a cottonmouth is near, but I have ever since I was a toddler, running around in the woods behind our house.

A water moccasin can be aggressive when it feels threatened, and I guess kicking pond scum in its face constitutes a threat in a snake's mind, although I doubt it was feeling any more vulnerable than I was at the moment, trying to keep a tight rein on my frightened horse, my eyes on that snake, and not getting dumped from my saddle, all at once and the same time, as they used to say. I heard Jim snap—"Put that gun away."—and saw Roy from the corner of my eye looking startled that a black man would speak up so authoritatively. Nonetheless, he slid his revolver back into its holster, and that snake, after a moment of floating there, hissing and exposing its fangs, hooked back over itself and started swimming away. I waited with my heart thumping hard against my rib cage until I saw it exit the pond about thirty yards away. It paused there on the bank for a moment as if waiting to see if I intended pursuit, then slithered off into the grass and disappeared.

The light was just about gone when we finally came to a grassy hammock not much bigger around than Dick Langley's little one-room cabin back at Lake Istokpoga had been—before the Yankees burned it—but we were all mighty glad to see dry land again. We crowded our horses onto grass as if there were prizes hanging from the tree limbs. I believe that was the first time we'd been out of water in several hours.

There was a large slough curving around two sides of our little island, and we could see alligators resting on the far banks like logs pulled up on shore and left there to dry. I'd guess there were about twenty of them lying there side-by-side, including a couple of old granddaddies, twelve and fourteen feet long.

"Them things decide to come for us, we're gonna be chin-deep in shit creek real fast," Roy said worriedly.

"Them 'gators ain't gonna be botherin' no one for a spell," Jim replied. "You can tell they's all be fed recent-like, and are just layin' up lettin' whatever they got in their bellies settle a bit."

"You willing to bet your life on that, Jim?" Casey asked.

"I wouldn't be leavin' one of y'all here if I thought they'd come huntin'."

Now *that* got our attention real fast.

"What do you mean, leave one of us here?" Roy demanded, his features scrunched up in a fierce scowl. "I ain't stayin'."

"Marse Boone," Jim said seriously. "We has got to go in on foot for a while, so we can check out what them Klees has waitin' for us."

"What makes you think they're waiting?"

"Because by now that Pablo fellow has told 'em we're followin'. They knows we're here, marse. We's got to count on that."

"All right," I said quietly, then waited for him to go on.

"One of us needs to stay behind with the horses, while the rest of us goes in on foot and see can we put a sneak on whoever they's got watchin' that north trail. Likely they's gonna be some deep water we'll have to wade, so we'll leave our rifles here and carry our gun belts 'round our necks. Won't do nobody no good was our powder to get wet."

I was unbuckling my belt before Jim finished speaking. Although I briefly debated who I'd leave behind, I think we all knew. Even Punch. His eyes grew wide as saucers when I turned to him.

"Boone, no. I ain't staying out here by myself. I won't do it."

"We ain't gonna be so far away we can't get back in a hurry, something happens," Jim said in a futile attempt to reassure the younger man.

"I don't care if you're within spitting distance. If I can't see you, it's too far." Pivoting in his saddle, he flung an arm toward the dozing alligators. "They could be here in five minutes if they set their mind to it, and I wouldn't even know it until one of 'em took a bite out of my rump."

"They won't," Jim said. "But even if they try, these here ol' horses'd let you know to skedaddle in plenty of time."

"You don't know that," the young man retorted.

"Someone's got to stay with the horses, Punch," I said firmly. "It can't be helped."

The kid's mouth hung open like he couldn't believe I'd make him do such a fearsome thing, but there was no way around it. Punch was the youngest man there, and the most inexperienced. He was the obvious choice.

"We likely won't be gone long a-tall," Jim said gently. "We just needs to see if they's waitin' for us, like I got a powerful itchy feelin' they are."

"How long is not long?" Punch asked in a small voice.

"Maybe an hour, maybe a few." Jim shrugged. "We be back soon as we can, though. You can bet on that."

"I'll shoot 'em if they come after me," Punch threatened, jerking his head toward the recumbent 'gators. "I don't care how much noise it makes."

I tended to agree with Jim. If even one of those big reptiles decided to make a move on the hammock, our horses would know it was coming before it got halfway across the slough— even after dark. A horse might shy away from a poisonous snake because it sensed the danger, but it'd know an alligator's approach meant life and death, and wouldn't wait around to see how Punch Davis intended to handle the threat.

"Stay in your saddle," I told him. "If you see a 'gator on the prowl, head for the road."

Punch flopped his arms in exasperation. "I don't know which way the road is, Boone. I'm so turned around now, I wouldn't swear the sun is really setting in the west."

"Dammit, Punch," Casey said impatiently. "Are you going to be a kid all your life, or toughen up? We need you to stay here and keep an eye on the horses. Do what you're told, and if something comes up, then handle it."

I guess what with Casey being family and all, it finally got through. Punch swallowed hard, then tightened his grip on his reins. "You boys put your lead ropes on your 'tackies," he said determinedly. "I don't want to have to haul them out of here with reins that'll snap when the going gets tight."

"Fair enough," Casey said, and quickly stepped clear of his saddle. He loosened the lead rope that hung around his mount's neck and handed it to his cousin. Giving the kid an affectionate slap on the knee, he added: "You'll be fine, Punch. We'll be back before you know it."

"I ain't gonna hold my breath waiting for you," the younger man said morosely.

I tied the bay's reins above its withers, then looped the loose ends around the saddle horn to keep them from sliding down the animal's neck. Then, one by one, we handed our lead ropes to Punch.

"Keep a sharp eye out," I warned him. "There's more than just 'gators in these swamps, and Fort Dallas ain't far away, either."

"I'll be OK," Punch said with more bravado than I suspect he really felt, although I admired his determination.

Leaving young Davis in the thickening twilight, we crowded close around Negro Jim.

"Single file," the black man instructed, "and don't make no noise. Them Klees is close, if I ain't mistook."

I stepped off that little hammock into the swamps with my heart in my throat, the water rising quickly to mid-thigh. It was a lot darker than I expected once we left the relatively open waters of the slough, and it made me feel bad for Punch. I'll tell you, I wouldn't have wanted to be left out there alone with night closing in so fast. It worried me, and after a while, I said: "Jim?"

He paused and turned. "Yes'um, marse?"

"Are you going to be able to find your way back?"

"I believe so, yes'um."

He waited a moment, but when I didn't say anything else, he started forward again. Following directly behind, I tried to ignore a feeling of doom that sat atop my shoulders like a small but chubby child. My eyes darted, but there was no longer much to see. The broad expanse of Jim's back under a faded blue shirt and his kinked, starting-to-gray hair were my only beacons. I kept my eyes riveted on them as we wound our way through the muck, aware of the others trailing silently behind.

We were in water nearly to our waists by then, and my boots felt full and heavy. Twice we had to alter course when the odor of cucumbers rose powerfully before us, and once we heard the hollow-tube huffing of a cow alligator, close enough to make my scalp crawl, and made all the worse because I couldn't tell from which direction the big reptile's warning came. Finally the earth started to slope upward beneath my feet, and in another few minutes we were back on dry ground, our chests heaving from either effort or anxiety, I'm not sure which. Flopping to our butts, we raised our legs to drain our footwear. No one suggested taking them off. To remove them at that point meant we wouldn't get them back on until they'd dried, which might have taken weeks in that humid country.

As our breathing returned to normal, we stood and shuffled about, moving our gun belts back around our waists and talking quietly about our recent adventure, reliving individually what we'd felt and thought when that cow 'gator cut loose. Then Jim, standing a few yards away, told us to hush.

We stood as statues, not knowing what was up, until Roy hissed: "Listen."

"It's them, I figure," Jim said softly.

At first I didn't hear anything other than the usual night

noises—the croaking of frogs, the cries of katydids, the occasional spine-chilling scream of a limpkin—but then I caught it, a feminine laugh echoing faintly through the swamp. Like a witch's cackle, it set my flesh to crawling.

"That ain't Lena," I said quickly.

"No, suh," Jim replied solemnly. "That there be a white woman laughin'." He looked at me, his expression unfathomable. "I believe we is there, marse, or mighty close to it."

"Miami?"

"Yes'um." He jutted his chin off to the side, and I realized with something of a start that I could see him do it, that there was light coming from somewhere. "Off yonder a ways," he volunteered.

I saw it myself then, a yellowish glow through the trees, followed by another burst of laughter, both male and female this time.

"Sounds like someone's having a high ol' time," Ardell remarked.

"Places like Miami, if what I been hearin' is true, they do a lot of high ol' timin'," Jim replied. "Lots of popskull to keep 'em in a mood for laughin'."

"What do we do now?" I asked.

"What me and your daddy used to do down in the 'glades. We go scoutin'."

"Lead off."

Jim hesitated. "No, I reckon I best go alone from here. I figure that Mistah Jacob, he probably got a man watchin' that north trail. It's him I want. Maybe we can ask him some questions, then tickle an answer outta him with the pointy end of my knife, if he ain't keen to talk." He looked at me. "That there guard, marse, he likely be a white man."

"I know, Jim. Do what you have to do. We want Lena back first, then the horses if we can find them."

"Yes'um. I'll be back in a bit, then. Y'all stay put, and don't make no noise. A guard ain't likely to be as drunk as that Miami bunch is."

I watched him fade from sight, and when he was gone, I realized I hadn't even heard him leave. Not a crack of a twig or the rustle of leaf. It made me wonder what stories Pa and Jim *hadn't* told me about their years fighting the Seminoles.

After a while we sat down to wait, rarely speaking as our ears strained at the darkness. Once, after we'd been there for what seemed like hours, I thought I heard someone calling my name. Casey and Ardell heard it, too, and Casey shoved to his feet.

"That's Punch," he whispered, starting for the swamp.

I rose and grabbed him by the arm and hauled him back before he could enter the black water.

"Even if it was Punch, you'd never find him in the dark," I said. "Besides, Jim told us to wait."

Casey stood like a dog on point, but finally allowed me to pull him back to where the rest of the crew waited. "If he's hurt . . . ," Casey said thickly, but didn't finish the sentence.

We grew even quieter after that, ceasing any comment on wet socks or how we might steal back our horses when we got the chance—typical nervous kid stuff, and meaningless since we had no idea where Klee was keeping the Flatiron mounts. It was another hour before I heard a thud in the dirt at my side, and scrambled to my feet with my hand clenched on the Navy's grips.

"Don't shoot," Jim called softly. "I's comin' in."

"Come ahead," I replied shakily, forcing my fingers away from the revolver. A few seconds later, Jim was standing before us. Sweat sheened his face, and his breathing was taut but controlled.

"Where the hell you been?" Roy demanded. "We figured you'd sloped."

"No, suh," Jim replied, keeping his tone mild. "I been scoutin', like I said I would."

"What did you find?" Casey asked.

"I found that guard, first thing, though I didn't bother him none. I figure they'll switch off soon enough, then we can take the mornin' man. That way they won't know anyone's missin' till daylight comes 'round, and maybe not then, dependin' on how much popskull whiskey they puts away."

"You reckon you can put a sneak on that morning man?" I asked.

"I reckon so, yes'um. They ain't likely to be no smarter than Indians, and your daddy and me put a sneak on a good many Red Sticks during the Seminole Wars."

I nodded, satisfied that Jim knew what he was doing.

"You boys need to be pullin' your charges, if you ain't already," he told us.

Jim's directive elicited a quick protest from Roy, but I held a hand up to stop him before he could work up a decent head of steam.

"We been traipsin' through a good bit of water, and your powder might've got wet," Jim explained, I suspect more for Roy's benefit than anyone else's. "Best y'all empty your pistols, then reload with fresh powder and ball. Make real sure what powder you pour in those chambers is bone dry, too. Then change your caps for fresh ones, and make sure they's sittin' tight on their nipples. It wouldn't do to lose a cap in the middle of a fight." After a pause, he added: "In them revolvers . . . make sure you load all six chambers. Likely we's gonna need 'em 'fore this mornin' is over."

"Have you had a look at the settlement yet?" Ardell asked.

"Yes, suh, I has. It's mostly south of the river, and I didn't cross over, but I saw a good bit of it from the north bank. They ain't much to the place, from what I could see, but it is full up to the muzzle with hardcases. The fort is on this side of the Miami. They's a dock there, in case some ship wants to tie up, but nothin' bigger than a sloop in harbor now. I didn't see no lights burnin' at the fort, though I reckon that don't mean much." He hesitated, then went on: "You boys do what I said 'bout them guns. I'm gonna go fetch Mistah Punch and the horses. I won't be long, but you be ready when I get back."

He turned, and within a few paces had once again vanished. I listened close, but didn't even hear him enter the water.

"Boone, that's one good Negro you've got there," Roy said in a heated whisper, "but if he calls me a boy one more time, I'm gonna be real tempted to take a whip to his black hide."

"Roy," I said evenly, "if you ever so much as lay a heavy hand on that Negro, I'll kill you."

I reckon that's the boldest statement I've ever made in my life, but I meant every word of it. I'd always respected Jim, even when I was just a toddler, and I liked him something fierce, too, but after that journey south from the Flatiron, I'd grown to admire him almost as much as I did my pa. To this day, I can't think of anyone outside of blood kin that I ever felt as close to as Negro Jim and Josie, and my eyes still get misty when I think of them. Ol' Jim's been dead a good many decades by now, but if I ever make it back to Florida, I'll look up his grave and tell him what I've been up to since leaving the state. I bet he'd be tickled I did, too.

Us boys, we'd pretty much cut our teeth on rifles and revolvers, and it didn't take long—even in that near total darkness outside of Miami—to pull our old charges and reload with fresh. I added a dab of bear grease to each of my caps to seal them in case I took an unexpected dunk in deep water, then returned the Navy to its holster and stood waiting with the others. Our ears were turned toward the swamps now, waiting anxiously for Jim's return.

It seemed to take forever, but of course it didn't. Finally we heard what sounded like that same cow alligator, huffing her warning to stay away. I figured she must have had a nest in there somewhere that she was protecting. Female 'gators are short-tempered when it comes to their eggs, and will tackle a full-grown bear if one gets too close.

"Bet that's them," Roy murmured, and, not long afterward, we heard the gentle splashing of several large animals moving toward us. Even though I knew it couldn't be anyone else but Jim, I ordered the boys to back off and fan out. A few minutes later I heard Jim's quiet call, telling us not to shoot.

"Come on in," I replied, then walked down to the water's edge as Jim led his cavvy ashore. Punch rode close behind him, no doubt as fearful as I'd been at the thought of losing sight of the African's broad shoulders in the swamp's pitch-like night. Punch had the extra horses strung out behind him, tied chin strap to tail, my bay bringing up the rear. As soon as the horses were on solid ground, we swarmed forward to cut our individual mounts out of the string and lead them aside.

"I thought you guys had forgot me," Punch accused from his saddle.

"Jim told you it might take a while," Casey reminded him.

"Them 'gators were stirring. I saw one swimming past not forty yards away, big as you please in the moonlight."

"Be thankful you had some light," Roy groused. "We been squattin' here in the dark like a bunch of constipated 'possums, waitin' for that Negro to do something."

"Hush," I chided, but Jim merely chuckled.

"Mistah Roy, you be gettin' your fill of doin' something real soon," he predicted. "Ought to clear up that constipation, too. Just see you don't get your head blowed off while you're at it."

Roy grumbled a little at Jim's response, but, hell, Roy was always grumbling about something. Turning my back on him, I walked over to where Jim was checking the cinch on his marsh-tackie.

"What now?" I asked.

"We be ready to ride or ready to fight, whichever comes our way, but if we ain't been seen, then you and me and . . . Mistah Casey, I reckon, is goin' to slip on over to where that Klee man is watchin' the north trail. It's well on past midnight now, and if they's going to spell him, it'll be soon. When I's sure it's the man I want, I's goin' to slip up on him and drag him into the bushes where we can squeeze some information outta him without being disturbed."

The muscles across my chest tightened, making breathing more difficult. "Do you intend to kill him, Jim?"

"No, suh, not me. It won't do for a Negro to kill a white man. Not if that Negro don't want his own neck stretched from a magnolia tree right quick. But I's goin' to make it real simple for you to do it." I swallowed hard, and I guess he heard me. "Ain't gonna be no different than what you boys did to them Yankees outside Punta Rassa," he added.

"No, I guess not."

"They got Lena, marse, and they got your daddy's horses. We let that slide, that bunch'll keep comin' back and takin' more."

"I said all right."

He nodded as if satisfied that he'd made his point. "You got your pistol reloaded?"

"Yeah." I took a deep breath, held it for several seconds, then exhaled loudly. "Then I reckon we're ready."

In a voice real low and real mean, like I'd never heard from him before, Jim said: "I been ready ever since I found my Josie out in them woods behind your daddy's house, scared near senseless for fear of what them men might do. What they might've already done to poor little Lena."

To be honest, I didn't remember Josie appearing all that

frightened when she came running toward us from the trees, but I suppose a man sees things differently when it's his woman who's been put through the ringer.

"I'll go get Casey," I said, and walked back to where the others were standing with their horses. I explained what we were going to do, then tipped my head for Casey to follow. We led our horses over to where Jim was waiting, but he shook his head when he saw our mounts.

"Best leave them horses behind. We'll go in on foot from here."

"Punch," I called softly, and when the younger man came over, we handed him our reins. "Keep 'em quiet," I instructed, then turned to Jim. "Lead off."

We made our way as quietly as possible over such rough terrain. Jim moved like a cloud shadow over the landscape, but Casey and I weren't as skilled, and, to my ears, at least, made enough racket to wake the dead. Twenty minutes after slipping away from the others, Jim stopped so unexpectedly I rammed into his back. He didn't look around or give me a reprimand, but just held up a hand in a "wait" gesture, and Casey and I froze in our tracks.

Swaying back to where I was practically standing on his heels, Jim said: "You boys stay put a spell. You'll know when to come forward, and you'll know where, too. Just don't make no noise till you hear my signal."

I nodded solemnly, blinked once, and then Jim was gone. Like he'd turned into smoke or something. Easing up at my side, Casey whispered: "I wish I could move that quiet."

I didn't reply, but I was thinking the same thing. Negro Jim was showing off skills that night I never had a clue he possessed.

The minutes dragged on and my nerves began to stretch toward the breaking point. So much so that, when I heard a sharp grunt, then the crackle of bushes from no more than fifty feet away, I nearly jumped out of my sodden boots.

"Easy, hoss," Casey breathed, then gave me a gentle push forward.

There were no further sounds, but I figured that had to be the signal Jim had told us to listen for. We started off in the direction it had come from, and Jim called when we got close. Shoving through a stand of arrowroot, I found him flat on his back, his powerful legs clamped around the mid-section of a heavily bearded man clutched in a bear hug. Jim's razor-sharp cane knife—kind of a machete with a barb opposite the tip to pull the cane stalks out of the way—was pressed tight against the look-out's throat, and I knew that a single, fiddle-like swipe from Jim would come awful close to severing the man's head. Judging from the wide-open stare of the guard, I suspect he knew it, too.

"Don't stand there gawkin'," Jim scolded. "Pull this 'coon's suspenders off and tie him up."

Casey and I didn't waste time. After yanking the man's revolver from its holster and tossing it toward a carbine lying in the dirt a few paces away, I grabbed his ankles while Casey cut the leather braces from his shoulders and bound him hand and foot. When he was securely trussed, Jim shoved him off and rose to his knees. He had a wicked grin on his face as he pressed the tip of his cane knife against the look-out's cheek. "Mister, you is gonna do some quick talkin', and you damn' well better make me believe you is tellin' the truth." He pressed in lightly with his knife. "You savvy, fish bait?"

"Jim," I said warily, half afraid from the expression on the Negro's face that he'd start cutting before we had the information we needed.

"That's all right, marse. I already explained to this boy how he can stay alive . . . assumin' that's what he wants. I'm just remindin' him that he ain't done what he needs to do yet."

"Jesus, mister," the look-out said to me in a panicky voice. "Is this your darky?"

"He ain't nobody's darky," I replied. "But he sure is mad about what you boys did at the Flatiron. That was his wife you scared into the trees, and his soon-to-be daughter-in-law you kidnapped and brought down here. He's been thinking about that ever since we started after you boys, and he ain't cooled off about it yet that I can see."

"Not one little peck," Jim agreed sinisterly.

"That gal of yours ain't been hurt, but she might be if you boys go stomping down there like you own the place." The guard was still looking at me, as if Jim no longer existed. "Ol' Jake's told us about you McCallisters and all the trouble they've had with your pap over the years. I'd say you're lucky your whole bunch hasn't been run outta the state before now."

"It ain't McCallisters or Davises that carry running irons in their saddlebags," Casey shot back. [*Ed. Note:* Running irons were generally straight iron bars, a foot or two in length, used like pencils to alter brands on cattle and horses; in many states and territories during the 19th Century, the mere possession of a running iron was considered an admission of guilt to cattle rustling and horse theft.]

"It seems you ain't takin' my warnin' serious," Jim said so softly I could barely make out the words; he was speaking to the bearded guard, and once again had his attention. "Let me be real clear on what I expect," Jim went on, and placed the cutting edge of his cane knife against the bottom of the look-out's nose. "You don't talk no more, 'less it's to answer a question I've asked, and you keep your opinions to yourself, too. Otherwise, I'm gonna slice your sniffer clean off your face and eat it raw. Then I'm gonna move on to other parts of your body,

and see how much gumption you've really got. You understand
. . . *boy?*"

The guard gave me a startled look, but—almost comically—
didn't utter a word.

"In case you're wondering," I supplied to his unspoken question. "Yeah, I'm going to let him do it. As a matter of fact, I'll
help hold you down."

Jim added just enough pressure to his knife to draw a thin
stream of blood, while clamping his free hand solidly over the
look-out's mouth. The man's eyes widened in terror. Pulling the
knife back slightly, Jim said: "You takin' me serious now?"

The man's head bobbed rapidly under Jim's palm, bringing a
hard smile to the black man's lips. "Good. Let's get started."

I guess it was all fairly anticlimactic after that. Jim asked and
the look-out answered, both of them speaking in low, terse
whispers. By the time they were finished, we had a fair idea of
how many men and women lived in Miami, how long the Klees
had been in town, and where they were holed up. Not surprisingly, the reply to that last question was the settlement's only
saloon, a cypress log building just up from the southern bank.
The only thing that surprised me was that old Judah Klee and
his part of the clan hadn't arrived yet. Led to believe that they
were already there, I was relieved to find out that I was wrong.
According to the look-out—whose name I never did get,
unfortunately—Judah and his bunch were still back in the
swamps south of Okeechobee, while Jubal Klee—Jake's
brother—had taken a gang north to do some raiding around
Jacksonville.

We also learned that Lena was being held in a slave shack at
the far end of Miami's single muddy street, the stolen horses
had been pastured somewhere south of the village, and that
Jacob had about a dozen men with him. The women, kids, and
old people were still on their way, dragging their belongings

through the swamps in canoes and dug-outs, which just shows you what kind of men they were, leaving the women and elderly to do all the hard work while they lazed around Miami's only saloon, raising hell with their drinking, gambling, and carousing.

After taking his cane knife away from the guard's nose, Jim crammed a kerchief into his mouth to keep him quiet, then stood and wiped his blade clean on a wad of coontie leaves. I became aware of the black man's quiet scrutiny and, with a sickening sensation in the pit of my stomach, knew what he was silently asking. Staring down at the bearded Klee—or at least a Klee man—I shook my head.

"Let him live."

"We do, we might someday regret it," Jim said.

I hesitated, but in my mind I kept seeing those Yankees we'd hung outside of Punta Rassa, recalling the fear and disbelief on their faces as we strung them up one at a time. It hadn't been the same with that detachment below Fort Pierce; they'd opened the ball on that one. Sighing heavily, I said: "We might, but I'm getting tired of fighting and killing. Make sure his gag is tight, then let's go get Lena."

After returning to where we'd left the others, I quickly outlined what we'd learned, then looked to Jim to take over.

"Best we lead our horses as far as the fort," he said. "Was a flat-bottomed boat tied up on the near bank when I was there earlier. We'll use that to cross the Miami. Once we get on t'other side, Mistah Casey and Mistah Punch can go after the horses, while the rest of us keeps an eye on the saloon. Soon as them two's got the horses, we'll slip in real quiet and find Lena, then swim the horses back across the river and light out for home." He paused and looked at me. "I reckon that's 'bout it, marse, 'less you gots something to say."

I shook my head, and Jim nodded. "Then I reckon we best

get movin'," he said, and started off through the darkness toward Fort Dallas, on the Miami River.

Excerpted from:
Views of Old Miami Town:
Reminiscences of a Former Resident
by
Patrick Kayne
Southern Pride Books, 1887

Chapter Seven
The War Years—1861-1865

In the early years of the War Between the States, life continued basically unchanged among Miami's founding residents. Still imbued with the resilience of a hardy pioneer heritage, they cheerfully forged ahead in their daily endeavors of harvesting the bounty of this singular niche in paradise, with the production of pine tar, turpentine, lumber, and Arrowroot starch [coontie] from the coastal pine ridge, which they sold primarily to eager markets in Key West and Nassau.

. . . [B]ut local industry, and Miami culture in general, was substantially and forever altered by this insidious act of antagonism [the Union blockade]. Although the Miami area was given low priority by the Federal military because of its isolation and what was perceived as a lack of commodities beneficial to Northern causes, Union ships regularly patrolling Florida's Eastern Seaboard continued a cursory monitoring of Biscayne Bay, and would frequently dock at the Fort Dallas wharf to take on supplies of wood, water, salted meat, and fresh produce.

. . . [H]owever, by 1864, the tenor of Miami's populace began to change dramatically with an influx of outlaws, horse thieves, pirates, blockade runners, and deserters from both sides of the conflict, desperate men one and all, seeking the locality's unique remoteness to hide themselves and their deeds, or to mask their otherwise cowardly identities.

This unexpected influence had several negative consequences upon the area's original settlers, not the least of which was a shuddersome dread of the outlaws' violently capricious nature. Furthering this trepidation on the part of Miami's more morally enlightened citizenry was an increase of Yankee aggression, affecting the area's original inhabitants as much, or more, than it did the community's less-refined denizens.

. . . While many of these scallywags preferred the jungles separating the Bay from the endless horizons of the Everglades, or the dense pinewoods to the south of our fair city, the bolder among them preferred to infiltrate the community itself, perpetuating their acts of anarchy in blissful ignorance of the damages they incurred upon the community.

The more notorious of this element were the men of the Eli Wilberson gang, made up largely of Southern deserters and thugs from the South's larger cities, and the multi-generational progeny of "Old" Judah Klee, whose clan ranged over most of southern and central Florida for several decades during the mid-19th Century, causing untold grief and havoc to even the most peace-loving settler and rancher.

SESSION NINE

Everything went pretty much as Jim predicted. Him and me and Ardell and Roy, we all took shelter among the trees lining the Miami's south bank, where we could keep an eye on the settlement, while Casey and Punch circled wide to the east to follow the beach in search of the horse herd. Although I was anxious to start looking for Lena, Jim held us back. He was afraid that once we entered the village, our chances of being discovered would "jump over the moon", as the saying goes.

"That happens," Jim had warned me as we crossed the Miami three at a time in a tiny skiff, "we'll have to forget them Flatiron horses and make a run for it."

Which is what we should have done to begin with, forgetting about the horses and focusing on grabbing Lena, then hauling our butts out of there as fast as our ponies could carry us. But I got greedy, wanting both the girl and the horses, and before the day was through—hell, before the sun came up all the way— we'd pay a hefty price for my avarice.

I saw a postcard of downtown Miami a few years ago that I found hard to accept. It was a night view, with streetlights glowing off wet pavement and automobiles parked nose-first along both sides of the street, like marshtackies hitched to cypress rails. There was a sizable crowd of men, women, and children— entire families—moseying along the cement sidewalks, peering into brightly lit storefront windows. Everyone seemed to be laughing or smiling, and save for the palm trees in the distance, it reminded me a lot of Fort Worth on a Friday night. The decent part of town, not the Acre. [*Ed. Note:* McCallister is referring to Fort Worth's notorious red-light district, known as Hell's Half Acre, often shortened to "the Acre".]

Miami wasn't like that when I was there in '64. Back then, there was but a single wide street, sheeted in mud from the recent rains, and maybe a score of buildings, most of them little more than shacks with palm frond roofs. There was a store on one side of the street and the saloon was on the other. Both were built close to the river, to catch the eyes of the sailors who occasionally docked at the Fort Dallas wharf. Dense jungles surrounded the settlement like a thin green rind, separating it from the sawgrass flats of the Everglades that stretched all the way to the distant Gulf coast.

Other than the store and the saloon, there wasn't much to see, and the sharp odor of damp rot, penned hogs, and human waste smothered any scent of fresh fruit or verdant gardens— and I'm just assuming there were some at that time. Although I couldn't see the hog pens from where we were crouched along the river, I could hear the low, discontented grunts of the swine as they moved about in their enclosure.

I was looking east, past the sloping palm trees to Biscayne Bay and noticing how quickly dawn seemed to be taking shape above the mangrove forests of an island way out across the water, when Ardell whispered: "Here they come." [*Ed. Note:* McCallister is probably referring to Virginia Key here, part of the barrier islands that form the eastern boundary of Biscayne Bay.]

Cautiously lifting my eyes above the lip of the bank, I spotted Casey and Punch entering the village from the south. Disappointment cut deep when I saw that they were still afoot, and my gaze slid resentfully toward the gray bulk of the saloon.

"We be out of time, marse," Jim said gently, then squeezed

the top of my shoulder as if in commiseration. "Come on. Your daddy's got plenty of horses, and we's already wasted too much time."

Well, there was no arguing that. Waving my hand for the others to follow, we surged over the top of the bank as a single entity and quickly made our way toward the center of the ramshackle community. As we exited the knob-kneed mangroves along the river, I began to realize just how late the morning had become. I have a kind of internal benchmark about what constitutes day from night, since "dawn" and "sundown" can often be ambiguous. For me, it's when there's enough light to read a newspaper, and not have to squint to make out the words. There wasn't any doubt about it as we entered Miami that day—it was a fine-print kind of morning.

Spotting a couple of Negroes stirring outside a hut at the southern terminus of the street, I told Jim to go see what they could tell him. "The rest of you spread out," I ordered. "If you find Lena, get her back here quick as you can."

While Jim headed toward the distant Negroes, I hurried across the street to intercept Casey and Punch. Casey started shaking his head while I was still some distance away.

"Couldn't find 'em, Boone," he said as I came up. "We saw some 'tackies about a quarter mile south of here, but nothing carrying the Flatiron brand."

"It doesn't matter," I replied, but before I could add any more, a scream pierced the air. I flinched, and all three of us—me and Casey and Punch—palmed our six-shooters. From the far end of the street, I saw a tiny figure burst through the sagging door of a palmetto hut and race down the middle of the street. Her cries rang over the slumbering village like church bells: *"Papa Jim, Papa Jim!"*

Jim ran to meet her, motioning desperately for her to keep quiet, but I guess she was too young, had been terrified for too long, to heed such good advice. She kept hollering shrilly until she just about crashed into Jim's arms, wailing in earnest now, her emotions breaking loose. It would have been heart-warming if not for the confused cries coming from the saloon, the certain knowledge that all hell was about to break loose.

"Find the others," I instructed Casey and Punch, then took off at a lope.

Jim was still hugging the sobbing young woman in his arms when I came up, but he knew we were in trouble. Although he kept telling Lena to hush, she seemed too far gone to reach with logic, and continued her terrified wailing. Meeting my gaze, Jim said: "We gots to get outta here, marse."

I glanced toward the saloon. A man with a scraggly beard nearly to his navel had stepped out of the building, carrying a brown jug in one hand, a rifle in the other. He stopped uncertainly on the roofless stoop, his gaze sweeping the street.

"Don't move," Jim whispered, easing his body around to shield Lena from the bearded man's view. I froze as well, knowing what Jim had in mind. If we didn't panic, if we just stood there like a couple of passers-by in quiet conversation, maybe the bearded man would decide there was nothing amiss and go back inside.

It might have worked, too, if a shout from the Miami hadn't signaled fresh trouble. It was the look-out we'd left tied up in the woods along the north trail, scrambling up the bank and raising seven different kinds of hell, all the while pointing toward me and Jim. If I hadn't been in such a rush, I might have cursed our poor luck. Instead, spotting an empty lot between a couple of nearby buildings, I said: "Over there. Let's get out of sight."

Jim peeled the trembling woman from his arms. "Hush, girl. We gots to *run.*"

But Jim didn't get to run. He'd barely turned toward the empty lot when a bullet caught him alongside his head. His body seemed to convulse in mid-stride, and he dropped limply to the ground. Blood spurted from his torn scalp. Lena screamed and threw herself across his chest. I think I might have cried out a hoarse protest myself. Then I spun toward the saloon with the Sharps coming up instinctively. But I didn't fire. A shot from Ardell had already sent the bearded man stumbling backward into the front of the saloon. Another from Roy spun the look-out into the river, clutching his chest.

I froze there for a moment, my finger taut on the trigger. Men were spilling from the saloon like rats off a sinking ship, and I'll make no apologies for the comparison. Within seconds it seemed like guns were blazing from every direction.

You know, I'd expected the Klees to fight, but I hadn't considered the possibility that the rest of Miami's lawless element would join the fray. It didn't dawn on me until later how our presence might be mistaken for an all-out attack on the village, something I suppose I should have anticipated, considering the settlement's population of deserters, murderers, cattle rustlers, and horse thieves.

My brief moment of paralysis broke at the sound of a bullet whuffling overhead. Grabbing Lena's wrist, I hauled her to her feet. She struggled against me at first, until I gave her a hard shake. "Let's go!" I shouted in her face.

She shook her hear. "No, massa, I can't leave Papa Jim."

"It's too late for him, Lena. We've got to get out of here before we all die. Come on."

I don't know how much weight my argument carried, but the bullet that cut through the shoulder seam of her gingham dress as neatly as a seamstress's thread ripper sure seemed to capture her attention. I pulled her forward, across Jim's body, and we began a mad dash for the empty lot between the two cabins.

Bullets splattered mud and sod at our feet, and whined past our ears like angry hornets. I heard a man cry out in pain, but didn't look around to see who it was. We were still several yards shy of the nearest cabin when something like a mule's kick tore the Sharps from my grasp. I did a little howling of my own at that, and actually stopped to retrieve the stubby rifle until I saw what the bullet had done to its lock.

"Massa, we gots to run!" Lena cried, and then it was her who was tugging on my arm, pulling me away from the broken weapon.

"Go!" I shouted, shoving her toward the closest building, and I was right behind her, my revolver in hand as we sprinted past the cabin's corner.

Lena fell to a crouch beside the wall, sobbing hysterically as she stared back to where Jim lay, a pool of blood shining wetly around his head. I stood with my shoulders to the same wall, my pulse thundering. Grief tore at my heart for the old man. Out front, the shooting continued unabated. It sounded like an army, like a thousand men battling for control of the city.

After we caught our breath, I took Lena's hand and led her around back. As I turned the corner, I was surprised to see nearly a dozen men and a couple of women fleeing toward the beach. Although the men were carrying their long guns, I could tell from the blur of their feet that they wouldn't be coming back anytime soon. And when you think about it, that also makes sense. Miami was filled with deserters from both sides of the war. They'd already fled once. Why wouldn't they do it again?

Hanging onto Lena, we cat-footed across the back lot to the next corner. Peering around the ragged edge of the log shack, I saw three men bent over a fourth, and knew instantly what they were up to. Even in southwest Florida, we'd heard about the two-legged scavengers that would slip onto a battlefield late at night to rob the corpses of whatever plunder they could find. If they were caught, they'd be hung or shot, but the word we got was that they were seldom caught.

I didn't care what they did to one another. I just wanted to get over to where the rest of my crew was pinned down across the street from the saloon. After warning Lena to be real quiet, we eased into the gap between the two buildings. I don't know. Maybe we made some kind of noise that I didn't hear. Or maybe that guy in the middle of the pack sensed us, rather than heard us. Whatever the reason, Lena and I had barely stepped into the open when he whirled toward us, clawing for a revolver thrust into the waistband of a pair of butternut trousers.

There ain't a doubt in my mind what that boy intended, but he had to draw his revolver first, and mine was already in hand. I fired before the deserter got his front sight clear of his pants, and my bullet caught him square. He crumbled like a marionette with its strings severed—straight down, limbs akimbo. The other two spun around, and I swear one of them snarled like a cornered wolf when he spotted me and Lena, but I bulled on, telling them to drop their guns quick if they wanted to live to see tomorrow.

Maybe it was something in my voice, but they practically flung those pistols away. Their hands went straight up without being told, as if this wasn't the first time they'd been thrown down on. In as mean a voice as I've ever heard come out of my mouth, I said: "Are you Klees?"

Both men shook their heads.

"Are you a bounty hunter?" one of them asked.

"No, we came here after Klees."

"Well, hell, son, you can have 'em," the other deserter said. "They been here barely three days, and they're already treatin' this place like it's their own private kingdom."

"You boys can run, or you can fight," I said. "What's your choice?"

"I'm running," the first deserter said, and the second one

started bobbing his head like a flathead piston on a short connecting rod.

"Then get," I growled, motioning toward the beach.

Well, they got quick enough, and I was already on my way when something snagged at my mind, bringing me to an abrupt stop. I remember just about wailing as I ran toward the man those sons-of-bitches had been robbing. Casey was sitting sloped into the side wall of the cabin, his feet splayed out before him, head tipped toward his chest. If I hadn't recognized his clothes, I probably would have passed on by. Blood covered the front of his shirt, turning what had once been deep yellow and cream into bright crimson.

Falling to my knees at his side, I put a hand on his shoulder and gently spoke his name. He raised his head with difficulty, squinting in the still gray light.

"Boone?" he said uncertainly.

"Where are you hit, Case?"

"Damned if I know. I got knocked off my feet by something, and when I come to, them buzzards were all over me." He grinned, revealing blood-stained gums, and I knew then that it was bad.

"Massa?" Lena said tentatively.

Grabbing her wrist, I pulled her down by my side. "Find something to bandage his wound," I said, my voice harsh with fear.

"Where?"

I jerked my head toward the body of the man I'd just shot. "Use his shirt."

Lena shook her head emphatically. For a second, I thought she was going to refuse. Then she flung the hem of her skirt out in front of her, and said: "Gimme a knife."

I handed her my folder, then gently pulled Casey forward to look at his back. I cursed softly when I saw the wound, and my vision turned misty as I eased him back against the wall.

Watching me with a sad smile, he said: "You're looking peaked, Boone."

"Shut up," I replied, awkwardly patting his shoulder.

"Ease up on yourself, hoss," he said mildly. "We all knew the odds when we came down here."

"We'll take care of you," I promised.

"No, you need to start scootin'. Right now, before Jacob Klee realizes how few we really are."

"I ain't going nowhere without you," I replied, then turned to Lena to ask what was taking so long with those bandages, but she handed me a strip of gingham sliced off the bottom of her dress before I could speak.

"It's cleaner than that thing he's wearin'," she said, tipping her head toward the dead scavenger.

I accepted the cloth without comment, but when I turned back to Casey, he was shaking his head. "Get outta here, Boone," he whispered in a voice so low I had to lean forward to make out the words. "It's just gonna hurt like a son-of-a-bitch if you try to wrap it, and won't make a damned bit of difference in the end. Those boys killed me, and there ain't nothing we can do about that. You've gotta get Lena outta here, so I don't have to think I died for nothing."

"Casey. . . ." I choked on whatever it was that I wanted to say, shaking my head in helpless frustration. Although I wouldn't have admitted it to anyone at the time, I'm not ashamed to confess now that I had tears streaming down my face as I tried to say good bye to probably the second-best friend I had in those years.

"Get movin', boy," Casey mumbled, but he was no longer looking at me or Lena. His face was turned toward the bay, an expression of wonder transforming it into something I'd never seen before. "My God, how beautiful," he whispered. "Like a river of gold running straight across its surface."

I twisted around to stare at Biscayne Bay, but didn't see anything that even remotely resembled a sheet of gold. There was just the gray dawn outlining the ragged cap of the distant key. Laying my hand atop his shoulder, I squeezed it probably harder than I should have, and said: "I'll come back if I can."

Although I waited for his reply, it didn't come, and his chest was no longer rising and falling. Pushing clumsily to my feet, I told Lena that we needed to go, and she took my hand and led me toward the rear of the lot.

I don't want you to think I was so incapacitated with grief that I couldn't function, but I do want you to know what a good girl Lena was. I'd liked her before the kidnapping, but I didn't truly admire her until that morning in Miami.

I also don't want you to think there wasn't a lot of shooting still going on while I sat there with Casey, because there was, although I noticed even then that its intensity seemed to be ebbing. I'd find out later that as the fighting continued between the Flatiron crew and Klee's outfit—most of that bunch holed up in the saloon—the town's less ambitious residents were busy slipping out windows and back doors to skedaddle into the swamps or down the beach.

I paused briefly at the rear of the empty lot for a final, backward glance. It was hard to believe Casey was gone, that our boyish adventures had come to a permanent end. I think for the first time I began to wonder if we wouldn't all be dead before the sun finally pulled free of that distant island.

Tight-chested, I turned my back on Casey Davis and slipped around the rear corner of the second cabin. My Colt pointed the way, and I had Lena's fingers wrapped in a too-firm grip with my other hand, although she didn't complain. We stopped again at the far corner, but before I could take a peek around the side, I heard the rustle of scrub from behind us, and turned with my throat nearly closing off.

"Drop the gun, McCallister!"

"Son-of-a-bitch," I said raggedly, using my elbow to nudge Lena behind me.

Pablo Torres stood about a dozen yards away, an already-cocked horse pistol—one of those old, single-shot percussion pieces with a massive bore—clutched in his stubby fingers. "I will shoot if I have to," he threatened.

I believed him, too, although I didn't drop the Navy, afraid that if I did, it would be all over for me and Lena. Not knowing what else to say, I blurted: "Why'd you do it, Torres?"

His reaction surprised me. I expected denial, or at the very least an attempt to shift the blame onto me or one of the others. Instead his head jerked back as if he'd been slapped, and his lips drew into a thin, taut line. "I said for you to drop your revolver," he repeated. "I do not wish to shoot you or the *niña,* but I will if my hand is forced."

I hesitated a long time, but that huge pistol never wavered in Torres's hand. Finally I opened my fingers, and the Navy tumbled into the grass at my feet. "You still haven't told me why."

Pablo hesitated so long that I began to think he wasn't going to reply, but then he started talking. "They caught me that day on the Caloosahatchee. I thought I was being quiet, but I was found and taken to where Jacob Klee was sitting in the shade of a cypress tree, waiting for his men to bring me in." Pablo bit at his lower lip, and his eyes took on a faraway expression. "They threatened to brand me if I did not do as instructed." He touched his cheek with his free hand. "With a running iron, like this." He made a trio of slashing motions across each cheek, and I could tell from the jerkiness of his fingers that he was reliving the moment. "I had no choice, Boone. I did not wish to be marked in such a way."

215

"What did they want?"

"To know where we were going, who your buyer was. Jacob wanted to know about you, too. How old you were, and if you had ever been in such a fight before, with guns."

"And you told him?"

"*Sí*, I told him, and he promised that when they stampeded the herd, I would not be harmed."

A flash of memory shot across my mind. "But you told us anyway, when you got back. You told us who it was, and . . . no, I guess you didn't, did you? You said Jacob only had six men with him, but he had nearly twice that number."

"I had no choice."

"Bullshit," I said softly. "You're through, Torres. You're through on every cow outfit across southern Florida. I'll see to that, or someone else will. Word of this will filter back to my pa and brothers, and your life won't be worth a lead plug."

"I will stay with Jacob and his men, and ride for the Klees."

I glanced at the huge pistol, still pointed at my mid-section. "Where are your revolvers? You used to carry a brace of them." Pablo's face flushed with humiliation, and I laughed. "Jacob took them away, didn't he?"

"I will get them back when I have proven myself," he replied defensively.

"By turning me over to him?"

"*Sí*. Jacob Klee wants you, and I will give him what he wants. Alive if possible, but dead if I must. The choice is yours."

"No," a voice said from behind Torres. "The choice is mine."

Pablo started to turn, but he was too slow. The shotgun's blast caught him dead center from less than five yards away, and threw him nearly halfway across the empty lot. At my back, Lena screamed and darted past my elbow. "Papa Jim," she squealed, racing toward the older man. "Papa Jim, you're alive." She just about bowled him over as she wrapped her slim arms around his waist.

Crossing the empty space between us, stepping over Pablo's torn and bloody corpse without a glance, I said: "I swear to God, Jim, I thought you were dead." Staring at the bloody gash across the side of his skull, I wasn't sure at that point that he wouldn't be.

"You done right, marse," Jim said.

"I wouldn't have left you if I'd known," I continued hoarsely, the horror of what I'd done filling me with raw emotion.

Easing Lena aside, Jim said: "Get your revolver, Boone, and don't ever take another step without it."

I hesitated, caught off guard by the authoritative tone of the older man's voice, his unprecedented use of my first name, without the familiar *marse* preceding it. Then I did as I'd been told. After we reloaded, Jim motioned for me to follow him back to where I'd left Casey. I had to resist the urge to double-check for a pulse. We stopped at the front corner, and Jim peered cautiously around the edge. I noticed that even though he was propping himself against the wall, he was still pretty wobbly. Like everything he'd done since crawling out of the road with his scalp laid bare was beginning to take its toll.

"Why don't you sit down before you fall down?" I suggested.

"No time for sittin'. Come here."

I moved up beside him, leaning out carefully for a full view of the street.

"They got our boys corked up tight inside that store," Jim said. "What we's got to do is get a man across the street so's he can come at that saloon from the rear." He gave me an appraising look. "I can't do it, Boone. I'm so twirly-headed now I can barely keep my feet. You is gonna have to do it, son. You is gonna have to get over there and give Jacob Klee and his boys something else to think about, while me and Lena sneak around behind the store. When you open up on the saloon, I'll pull our

217

boys out the back way. If we can get down to the river, we ought to be able to hold 'em off long enough to get ever'one across. You savvy?"

"Yeah, I savvy."

"Boone."

I looked at him, puzzled by the strained tone of his voice. "Yeah?"

"Once we pull outta that there store, you is gonna have to find your own way to the river. Think you can do that?"

"I can do whatever I have to do. Just tell me what it is."

"I wish I could, son, I surely do, but when you get over there, you gonna be on your own."

I nodded grimly, determined not to let him down a second time. "I'll do it," I vowed.

"Lena, honey, grab me a couple of them revolvers, will you?"

Lena rushed to comply, returning within seconds with all three of the handguns I'd ordered the scavengers to leave behind. Jim took the guns one at a time and checked their loads. Then he shoved two inside his belt and handed the third to me.

"Shove that in your britches," he instructed. "It's loaded. When it's empty, don't waste no time reloadin'. Just give it a toss and keep runnin'. The only revolver you needs to hang onto is your own. Understand?"

"Yes, sir," I replied, unaware at the time of the irony of my response—a white man calling the family slave *sir.*

Then Jim did something I never would have expected. He handed me his double-barreled shotgun, the one Pa had given him so many years before. "That there scatter-gun is loaded full-bore, Boone. She'll kick like a mule when you pull the trigger, but she'll do the job."

I nodded solemnly. I knew Jim loved that old smoke-pole. It represented something between him and my pa that I couldn't begin to fathom.

"You be ready, son?"

"Yes, sir."

The old man smiled affectionately. "You'll do fine, Boone. Just remember to duck when you see someone shootin' your way."

I swallowed and nodded and moved out in front of him. The firing from the saloon seemed to intensify, and I sensed that time was running out. Taking a deep breath, I bolted from the shelter of the log cabin like a rabbit startled from its hedge. I was heading for a small lean-to stable just south of the saloon, and was just about there when a man stepped out from behind a corner of the stable and pulled the trigger on a large-bored carbine.

Getting shot was like running full-tilt into a chest-high log placed across my path, with about the same results. My top end stopped instantly at the bullet's impact, but my legs kept pumping. I believe if there had been a wall in front of me, I might have made good progress going up its side. Unfortunately there wasn't, and I landed hard on my back and shoulders, rapping my skull in the process.

I laid there for a good long bit, listening to the roaring in my ears while the sky danced and shimmied overhead. I don't know why the man who shot me didn't finish the job. Jim said afterward he'd taken off like a scalded cat as soon as he saw me go down. It was Jim's speculation that the shooter wasn't a Klee man, just some deserter caught up in the fight.

After a while I became aware of a distant ache in my shoulder, and soon came to wish that it had stayed there. But you don't get your hide drilled without paying a price in pain, and mine wasn't long in coming. Groaning, I pushed over on my right side, protecting my left shoulder as best I could under the circumstances. I was starting to become aware again of what was going on around me, and took notice when a bear-like roar from the saloon was following by a ragged cheer. A knot of men burst out the front door with their guns blazing, fat Jacob Klee waddling swiftly at its head. They were rushing the store, pouring lead into the building like they meant to blast it off its limestone foundation.

Swallowing back the bitter taste of bile, I shoved awkwardly to my feet, drawing my Colt as I did. I wouldn't have been able to handle Jim's shotgun even if I knew where it had flown, and I clean forgot about the spare revolver that had bounced out of my waistband on impact. I don't know what came over me in that moment, but I'd suddenly had a gut-full of Jacob Klee and his lawless clan. Drawing a deep breath, I bellowed his name into the street.

You know how when the action is going fast and furious and everything seems to be happening all at once and then, in the middle of it all, there's that tiny fraction of time when complete silence falls over the scene? That was the void my challenge filled, and I truly doubt that anyone would have ever heard it if not for that brief moment of quiet. But they did, and Klee's men came to an uneven stop in the middle of the street, half turning toward me while still keeping an eye on the bullet-riddled storefront.

"Jacob Klee!" I yelled again as loud as I could.

The shooting tapered off, then ceased. Klee's men—maybe ten of them altogether—backed away uncertainly. At the store, Ardell and Punch stepped outside with their revolvers drawn, though sloping toward the ground. Nobody spoke. Every eye was locked on me.

"Jacob, if it's me you want, then come and get me."

The old man pushed to the front of his crew, and, as much as I despised that belly-jiggling skunk, I have to admit that at least he'd been out front leading the charge. It was more than a lot of those generals up north were doing.

"You killed my nephew, McCallister!" Klee shouted.

Just so you know, all of our conversations that day were spoken in loud voices, what with the distance and the ringing in everyone's ears from the gunfire.

"You killed your own nephew," I retorted.

"That's a damned lie."

"Is it? If you hadn't been following us to steal our herd, he never would have died. He never would have even been there."

Klee started forward, and I have to admit he seemed to be moving fairly nimbly for a man of such girth. He was grinning as he approached, like he'd already finished the job and was anticipating the celebration.

"You don't look so good, McCallister."

Well, I don't know what I looked like, but if it was anything close to how I felt, I suspect Jacob was being kind in his assessment. I know I was swaying on my feet, and that the entire left side of my shirt was sodden with blood. Lena said later on that I looked as pale as a ghost, and that she'd been half afraid that's what I was, standing there to take revenge on the men who'd killed me.

"I've got ambition enough to finish this chore, if that's what you're wondering," I replied. "You and your kin have been a burr under the Flatiron's saddle for long enough, Klee. I'm going to end it here."

Laughing, Jacob said: "That's brassy talk, boy, but I'll be your huckleberry. Lift that pistol anytime you see fit."

Jacob had been walking steadily toward me, but then he stopped about forty yards away. Gritting my teeth against the deep throbbing in my shoulder, I started forward. He looked surprised by my move, but held his ground. We both had our revolvers drawn, though hanging, muzzle-down, from our fists. I'd covered maybe twenty feet when I stepped on a clod of dirt no bigger around than my fist, something so slight and soft I wouldn't have even noticed it if I hadn't been so foggy-headed. As it was, the clod staggered me to my right.

Laughing, Jacob took a half step forward. "The hell with you, you little pup," he called, and began to raise his revolver.

The difference between me and Jacob that day was that Jacob tried to bring his gun up to eye level so that he could aim—which is smart if you've got the time. I didn't. Jerking the Navy to waist level, I snapped off a round before Jacob even knew what I was doing.

I still remember the look of astonishment on Jacob's face when my bullet struck him in the gut. Jim said he grunted loud enough to wake the dead, although I didn't hear it. Then the look of surprise vanished, and Jacob raised his gun with an oath vicious enough to peel paint. I got off a second round before Klee could fire his first, but my aim was all out of whack by then, and my bullet plowed into the dirt between the big man's feet, doing no harm.

Klee's luck was better, and his slug caught me just under and to the outside of my ribs. It wasn't a bad wound, as far as those things go, but I was so addled by the first that I went down instantly.

Klee stood where he was, one hand covering the wound in his belly, the other still hanging onto his revolver. I could see blood seeping through the fabric of his shirt between his fingers, but he didn't look especially weakened. Raising his head from where he'd been staring at the wound, he started cursing me for a trouble-making fool whose family thought they owned all of southern Florida—the usual trash you'd expect from a horse thief and slave stealer—but he was also lifting his gun for a second shot, and I knew I couldn't just lay there and let him take it without challenge. Pushing to my knees, I brought my revolver around in a slow arc, settling the tiny brass post at the muzzle end on Jacob's chest.

Klee got his shot off first, and I swear the bullet came close enough to clip off some of the hair above my ear. But it didn't hit me, and my shot sailed true. The Navy's ball struck Jacob solidly in the chest, but the son-of-a-bitch *still* didn't fall!

"God dammit," I shouted in frustration. "Klee, drop your gun!"

Instead, he spat a bloody glob into the dirt at his side. Looking at me with those little pig eyes blazing, he started to bring his revolver up one more time. That ol' boy was determined, but so was I, and I got my final round off before he could pull his trigger. This time, Jacob Klee went down hard, a hole about the size of a dime centered just above the bridge of his nose.

It's taken me a lot longer to tell you about this than it did for it to happen. I suspect the whole thing—from the time I shouted for Klee to come and get me, until he hit the ground like a load of bricks—didn't take more than a couple of minutes. What I didn't know at the time, as focused as I was on Jacob Klee, was that Ardell and Punch had taken that opportunity to walk out into the street behind those Klee boys, so that after the old man fell, they were standing right there with their guns drawn. I don't think Klee's gang knew they were there until Ardell told them to drop their guns or get the same treatment as the old man. I guess with the snake's head chopped off, those boys had lost their will to fight, because they threw their weapons down without protest. That much I saw. Then I keeled over unconscious.

SESSION TEN

If you're thinking about ending this interview anytime soon, now might be a good time. That last disk is full, and Lord knows I've about run out of story. I don't mind going on if that's what you'd like, I just don't want you to think there's enough left of this tale to fill another disk.

Fair enough, I'll keep talking as long as you keep recording.

First off, I need to confess that I don't recall a whole lot about what happened after I hit the dirt out there in the middle of Miami's solitary street. Most of what I'm going to tell you about the following few days is what I gleaned afterward from Ardell and Jim and Lena and Punch.

I reckon it's safe to say I got hit pretty hard by that deserter I scared up out of the lean-to. His bullet poked a hole in the hollow of my left shoulder so close to my lung the boys were half afraid to move me. Not that they had much choice. Although most of Miami's leading citizens had scattered like their britches were afire when the fighting broke out, Jim figured they'd be back as soon as they realized it wasn't a cavalry regiment swooping down on the place, but just a bunch of cow hunters, most of whom weren't quite dry behind the ears.

Feeling a need to move fast, Jim sent Ardell into the shot-up store to fetch a coil of hemp that they used to hog-tie all but one of Klee's gang. With the clan secured, Jim told Punch and the man they'd left untied to bring in those stolen Flatiron horses, including that little gray filly of Pa's.

I probably ought to mention that, of the whole bunch, Ardell and Lena were the only ones to come through that Miami fracas unscathed. Roy had taken two serious wounds to his chest and was laid up inside the store, where Lena was doing her best by him, and poor ol' Punch really earned his nickname that summer; besides the piece of buckshot he'd collected at Chestnut Thumb, he caught a second bullet in the calf of his leg and another—more burn than gouge—across his ribs there in Miami. Ironically it was that deep scratch over his ribs that he complained about the most, claiming for years afterward that it never stopped itching.

Ardell brought a chair out of the saloon for Jim to sit in and keep an eye on the prisoners, then hurried down to the river to commandeer another skiff for our return to the north bank. He told me on the ride home how a bunch of Yankees in naval uniforms had stood outside the main entrance to Fort Dallas and watched as he readied the tiny craft. He said he'd been worried they might come over and try to put a stop to his efforts, but thankfully they'd seemed content to stay where they were and mind their own business. By the time Ardell had everything arranged on the river, Punch and Klee's man had returned with the horses, including Pa's filly.

With Lena's help, Ardell got me and Roy into the skiff, then went back to fetch Casey's body, wrapped in a quilt stripped from some hardcase's bedroll, and placed it in the boat at our feet. I don't know if Ardell sailed us across the Miami or rowed, but he did mention some weeks later that, although the river was wide at its mouth, the current wasn't bad because of the incoming tide.

If you want more details about the next few days, you'd need to hunt up Ardell and ask him, since I was more out of it than not. The last I heard, he was living in a nursing home in Tallahassee, so if he ain't kicked the bucket over yet, he shouldn't be hard to locate. Ardell Hawes. If you talk to him, tell him I said howdy. Hell, tell him to write me a damned letter. I ain't heard from that ol' boy in a many a year, and I'd like to know what he's been up to.

Anyway, Ardell and Lena got everyone back across the Miami, including the stolen horses. I came around a little as they were packing us onto the mounts we'd ridden south on. They'd strapped Casey belly-down over his saddle, and put Roy on my bay so they could tie him horn to cantle. Even with that, Lena had to ride up behind him to keep him from falling off. They sat me atop Casey's little marshtackie, where I guess I swayed like a clump of sea oats in a brisk wind. Although I didn't fall off, I sure wasn't much help. Mostly I just sat there in a fevered daze, the world spinning every time I opened my eyes.

Jim brought the column to a halt a few hundred yards down the trail, and ducked into the woods where we'd left the look-out the night before, bundled up like a sack of flour. He returned several minutes later carrying the look-out's suspenders, the ones Casey'd used to tie the man's wrists and ankles while me and Jim held him down. Jim figured the guy must have had a small knife hidden somewhere, besides the heavy belt knife Jim had tossed into the bushes. We'd been careless not to check, and paid a grievous price for our mistake.

To Jim's credit, he never brought up my decision not to cut the look-out's throat when we had the chance, but the old black man's words to my decision to—"Let him live."—haunts me to this day.

We do, Jim had said, *we might someday regret it.*

He was sure right about that.

I was hurting real bad that first day on the trail. Every muscle and joint in my body seemed to protest the slightest movement of my mount, and sweat soaked through my shirt and trousers and socks, turning my hair as wet as if I'd been caught in a summer downpour. Finally I became aware of Ardell standing beside my saddle, shaking me awake and saying I needed to let go, which was about the easiest chore I had to do that day. I tipped outward and Ardell helped me to the ground, then passed me on to Lena, who led me over to where my blankets were already spread out on the ground beside a cabin I didn't recognize. I remember Lena talking to me, but I couldn't tell you what she said, nor did I attempt a reply. I just fell back in my bed and slipped into sweet unconsciousness. I'd hear voices from time to time, or feel fingers prodding at my shoulder that I'd weakly try to swat away, but I don't think I ever opened my eyes to see who it was doing the talking or poking. When I finally did pry my eyes apart, the sky was once again gray with dawn.

"You awake, massa?" a voice asked.

I nodded weakly, and Lena shouted loud enough to make my head throb: "Mistah Ardell, Massa Boone be awake now!"

Squinting, I let my head loll to the side. Lena was sitting on her calves beside my bedroll, dipping a remnant of her skirt in a bucket of water. She brought the rag dripping across the grass to my forehead and, oh my, did that feel good.

"You thirsty, massa?" she asked. "Papa Jim says I'm to give you all the water you wants, on account of that fever."

"I could drink," I admitted. Truth is, I was so parched I could have emptied the Miami, or at least exposed a good deal of its banks.

Lena dipped a cup from the same bucket she was using to soak her rags—something that would make a lot of people squeamish today, but which we didn't think too much of at the time—then lifted the back of my head with one hand and tipped the tin mug to my lips. I swallowed it down quick and grateful, and could have drunk more, but decided the effort wasn't worth the way moving woke up all the aches and pains that must have been slumbering with me.

With my head back on a folded blanket that served as my pillow, I looked up to see Ardell leaning over me, his face a mask of concern. He didn't waste any time getting to the point.

"That wound in your side isn't much more than a scratch, but we've got to get that bullet out of your shoulder. It's going to go bad if we don't."

By bad, he meant infection.

"Get it," I said in a voice still raspy and dry.

"It won't be easy. Jim thinks it might be sitting close to a lung. If I go digging around in there with a knife, I'm liable to puncture the damned thing, and I don't want to do that."

"Well, that makes at least two of us," I replied, "but the odds are likely better now than if it does get infected."

Without much enthusiasm, he said: "We could put you on a boat, sail you up the coast to Jacksonville. They'd have a doctor there."

"Yeah, a Yankee doctor. If he don't cut off an arm or a leg, he'd still throw me in a rock coop. I ain't going to Jacksonville, Ardell."

The young cow hunter sighed loudly. "I didn't think you would. All right, I'll do the best I can, just don't die on me, you hear?" He was glaring like I'd have anything to say in the matter.

"I'll do what I can," was my reply.

"Good. I've got everything just about ready. Lena, start pouring as much of that popskull down his throat as you can, while I go get my knives. I don't want him feeling anything he doesn't have to."

"Yes, suh," Lena replied gravely, then looked at me after Ardell walked off. "I ain't never done nothin' like this afore, massa."

"You'll be fine. Just listen to Ardell and do what he says."

"Mistah Ardell ain't never done nothin' like this afore, either. He was talkin' to Papa Jim at breakfast. Papa Jim says he's seen wounds durin' the Indian Wars like what you got, and says it'll go bad if that bullet ain't cut outta there real soon. Mistah Ardell wanted Papa Jim to do the cuttin', but Papa Jim says he's too woozy yet, and sometimes sees two of ever'thing. He can't do it, and that poor Mistah Punch is as weak as a half-drowned kitten after that long ride outta Miami with his leg all swolled up from that bullet in his calf. Papa Jim says Ardell be the only man here what can do it, but Mistah Ardell, he sure don't want to."

"Just do what Mister Ardell says," I replied, growing aggravated by the woman's nervous talk.

Well, I don't guess you need to know the particulars, not that I could give them to you if you did. I will say it wasn't an experience I'd ever want to repeat, or wish on an enemy, but I obviously lived through it. Ardell pried a .44-caliber slug out of my chest that day, and later on asked if I wanted it, but I told him no. What the hell kind of a Miami souvenir would that have been?

I was in and out of consciousness all day, but woke up toward evening feeling better—"better" being a relative term, of course. Turning my head slow and careful, I found Jim sitting by my side. There was a ragged strip of cloth from the hem of Lena's skirt—that gal was going to end up bare-assed naked if she didn't soon find another source for rags—wrapped around his head, hiding what would eventually become a long, ridged scar just above his ear. Jim had his back to the cabin's wall, and was staring in grim reflection at a dense wall of mangrove forest that rose fifty or so yards away. He was drinking something from a tin cup that steamed gently in the softening twilight, and didn't realize I was awake until I spoke.

"How you feeling?" I asked, the words kind of choppy on that first sentence, but smoothing out afterward.

Smiling, Jim put his cup down and scooted closer, placing a cool palm to my forehead. "You still warm, marse, but you ain't burnin' up like you has been the past couple days."

I had to think about that for a moment. Frowning, I asked: "Two days?"

"Yes'um. We's been here in Fort Lauderdale two full days now, waiting for you to get better enough to go home."

"Lauderdale?" I was really confused then. Lifting my head, I took a quick peek around. I spotted the ruins of the old fort off to my right, then heard the lapping of the surf not too far away. It was the gentle breaking of waves that finally gave me a sense of direction, and made the rest of the world seem real again.

Although the settlement that had grown up around the fort had been deserted when we came through a few days earlier, there were people in sight that evening, going lazily about their business in the oppressive humidity.

"They come back," Jim explained, seeing my questioning look. "They was down to the coast salvagin' a wreck, last time." He reached behind him to hold up the cup I'd seen him drinking from earlier. "Was a Yankee ship they found, with a good supply of coffee and tobacco on board. Mistah Ardell bought up a whole sack of both, and some medicine, too. He'll have you feeling pert again in no time."

Letting my head roll back into the sweat-soaked cradle of my pillow, I didn't reply. We were in Lauderdale, and had been for two days, rather than just one. But there were other things I found even more disconcerting, and the biggest was the return of Jim's subservient attitude. Apparently with the worst of the danger past, he'd instinctively reverted to his old mannerisms. I found it annoying, yet I also understood that for Jim—and for me, to a much lesser extent—anything else would have been impossible. There were never a lot of slaves in southern Florida in those early years of the cattle trade, but there was still that attitude of dominance and superiority over the darker races. Roy was a good example of that, but there were others a whole lot worse. Although it bothered me, I decided not to bring it up until I had a chance to talk with Pa.

"How are the others?" I finally asked. "Punch and Roy?"

"Mistah Punch is doin' right well," Jim replied. "That bullet was a tiny thing, no bigger'n another piece of buckshot. It went all the way through his calf and didn't tear up too much meat a-tall. He's sore, but gettin' around." He hesitated, and I felt a sinking in my stomach. "Mistah Roy didn't make it, marse. We buried him and Mistah Casey over close to the river, where they's others been laid to rest."

"A cemetery?"

"Yes'um." Jim nodded. "He was hit real bad, marse, and hurtin' real bad, too. I'd've give just about anything for him to live, but . . ."

When Jim's words trailed off, I filled in what he'd left unspoken. "Sometimes dying is best."

"Yes, suh, I surely believe it was for Mistah Roy."

I closed my eyes.

"You wants something to eat, marse? Lena fixed a pot of turtle soup."

"No, not now," I replied without opening my eyes. "Maybe later."

"Yes'um, but you gots to eat. Needs you some food down your belly to get you well again."

"I know, but . . . later."

Leaning back, Jim sighed. "All right, but next time you wake up, you gots to."

I nodded weakly, already drifting off.

We stayed in Lauderdale three more days, until Ardell

deemed me well enough to fork a saddle. I was the last of the wounded to get back on my feet, and even then I was as shaky as a three-legged goat. I was more than ready to go home, though.

I don't guess there's much point in telling you about our return, since nothing really exciting happened, and sure as Hades there wasn't much conversation between us. We all kind of slipped into a blue funk on the ride back, the memories of Casey and Roy riding vividly right alongside us, as painful as broken teeth.

We were all bone weary and sick of the saddle by the time we rode into the Flatiron. Josie met us in the yard, and the reunion between her and Lena brought tears to my eyes. After the greetings were over, she put me and Punch straight-away to bed, and neither one of us protested. Jim went to his own house, and Lena said the snores coming from his and Josie's bedroom made her fearful of the cypress shingles flying off the cabin roof.

Ardell hung around for a couple of days, but he was anxious to get back to his own place. I didn't blame him. He said he'd stop off at the Turners on the way and tell Roy's mama and sisters what had happened. He obviously wasn't looking forward to it. If I'd been in better shape, the chore rightly should have been mine, but I didn't think I had another hundred-mile round trip left in me. I felt kind of guilty for my relief at not having to talk to Missus Turner, but not enough to volunteer for the task.

Punch left the day after Ardell did, promising to swing wide on his way home to inform Casey's folks of their son's death. I was glad to avoid that one, too, although in fairness, Punch was family, and by rights the chore was his to complete. Punch was mighty young for the task, being just fifteen when we started that drive to Punta Rassa, although I reckon he grew up fast that year.

I wrote a letter to Calvin Oswald's folks in Kissimmee, probably the most difficult missive I ever had to put down on paper. Later on, after the war, I went to Punta Rassa with Calvin's pa and older brother to help them retrieve the body. They buried Cal in the Kissimmee Cemetery, and I stayed for the funeral, although I didn't feel welcome. I think his folks—his ma in particular—blamed me for the boy's death, rather than the Yankee invaders who'd shot him in the back. But what can you do in a situation like that except steel yourself to the icy stares and hang on until it's over?

It was a full week after our return to the Flatiron before I started taking on light chores around the place, but I couldn't work up much enthusiasm for it. Pa and the others were overdue by then, and I was starting to worry. Jim and Josie and Lena were feeling equally fretful, like a sense of doom had drifted cloud-like over the Flatiron and refused to budge.

It was Joe-Jim who finally showed up, nearly six weeks late by my reckoning. He was riding a little Flatiron marshtackie and trailing an extra horse and a pack of catch dogs, my own Blue-Boy among 'em. Although skinny and worn-down, Joe-Jim beefed up real quick under his ma's and Lena's cooking.

The first thing Joe-Jim did on his return was ride over to where I was toiling at the burned-out wreckage of the barn and hand me a letter from Pa. Although my fingers trembled as I opened it, I don't believe I was really surprised by the news. Pa had decided to stay in Georgia and help drive a wagon train of supplies to our boys fighting in Tennessee. When my brothers elected to go with him, Pa sent Joe-Jim back with the catch dogs. [*Ed. Note:* Jefferson McCallister's letter, along with the note from W.B. Ashworth, are available for viewing in the Mc-Callister Papers, archived in the Arcadian Historical Association files; the letter Boone McCallister received that day reads: *Deer Boon me and your bothers have desided to stay in north and fit yankees for awile. you are in charge of flatiron until i get bak, hopfuly in the spring your pa, jefferson t. Mccallister*]

That was the last correspondence I ever received from my father, although I got a letter from Bud in May, more or less repeating what Pa had said. [*Ed. Note:* Bud is Kenton Simon, Boone's older brother.]

There'd been a time when being put in charge of the Flatiron would have swollen my chest with pride, but I found myself feeling strangely ambivalent in the weeks following my return from Miami. Finally I decided that if that was what Pa wanted, I'd do the best I could until his return. I even started putting together another herd to take north, although it was Frank Turner who ramrodded that drive, while I stayed home to look after the ranch.

Even though Pa never came back, I'm pretty sure he would have approved of what I did later that summer. Leaving Jim in charge, I saddled my bay and rode down to Pete Dill's trading post on the Caloosahatchee. Like before, Pete got a startled look on his face when I walked in, but a grin wasn't far behind.

"Howdy, Boone," he called, his voice booming hollowly across the nearly empty trade room. "Belly up here and sample a dose of Norm Wakley's latest. Tell me it tastes better than gopher spit."

"It'd be an improvement if it does," I allowed.

"Ain't that the God's honest truth," Pete replied solemnly. He brought a jug and two mugs out from under the counter. "Dang if it ain't been a 'coon's age since I seen a Flatiron rider."

"It kind of feels like a 'coon's age," I agreed, leaning into the counter. "How have you been faring?"

"I been lonesome. Can't even get some wild buck from the 'glades in here to trade for the merchandise I've got left. Tell me you're wanting some ink or writing paper, and the next drink is free."

Pete's offer made me laugh. "That's exactly why I'm here.

Klee's boys burned all the spare writing paper we had at the ranch."

I don't think he believed me at first, but his expression sobered noticeably when I told him why I wanted it.

"What's your daddy going to say when he gets back?"

"I believe he'd say it was past time and then some, but even if he doesn't, he was the one who put me in charge. I'm set on this, Pete, and need you to witness the transaction."

Dill shrugged uncertainly. "I'll witness the signature, although I think you're wrong to do it."

"You got that paper and some ink?"

"Yeah. Need a quill? I got some turkey that nibs down to a fine point."

"Bring it out," I replied, setting my drink aside—and in case you're wondering about that latest batch of Norm's, it wasn't a damned bit better than what he normally brewed—raw as kerosene, and probably just about as deadly.

After conducting my business and having Pete add his signature as witness, I returned to the Flatiron and told Jim and the others to come into the winter kitchen. I handed out the contracts I'd put together at the trading post, and explained what they were.

"Those papers mean you're free," I told them.

All four of them were watching me gravely, like they were expecting some kind of stipulation, but there wasn't any.

"Up north, Mister Lincoln has signed something called an Emancipation Proclamation, which basically says the same thing these papers do, and probably a whole lot better. But even though these are hard times for the South, it ain't yet a given that the North will win. If the Confederacy survives, these papers will guarantee your freedom. Soon as things ain't so dicey, I'll ride up to Tallahassee and register them proper-like at the capital."

I don't recall what kind of reaction I was expecting, but I'm pretty sure it wasn't the subdued thank-yous I was given. Holding their papers in front of them like hats removed for prayer, they filed out of the main house and returned to their cabin. In time the reality of what I'd given them sank in, and they kept those papers wrapped in oilcloth and parchment to protect them from bugs and humidity, but they never spoke of them openly. It was like they were afraid someone might come along and take them away if word got out.

After the war, as a wedding gift to Joe-Jim and Lena, I deeded them one hundred acres and a team of mules, and helped them register their own brand—the Flatiron mark, with the letters J-L inside the triangular figure. I thought a connection to the Mc-Callister spread might help if some carpetbagger tried to wrestle ownership away from the happy couple. Joe-Jim and Lena prospered on their new place, and according to Bud, who would write from time to time, they eventually had seven youngsters to pass the place on to. Although I offered Jim and Josie a similar parcel of land just north of their children, they declined.

"We's settled good enough right here, if that be all right with you," Jim said, and Josie, standing behind him, had nodded emphatically, as if they'd already discussed the possibilities.

"You ain't slaves no more," I reminded them. "You can stay forever, and I hope you do, but you don't have to."

"We know, marse," Josie replied. "But this here be our home, and I don't hardly know what we'd do som'wheres else."

I probably told them a dozen times in the years that followed that I didn't want them calling me *master* any more, nor any of its kin—like massa or marse or boss.

"From here on, I'm just Boone, OK?" I'd say, and they'd always agree, but I guess old habits are the hardest to break. In time they started calling me Mr. Boone, which was a little better, although, now that I'm older, I can see it was more important to me than it was to them. Guilt, I guess. I remember Josie saying—"We'd rather."—the last time I tried to get her to drop the *mister,* and I finally decided to let it go. Hell, if they were free, then I reckon they could do whatever they wanted. The South itself had other ideas, though, and there were rocky times ahead for Negroes all over the former Confederacy. Up north, too. But I'd done what I could for Jim and Josie and Joe-Jim and Lena and their seven, and so did Bud, after I left for Texas.

Bud was the first of my brothers to return home after General Lee's surrender in April of 1865. He showed up in June of that year, barefoot and half starved, armed with just a rusty musket instead of the Sharps carbine and Navy revolver he'd gone off to fight the Yankees with. It was Bud who told me about Pa and Stone, both killed by an artillery shell at Bull's Gap in Tennessee. Other than confirming that they were gone, it was several more months before I learned from Clark what had happened. I'm not going to tell you about it, though. Clark was there and saw it, and his description is a dog that needs to be left to sleep.

Lew came home later that summer, and in not much better condition than Bud, although they would both pale in comparison to the scarecrow that showed up a few days before Christmas. Clark had been captured at Bull's Gap, and spent the remainder of the war in a prison camp near Washington, D.C., in conditions that would make your blood run cold to hear about.

Crockett never returned, and no one seemed to know what became of him. Lew said he was still alive after the first day's fighting at Bull's Gap, but he lost track of him afterward. There were rumors that Crockett joined a band of partisan fighters, rangering all through Tennessee and Kentucky, and even up into Indiana and Ohio on occasion. Another tale had him joining Mosby's Rangers, which is close enough to the first rumor to make me wonder if there wasn't a kernel of truth in those stories. If you ever run across any information on Crockett Mc-Callister in your travels around the country, I'd appreciate you dropping me a letter about it. Ol' Crock would be well into his nineties by now, but he'd be McCallister tough, too, and likely still kicking if someone didn't put a bullet in him.

Of the kin that did come back from the war, I don't think things were ever the same. We all stayed on the home place through the winter of '65 and '66, but, after that, we kind of drifted apart. Clark went to Tampa and married a Turner, distant kin to Roy. They had two kids, but later divorced when Clark fell too heavily into a bottle. He died in 1909, struck by one of the first automobiles ever to ply the dusty streets of Tampa.

Lew fared better, although he also had his troubles with the bottle. He moved to Orlando, where he eventually married a local girl. After clerking in a store for some years, he started buying up land west of town and putting in citrus trees. It didn't pay much until the railroad came through in the early 1880s, but, after that, Lew became a wealthy man, easily the most prosperous of all us McCallister boys.

Like I've mentioned more than once over the past few days, I left the Flatiron in '66, but my feet must have been itchier than my brothers', because I didn't stop until I reached Texas soil.

It was Bud who stayed on to run the Flatiron, and would have his share of trouble with the Klees off and on for the next forty years, but that's his story to tell, not mine. I'm glad one of us stayed, though. The Flatiron ain't a tenth of what it was before the Northern Invasion, but it still covers eight sections of prime cattle country, and is a force to be reckoned with along the Pease River of southwest Florida. [*Ed. Note:* A section of land equals six hundred and forty acres, so the Flatiron's eight sections would represent five thousand one hundred and twenty

acres between the headwaters of the Pease (Peace) and Caloosahatchee Rivers, west of the Florida Highlands.]

Me? I kept on cowboying, as they call it out here. I did that
for a good many years, before finally settling down in Fort Worth
in '89. Too old for the range but too stubborn to quit the trade,
I became a buyer for the Armour brothers out of Chicago and
Omaha, one of the biggest meat packaging companies in the
nation today. I was personal friends with old Phil Armour, and
a guest in his house in Chicago several times throughout the
1890s. I only quit the company when I got too slow to get out
of the way of charging steers. After getting knocked on my ass
that last time and busting a hip in the process, I decided to
hang up my stockman's cane and retire. Mostly I have, too,
except every once in a while I like to go down to the Fort Worth
stockyards and do a little dickering on the side. Just small-scale
stuff, for old times' sake.

I'm going to go down there this afternoon, as soon as you say
you've got enough of my story on your disks. I'm going to look
up a guy named Harry Walton, who was telling folks just last
week about how me and Casey Davis threw a man named Klee
into a 'gator hole just to watch him get et. When I find Harry,
I'm going to tell him about these recordings, and how the truth
of those days has finally been told. Then I'm going to punch
that son-of-a-bitch square in the nose. You can come along if
you'd like, and see if I don't.

End Transcript

Letter on File in the McCallister Papers
Arcadian Historical Association
Arcadia, Florida

From the Offices of Massey, Hibbard and Gelms
Re: McCallister, Boone Daniel—Last Will and Testament
To: William Mills
Attorney At Law
Arcadia, Florida

My Dear Mr. Mills:

It is with deep regret that I inform you of the passing of my client, Boone D. McCallister, of this city, on Six January, Nineteen Hundred and Thirty-Eight. As you know, Mr. McCallister was quite advanced in years, and had been in ill health for some time prior to his demise.

There was a will, about which you inquired, but it was trifling, and consisted largely of the disposition of mementos. The most valuable asset in probate was a "Texas" saddle, which I understood he had owned since youth. The recipient of his estate was a Miss Helen Geiger, also of this city, a longtime acquaintance of Boone's.

There was no mention in the McCallister Will of the Flatiron Ranch of Arcadia, Florida, nor had he made any reference to the property in the years I knew him as a client. It would appear that your concern regarding the legal disposition of the property to the sole heirs of Kenton S. (Bud) McCallister will remain unchallenged by Texas courts.

I Remain, Sir, Your Most Humble Servant,
[SIGNED]
Troy Hibbard
Fort Worth, TX

Post Script: If I may, without jeopardizing client/attorney confidentiality, I wish to state that my association with Mr. McCallister, while at all times professional, was one of utmost enjoyment for myself and associates. Mr. "M." was a colorful character of a time rapidly vanishing, and earned my respect and admiration for his contributions to our unique American Heritage. His periodic visits to our offices will be missed.

R.I.P., Old Friend

ABOUT THE AUTHOR

Michael Zimmer grew up on a small Colorado horse ranch, and began to break and train horses for spending money while still in high school. An American history enthusiast from a very early age, he has done extensive research on the Old West. His personal library contains over two thousand volumes covering that area west of the Mississippi from the late 1700s to the early decades of the 20th Century. In addition to perusing first-hand accounts from the period, Zimmer is also a firm believer in field interpretation. He's made it a point to master many of the skills used by our forefathers, and can start a campfire with flint and steel, gather, prepare, and survive on natural foods found in the wilderness, and has built and slept in shelters as diverse as bark lodges and snow caves. He has done horseback treks using 19th Century tack, gear, and guidelines. Michael Zimmer is the author of twelve previous novels. His work has been praised by *Library Journal, Historical Novel Society,* and *Publishers Weekly* among others. Zimmer's *City of Rocks* (Five Star, 2012) was chosen by *Booklist* as one of the top ten Western novels of 2012, the reviewer saying of the first-person narrator that "at times we can hear the wistfulness in his voice, the bittersweet memory of a time when he and the country were raw, young, and full of hope and promise. A stirring tale, well told." Zimmer now resides in Utah with his wife Vanessa, and two dogs. His website is www.michael-zimmer.com.